Verja

Michaela Daphne

THE HIDDEN GROVE SERIES: BOOK 2

VERJA

Be The Good Publishing

Copyright © Text Michaela Daphne 2020
www.michaeladaphne.com

Cover by Gabriel Akinrinmade 2020
www.boxofwolves.com

Edited by Ocean Reeve Publishing
www.oceanreeve.com

All rights reserved. No part of this book may be reproduced in any form by any electronic or mechanical means including photocopying, recording, or information storage and retrieval without permission in writing from the author.

This is a work of fiction. Names, characters, places, and incidents are the products of the author's imagination or are used fictitiously. Any resemblance to actual events, locales, or persons, living or dead, is entirely coincidental.

ISBN 978 0 6482241 5 0 Paperback

First Edition.

DEDICATION

To my dad, my hero. You know what you did.

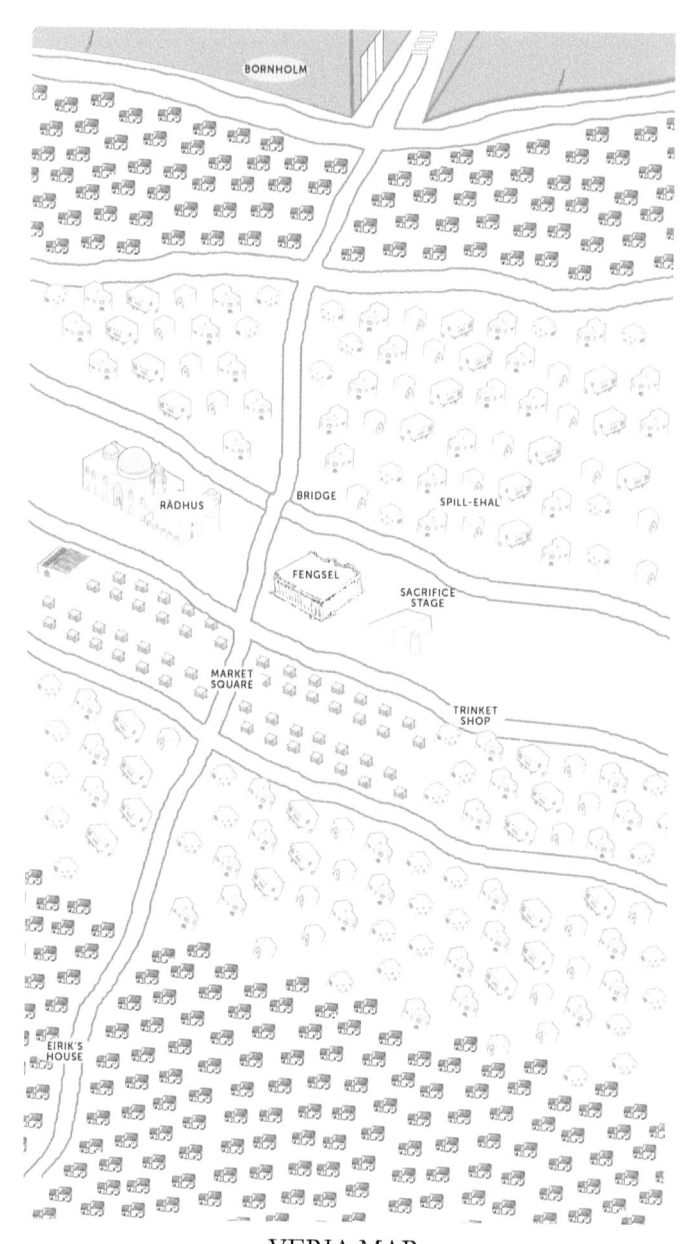

VERJA MAP

1

LIGHT STREAMED THROUGH the kitchen window, warming my cold skin. I stepped back into the shadow. It was too bright; always too bright—like I was standing naked in an interrogation room about to be scrutinised, my secrets laid bare. But I wouldn't share my secrets. They couldn't make me. Not even Dad.

He watched me from the dining table, riddled with heavy-set lines beneath his eyes like a Rembrandt self-portrait. He did that a lot these days, tired eyes poring over me as though I might disappear on him all over again. But I had no plans to do anything of the sort.

He rubbed his weary eyes and sighed, "I'm going to weed your mother's garden this weekend."

I don't know why we still called it that. It had been eighteen months since her death and whilst I could never forget that horrid summer day, I had mourned for her enough to not be so attached to what had once been hers.

His gaze returned to my aikido uniform.

I tightened the white belt around my waist and wound up a mock karate-kick to distract him, stopping just in time to pinch the cheesy toast from under his nose. I cheekily took a bite.

He chuckled a moment before grabbing it back, his face becoming earnest. "You did something to your hair," he said.

"I just straightened it," I said, blushing.

"But aren't you going to your aikido class?"

"Yeah."

He looked at me sidelong and shrugged. "My shift ends at 7 am," he said.

I shuffled over and gave him a kiss on the cheek.

"See you in the morning, Dad."

I slung my sports bag over my shoulder and headed outside. A gust of wind lifted my hair as I crossed the threshold of the rickety old front door, undoing what I had spent the better part of forty minutes in the bathroom perfecting. It knotted back into a wavy mess.

Storm clouds were brewing as the sun slipped below the horizon—an unusual sight for a Queensland winter.

Another gust blew, rippling at the chipped and flaking maroon paint of my car. It wasn't much, but it was mine—for the next twenty-four hours, anyway. Mum's life insurance was now well and truly dried up, so Dad was working extra shifts on weekends. It barely got us by. The little money from the car sale would do its bit in helping to keep my final year's worth of Mianjin Arts College fees in check.

I jumped in the car and jabbed on the music. I needed to drown out the memories of William that had all started flooding back: how I had run away with him when I should have run from him. How he had slowly unravelled from a charming gentleman living a simple life on a farm to a cruel puppeteer, intent on making me into his idea of the perfect girlfriend and mother of his children.

The memory of his twisted body at the foot of the tree portal back to Earth flashed across my mind. Blood slowly pooled beneath his broken leg.

I could never return to the Hidden Grove and venture

to the tree portal into Purlieu. I couldn't risk him being there, biding his time to finish what he had started. That is, if he was even alive.

I swerved on the road, the wind forcing the car about, just as it started to rain.

"Come on, Evelyn. He can't get you here," I said to myself.

My left hand clung onto the steering wheel; I made to pick at the dried paint on it, but found my skin clean. I hadn't painted since Purlieu.

I turned the volume knob up to drown out the noise and let the bass pulse through me as I drove into the heart of the storm, gripping the wheel tightly with both hands. The scar across the palm of my weak hand pulled taught. I gripped tighter.

"He can't get me here," I repeated.

I wound down the window a fraction and let the rain lick my face and start to soak my hair, springing it free into its wiry auburn chaos. Vân wouldn't care if I had hair as straight as my aikido jo staff or not, just so long as I was partnered with him in class.

I pressed on into the storm.

My hair was slicked to my face obscuring my vision. I pulled it back into a ponytail and stepped up to the basketball grandstand to dump my bag, shielding my eyes from the harsh fluorescents overhead. Wet shoes squeaked and echoed on the waxed flooring behind me as parents brought their children to the class before mine.

I was always the first to arrive for class, so I sat down and watched the primary-schoolers tumbling around the blue gym mats and squealing with collective delight. I may have been training for only just over a term, but both my fitness and technique now surpassed their skill level. I'd gratefully been training with people my own age for the past few weeks.

After traversing the eccentric and dangerous worlds of the Hidden Grove, my previous desire to travel abroad as an artist had been sucked dry. I could barely stomach to pick up a paintbrush these days. Panic hung over me about what I would do next, with graduation from high school on the horizon.

Without my nights filled with aikido class at the community centre or training at home, I would be swallowed up with despair for the future. It was nice just to focus on the here and now—and even nicer that I didn't have to go it alone. Tiffany had signed up along with me. Then her boyfriend, Darius, followed suit with his bestie Cameron in tow. Cameron and I were still not really on speaking terms.

He snapped me from my thoughts as he slumped onto the step below on the stands. He grunted in my direction. I gave a strained smile.

As he pulled off his expensive leather loafers and stuffed them into his bag, he glanced at me again. "You should get stuck in the rain more often," he said.

I felt heat gather in my cheeks.

"How else was I supposed to get from my car into here?" I snapped. "Just 'cause I don't have some maid carrying an umbrella over my head and unrolling a velvet carpet at my feet, Cooba Corowa."

I guess he only put up with me because of Darius, just like I only put up with him because of Tiffany.

"It's Cameron," he said.

"That's not what your bag says." I motioned to the iron-on label.

He turned the bag around and went back to preparing for class. I crossed my arms and returned my attention to the primary schoolers.

Across the court, a cheeky smile and dark, straight hair caught my eyes. It was Vân Vũ and he was looking at me.

In my mind, I drew lines down his hair with a graphite pencil. Sharp, thick, heavy lines cascading across his forehead.

My cheeks flushed again. I gave him a small smile back. This had been going on for weeks—in aikido class and at school—but he'd not done anything about it, even when we were partnered up to practice defensive moves. Maybe he was worried because I was older than him?

I wished Cameron would go away and give Vân a clear path.

If it weren't for Cameron and how he had treated me, I never would have followed William into Purlieu. What I had been through, and still carried with me, was essentially as much Cameron's fault as it was William's.

I glared at the back of his head. His brown ears had turned a tinge of pink. He must be just as mad for being stuck in this situation as I was. If Tiffany and Darius weren't dating, he could go right back to ignoring me.

"Right on time," Cameron said under his breath, as Vân dodged around the edge of the court, headed straight for us.

I breathed a sigh of relief—I wouldn't have to endure being paired up with Cameron for the class at least.

I couldn't believe my luck that Vân had shown an interest in me these past few weeks. Even though I had a scarred, weak hand, he didn't seem to notice or mind; his eyes always on mine.

"What's that supposed to mean?" I said.

Cameron turned to look at me. "You're better than him, Ev."

"Don't call me that," I said. He had no right to call me by a nickname.

Vân was within earshot now.

"Oi—leave her alone," he said.

Cameron got to his feet and balled his fists. Vân stood up a little taller. I got up and towered over them both from my vantage point on the basketball stand.

"Cameron, just go away," I said.

His dark eyes searched me for a moment. He shouldered his bag and slumped off to the other side of the basketball stand, fists still balled.

"You are one impressive woman, Evelyn," Vân said, shaking his head with a smile.

I smiled back at the compliment of being called a woman at the age of eighteen. He stepped up onto the grandstand beside me, pulled out his phone, and took a selfie with me.

Haruto Sensei started clapping his hands and the children dashed off to their parents, buzzing. The boy nearest me slide-tackled his little sister with so much enthusiasm that she promptly sucker-punched his stomach in return. Their mother watched on with a smile, shook her head, and turned to leave.

"All right *deshi*, partner up," said Haruto Sensei.

Vân turned to me and smiled. "I guess you're stuck with me," he said.

My heart skipped a beat and I smiled back, following him onto the basketball court.

"Such an unfortunate turn of events," I replied.

"Don't worry. I'll make it worth your while. You might actually learn something." He motioned to his blue belt and then to my white belt. I stuck my tongue out at him.

The door to the basketball courts opened and amidst the bucketing rain beyond, Tiffany ran inside, followed dutifully by Darius sporting an oversized green umbrella. They were thoroughly soaked, squelching water onto the court as they left their things at the grandstand, kicked off their shoes, and raced into place for class.

Sensei proceeded to take us through the traditional series of warm-ups where we were tasked with mirroring one another. Vân kept pulling faces that made me giggle and gave Tiffany plenty of reason to keep looking at me questioningly over Darius' shoulder.

We moved into our first defensive move of the class—a simple backwards step to get our partner off-balance. Vân was up first and put me off-step with a few quick placements of his hands on my arms, landing me roughly onto the gym mats.

Heat flooded my cheeks. I hadn't expected him to be so harsh.

I slowly got back up and stood a little taller. I couldn't let it be so easy to floor me.

It was my turn.

Vân smirked. I grimaced in return, quickly skipping through the standard grips on his arm until I moved him into a state of imbalance. He let out a small yelp of surprise at how quickly I'd gotten him into a compromising position. But it wasn't enough. I whipped him over my body, onto his back.

I made to let go of his hand but his grip tightened and he pulled me down with him. He rolled on top of me. Breath escaped me. He was towering over me, both hands now on my face and he was looking at my lips.

"Kiss me, Evelyn," he said.

Vân's slim face transformed into the repulsive green eyes of William, bearing down at me with the power of his command, telling me how I should best please him; telling me how I could make up for every fault of his parents by creating a new family with him, with a child conceived by rape.

Before I knew what was happening, my bent knee was moving skywards, socking him in the groin. Vân collapsed to the side, groaning in agony.

My feet found the gym mat and I ran from the class, desperately hiding my face and the tears that I barely kept at bay.

What have I done? What have I done!

The rain hit my head with a shock and sent the tears rushing from my eyes. I stumbled around in the dark, tears and rain filling my vision as I weaved my way between the cars. The wet cold reached my bones and I started to shiver.

"Ev! Evelyn!" It was Tiffany.

She took my hand.

"Come on, your car is back over here."

She pulled me into a jog and within a few moments we reached my car, which I'd apparently walked straight past.

"I left my keys inside," I choked as I wiped my eyes.

She pulled a bag off her shoulder. It was my bag. She gave a kind smile, took my keys out, and we piled in.

I turned the ignition and prodded on the heater with a shaking finger.

Palms sweaty, I hugged myself, watching the droplets of rain fall from my body onto the old velveteen upholstery.

The shocked look on Vân's face went round and round my head. My stomach constricted. I hadn't meant to hurt him. It was like my body had taken over while I watched the scene from afar. Like a switch had been flicked when Vân had tried to control me as though he were William. But Vân had a different kind of power to William—a charming smile and flirty words that lulled me into a romantic stupor. I wouldn't let him—or any other man for that matter—try to control me ever again.

"What happened back there?" Tiffany asked.

"Vân. He—"

I couldn't finish the sentence. I couldn't put words around how he had acted just like William because Tiffany didn't even know about what William had done. Not really, anyway.

"Evelyn, you can tell me."

I tried to form the words but they didn't come. I shrugged my shoulders, silent tears rolling over my cheeks.

"I don't want to talk about it."

"But, Ev—"

"You don't want to talk to me about it either," I said. "You talk to Darius about it, but not me."

All I knew was that she'd followed me into Purlieu and William had imprisoned her in a dugout behind his bookcase. That she'd been trapped in the dark for days, scratching the back of the bookcase until her fingers bled. That she had no idea where she was or why she was being held captive or if she'd ever get out. It still made me sick to think of it, to think of the sight of her face when I tore that bookcase down. At that moment, she was a mere shadow of herself.

Her mouth hung open. She knew enough to realise that this was bigger than Vân.

"You've got your own stuff to deal with," she said. "Besides, when I tell Darius, it's like I'm a fly on the wall, like it didn't really happen to me. It's like a story. But when I look at you, it's just—it's just too real."

Her words hung in the air, creating a chasm between us. I tucked my knees up under my chin and watched the rain slow to a trickle down the glass.

"My Ya-Ya liked Darius, by the way," Tiffany said after a while.

"Oh, I totally forgot," I said. "Sorry, Tiff. How'd it go?"

"Well, when Dad came to pick us up from the home, he started talking himself up in front of Darius again and then Ya-Ya shared this super embarrassing story about how Dad couldn't get into the army, not because he was short or a wog, but because his teeth were fake from a cricket accident! Dad went bright red. Was hilarious. That was when he decided it was time we went to aikido."

I squeezed her hand.

"I'm sorry he sucks so much," I said.

"Me too," Tiffany sighed. "Anyway, do you want to go back inside?"

The thought of facing everyone made my stomach turn over. I shook my head. Tiffany reached over and wrapped her arm around me, pulling my head to rest on her shoulder.

"Okay," she said, and we watched the storm pass together.

Thirty minutes later, Darius and Cameron both sidled into the back seats of the car, making a point to dodge my eyes.

"Hey, boys. Ready for one last hurrah?" Tiffany said,

leaning across me to give the horn a nice long toot.

It had become our post-class habit to pile into my car and hang out over dinner on Wednesday nights. We'd have to find a new ride after the holidays, what with my car getting sold and the others not having their own. Well, Cameron used to have a car, until he totalled it in the school car park last month, and Darius had already lost his license.

"My vote goes for the snack bar next to the library," Tiffany continued.

There was a chorus of grunts in agreement, so I moved the car into drive and gladly left the dojo behind. Because of Vân, my new sanctuary had been ruined.

And now, how was I supposed to act around him? What could I possibly say to him tomorrow at school?

My stomach grumbled in hunger. Or was it tension?

I felt, more than saw, a general murmur ripple around the classroom when I stepped into English. At the paired tables girls huddled and a few brave eyes looked at me while they whispered to their neighbour.

"I heard it wasn't her first time," Jessica, the star pianist, said. She was standing with her back to the door. "Such a slut," she said, laughing.

Her friend gave her an elbow in the ribs that made them both sit down in a hurry.

I moved to a vacant table. Tiffany slipped in beside me a moment later.

"Ev, I need to show you something," she said, getting her phone out.

Mrs Patel, in her pressed winter pinafore, entered the classroom and raised an eye at Tiffany's phone. Tiffany stuffed it in her pocket and gave an apologetic smile.

Mrs Patel moved about the classroom, handing back our *Looking for Alibrandi* essays. She paused a moment too long at my desk as she placed my essay down. It had 'low achievement' scribbled across the top. I slumped back in my chair.

English had always been a necessary evil despite attending an arts high school, but I used to get by. These days, however, I was essentially failing or near-failing every subject and I couldn't seem to be able to do anything about it. It was like I was walking down a dark narrow path and could do nothing but keep going. No matter how hard I tried to focus in class, how many hours I poured over research and textbooks, the information just failed to stick, and so I carried on down this path of desolation.

What was the point of scrounging our money together to send me to this school if I was only going to fail? How would I get into art college then?

I tried to distract myself from the spiralling feeling that had overcome me by turning my attention to the view beyond the classroom windows. There was a rhythmic drumming increasing in volume, like someone was battering the metal railings of the walkway outside. A dark figure emerged from the frosted glass into view of the open window beside me. It was Vân, slapping his drumsticks along while taking a good gander at my English class. His eyebrows crumpled into a frown, which quickly turned skyward into a wicked grin as he set his eyes on me. Heat shot up my neck. I looked away. The rhythmic drumming grew distant.

Mrs Patel had moved to the back of the classroom. Tiffany pulled out her phone again, hiding it in her lap. It cast blue light beneath her chin as she navigated to a post.

"Ev, look," she hissed. "Vân just posted this."

It was the selfie of Vân and me from aikido last night, captioned "Guess who got some? Redheads are the best."

Heat flooded my cheeks. He wouldn't!

"But everyone saw me own him at aikido. No-one in their right mind would believe this," I said.

"You guys have been flirting incessantly for weeks."

He'd seemed so nice. How could I be so stupid, so trusting? Again.

"I could get Darius to take him out, steal his phone, and we could delete it? Or I could write a comment about how his mother is a natural redhead?" she said.

It wouldn't work. Apparently, people already believed it was possible. And the worst part was that Jessica was right: I was no longer a virgin.

I think I had this idea of who I was—a good girl who did what she was told and diligently did her school work and was going to be this extraordinarily creative artist. But I wasn't that 'good girl' anymore. Maybe I had never been.

Tears welled in my eyes but this time I kept them at bay. I wouldn't give them the satisfaction. I picked up my books and made to get up.

"Where are you going?" Tiffany hissed.

"Where do you think?"

"But class isn't over yet."

"Screw that, let's go get him," I said.

Mrs Patel crossed in front of my path. "Evelyn, class is not over yet," she said.

I chewed on my lip and glanced at the clock above the whiteboard. Forty minutes. I could survive another forty minutes. And then Vân would have a lot to answer for.

I sat down again.

Mrs Patel continued on about the final assessment piece for Year Twelve due the following semester.

By the time the bell rang, I felt frazzled and anxious, my heart beating uncomfortably in my chest. I took a deep breath, steadying myself to face Vân, and made to leave the classroom.

"Uh, Evelyn, can I see you for a moment?" asked Mrs Patel.

I internally groaned and approached her desk. Tiffany waited by the door until Mrs Patel shooed her on.

"It's about your essay. I showed it to Miss Daniels, the counsellor, and she agrees with me that you should take some counselling," she said watching my face carefully. "Don't worry. It's normal protocol for any student who brings up topics such as suicide, substance abuse, or promiscuity in their school work."

She had to be kidding. That was what the book was about, after all.

"I don't need to see a counsellor."

"That is not up for debate. Miss Daniels is available to see you at lunchtime on Friday."

I crossed my arms. "You can't make me go."

Mrs Patel raised an eyebrow. "I'm afraid you don't have a choice in the matter," she said, pursing her lips. "Evelyn, this is very unlike you. You used to be such a good girl."

I rolled my eyes and immediately regretted it, heat hitting my cheeks with embarrassment at my own insolence.

It was looking to be the perfect end to term two.

Tiffany was waiting for me at the bottom of the stairs. Vân was ahead, chatting with his friends, still happily hitting his drumsticks on anything and everything within arm's reach; this time his target was the bag rack. I used to think it was cool when he did that.

One of the guys looked up and saw us coming. He nudged Vân, whose drumming promptly stopped and suave demeanour faltered. He looked uneasy, eyes darting from me to his friends and back again. The rest of the guys parted their circle to make way for me. Tiffany hung back.

I scrambled for the right words to convince him to step aside privately with me and avoid embarrassment for either of us.

"What is wrong with you?" I said instead.

I gulped, unsure where my words had come from or how to follow them up.

"How could you lie like that?" I continued.

Vân took a step backwards, clearly taken aback by my strong start. He recovered fairly quickly, resuming that wicked smile across his face.

"Oh baby, it's okay. I know I promised to keep it

between you and me but I just couldn't help myself," he said.

He reached out to take my hand but the moment our fingers touched, I twisted him around and slammed his body into the bag racks. His head hit it hard with a dull thud that made me feel hollow inside.

We stayed like this for a moment; I think each of us as shocked as the other. Again my body had acted on my behalf.

I could hear murmuring behind me as his friends came out of their own stupors, and their glee turned to shock.

Vân pushed against my hold, struggling to break free like a fish on a line.

"Ger—off me!" he said. "You watch. I'm gonna make sure everyone knows what a slut you really are."

I slammed him one more time into the bag rack. I'd been right not to trust him.

He pushed me off him, his lip a little swollen.

He spat at the ground by my feet, the eyes of his friends returning to glee. Following behind Vân, they marched off towards the tuckshop.

I breathed in long, deep breaths, my body shaking. What had I just done? Had I just made it worse?

As their footsteps became distant, they were replaced by another set of heeled, purposeful ones.

"Evelyn! Responsible Thinking Classroom—now!" said Mrs Patel.

Her face said that she'd seen the whole episode.

"You mean detention?" I replied.

She looked like she didn't want to be messed with so I hurried past Tiffany, past Mrs Patel, to RTC.

The aging RTC Monitor, Mr John-Jacobs, made a rhythmic high-pitched whistle with his nose as he breathed. It was the only sound in the room because we were the only two people in the room. After all, who was stupid enough to get sent to detention on the last week of school? Apparently, I was.

The Comic Sans font asked me to determine what I had done wrong, how I would act differently next time, and whose fault it was that I was in RTC.

What had I done? Not pushed Vân hard enough. What would I do next time? Push him harder.

I grabbed the pen with my weak hand and started colouring in the loopy letters on the page, scoffing at the whole process. It should have been Vân in RTC, not me.

The shiny scars on my weak hand stretched and flexed as I attempted to stay inside the lines. No matter how hard I tried after the accident, I'd been unable to regain fine motor skills in my right hand, all except for that brief period in Purlieu when William had used his powers to melt the scars away, leaving behind an unnaturally smooth, undamaged hand with full function. But it wasn't really my hand, and as soon as I crossed the threshold out of Purlieu, the damage returned, as though it had been hiding from sight the whole time. Just like now—on the outside, I seemed perfectly fine; normal, even. But there lurking beneath the surface, just waiting to rear its ugly head, were the emotional scars left behind by William.

Mr John-Jacobs continued his incessant whistle.

I knew well enough from my last visit to RTC that the noise would never cease, so I moved to fill out the form in front of me as quickly as possible, desperate to escape that sound that was bound to drive me to insanity.

I took a fresh look at the form.

What had I done? Pushed Vân. What would I do next time? Not provoke him. Whose fault was it that I was in RTC? My own.

I took the form up to Mr John-Jacobs and handed it over. He breathed in through his mouth as he scanned over my responses. I relaxed a little, finally getting a reprieve from his rhythmic whistle.

He sighed. "I remember when I used to be your English

teacher; you were such a good girl, a nice girl," he said.

I wished he'd go back to the whistling. I tapped my foot impatiently, awaiting his signature so that I could return to class.

"You know, you should pull yourself back into line. You could get suspended," he said, signing the document and passing it back to me.

He had no right to tell me what to do. I snatched the document from him and sped out of the room.

The car revved as Stephen Sawtell—the buyer—gave the clutch of my car a good stomp in the school car park. A small crowd stared from afar at his crumpled, olive green cargo jacket and weathered skin while they waited for their bus or their parents to collect them. It was a sight to see in such an expensive school. I winced and gripped a little tighter to Tiffany as we watched from a distance as he wrapped his oil-smeared hands around the steering wheel.

Dad finally pulled up in a cop car. He was late. Stephen looked uncomfortable at his late arrival—or perhaps it was the police uniform?

"Why didn't you wait for me?" Dad said out of the side of his mouth as he went to greet the buyer.

They exchanged some words. Dad laughed but Stephen just looked wary. I couldn't quite hear what they were saying—something about the missing rear spoiler and the rego?

Stephen pulled a yellowing envelope from his pocket and pushed it into Dad's hand. He seemed eager to end the transaction. Dad quickly counted out the cash and gave me a toothy grin and a thumbs up, as Stephen signed the paperwork.

He got into the car, gave it another rev, and drove away.

I squeezed Tiffany's hand and went to join Dad in the cop car.

"Poor fellow got a nasty shock when he realised that

'derryoshea_1979' was a copper!" Dad said.

I giggled. Just as well Stephen Sawtell's friend hadn't stuck around in the beat-up Land Cruiser he'd arrived in. It definitely didn't look roadworthy. Stephen probably only went through with the transaction with Dad because he had no other way of leaving the school car park.

Dad tried to pass me the envelope but I pushed it back at him.

"Dad, you keep it. You're the one who's paying the school fees."

I looked at his overgrown stubble as he exited the car park. After thinking I'd never see him again in Purlieu, these days I savoured every opportunity to look at his face, even if it made me feel guilty that he always looked tired, working too many hours and too many days a week.

We stopped at a traffic light and he rubbed his face.

"I'm sorry you have to work so much because of me," I said.

He glanced over before heading off again.

"What? Sweetheart, no, that's not it at all. Never you mind—it's just … it's just a case I'm working on at the moment."

His hand reached for the gold locket—Mum's gold locket—around his neck and thumbed across the surface of it.

"I got a call from your school today," he said, changing the subject. "RTC again?"

I bit my bottom lip.

"You hit a boy? And you have to go see the counsellor?"

"I only pushed him, Dad."

The sound of the gear changing from third to fourth filled the silence between us.

"Why?" he asked.

I sighed. It was too complicated to try to explain. "I dunno."

"Work with me here, Evelyn. I'm on your side. I'll always be on your side."

I sighed again.

"Because, well, he started a rumour about me."

"Evelyn. When someone attacks you with words, you don't attack them back with physical violence."

"It was a really bad rumour."

"Okay," he responded, slowly, pensively. "What was the rumour about?"

My cheeks flushed hot.

"That I had sex with him." I let the words tumble out on top of one another quickly. "But really he's just embarrassed because I rejected him and easily floored him at aikido last night. And now he's calling me a slut."

"He did what?" Dad asked. His face had turned pink too. "Which boy?"

He moved the car back down into third, approaching another red light ahead. A girl walked her bike across the road in front of us as the green man turned to amber.

"Vân Vũ. He's in the grade below me. A blue belt at aikido."

"Blue belt? I could take him on."

Dad still hadn't asked if the rumour was true.

"What's the school doing about it?"

I shrugged.

"Do they even know?"

I shook my head. He clenched his jaws.

"That principal of yours is hopeless. I oughta give him a piece of my mind."

"Dad, please don't make a big deal out of it."

My cheeks continued to burn red hot like the pedestrian crossing light that was now flashing. Heat ran down the back of my neck. Dad glanced across at me and his indignant facade crumpled. He drummed the steering wheel with his silver wedding band for a moment but stopped suddenly.

"I'm sorry he did that to you, sweetheart. But you don't have to fight this alone. I'm here for you."

I nodded as the light turned green and we headed off

again.

"Now," he said, breaking the silence. "Has any of this to do with William?"

"What? Dad—no! And you promised you wouldn't ask any questions about that."

I folded my arms and felt my eyebrows crinkle up into my forehead and all at the same time, panic rose in my chest. If he knew what had happened in Purlieu—all that I had done, all that William had done to me—there was no chance he'd still want me, that he'd still love me.

Up until now, he'd respectfully stayed silent and hadn't asked any questions about those four days where I'd gone missing from the art excursion, and it needed to stay that way. As far as my dad was concerned, I'd wagged the excursion to run away with my boyfriend, it hadn't worked out, so we broke up, and I came back home. He didn't know that William was from another world. He didn't know that William had trapped me in Purlieu. And he certainly didn't know that William had raped me.

"We are not going to talk about—about him," I said.

Dad's shoulders dropped a little.

He didn't deserve to be treated like this. He worked too hard for my sake only to be left in the dark and then bear the brunt of my school delinquencies and inadequacies. If only I had a shining report card to bring home at the end of the semester, to prove to him it was all worth it. All I had instead was a platter of shame.

"I'm sorry I keep messing everything up and making things harder for you, Dad," I said.

"It's okay, sweetheart. I know you're trying your hardest."

We shared a grim smile.

"Just promise me you'll go to that appointment?"

"But I don't want to go," I whined.

"Yes, but the school has said it's necessary. If you don't follow their rules, they could suspend or expel you. Now what good was us selling your car if we don't need to pay fancy school fees anymore?" he finished with a cheeky smile.

We exited the main town area into open country, the silver-trunked gum trees lining the road blurring into one. I felt at ease here in the country.

"Okay, I promise," I said.

We'd certainly come a long way on the whole communicating thing since I got back from Purlieu. That was something.

The class was quiet, busy at work creating their final artworks for Year Twelve.

I was forever grateful that Tiffany had continued to choose to sit with me in art class, despite the fact that we shared the class with both Darius and Cameron and I knew she wanted to sit with her boyfriend. Today, in particular, her presence helped to quell my rising anxiety about the looming counselling session with Miss Daniels following the end of the double period.

"Darius should have his licence back after the holidays, so we can keep up our Wednesday night tradition after aikido!" Tiffany said.

I hated not having the freedom of my own car anymore and I didn't much fancy carpooling with Cameron more than I had to, even if he would now serve as a good buffer from Vân at aikido. But the extra time driving with Dad would actually be really nice.

"I still can't believe that Vân would do that," I said.

Tiffany's mouth bobbed open then shut again.

"How did he think it was going to end? That I'd just smile and play along with the lie?" I continued.

He was deluded. And he'd gotten away with the entire thing. Not only that, but even after I'd taken him out for a second time with countless witnesses, people still believed it was true.

"Don't worry about it, Ev. They're a bunch of goldfish

around here—remember, they all used to think we were uncool."

I raised an eyebrow.

"Are you suggesting that we're now popular?"

"Well, I wouldn't go so far as to say 'popular', but at least we're not uncool."

"We have a lot to owe to Darius, then, don't we?" I said, rolling my eyes with a laugh.

Tiffany sighed dramatically.

"He is just the best, isn't he?" she said. "And it's forced my dad to take more of an interest in me—you know, play the intimidating father role."

It sucked that it took her having a boyfriend for her dad to remember he had another family and not just drop Tiffany for his new one.

She glanced across at me sheepishly. I raised an eyebrow.

"Yes?" I asked.

"I think I love him."

"Gee, Tiffany, I would have hoped so—you are sleeping with him, after all," I said.

She shoved me and we shared a smile. I couldn't say that I was particularly thrilled with her choice of partner, but I had to admit that Darius had been really good for Tiffany. And whilst he hadn't taken what he wanted from her and dumped her like I'd suspected he would, I still didn't really trust him. It was like I was waiting for his true colours to show.

Tiffany returned to covering the potted olive tree on her desk with shades of blue paint. It was her idea of marrying her Greek heritage and her inherited Australian culture. It was pretty clever, actually—as the paint dried and the little tree continued to grow, the two would become more and more the one.

On every desk, my peers flexed their creative prowess on the subject matter of identity in art—from skateboard decks to intricate imagery of doughnuts and croissants—painting away the ninety-minute lesson.

I stared down at the lined notebook in front of me and the ideas I'd jotted down about where to take the assessment, just like I had most art lessons of the term. Art reference books were stacked around me, hiding me from Mrs Dawne's kookaburra-like eyes. She had already moseyed three times around the classroom, hovering at my desk at each turn.

I checked back to the decaying text on Scottish artist Waller Hugh Paton and his landscape pieces, having forgotten my train of thought to the conversation with Tiffany.

"Most people create art before writing about it," said Mrs Dawne.

She had returned to my desk and finally decided it was time to say her piece after weeks of watching on in silence. I bit my tongue and chose the dip in her bronze nose as the ideal place to turn my attention while she berated me. Not that she was particularly good at berating.

"It's the last day of semester one, Evelyn," said Mrs Dawne. "Everyone else's final works are coming along nicely but you haven't even started. At first I thought you were being clever, doing the research first, but I think you're actually procrastinating, aren't you?"

I knew I'd have to eventually create something if I wanted to graduate. After all, what was the point of applying to get into art college if I couldn't do art anymore? But every time I tried, I felt emptiness. Utter emptiness. I tried to push through, but nothing ever came. And fruitlessly I had hoped Mr Waller Hugh Paton and co would offer inspiration but nothing seemed worth creating anymore.

"I look forward to seeing you pull this off," she said.

You and me both.

The Kepu twins sitting in front of us turned and gave me a haughty look. I'd been getting a lot of that since Vân had started the rumour and it didn't seem to be dying down. I ignored them, my present dilemma more desperate—that I really wanted to be an artist. Granted, I had lost all desire to travel the world and paint but the idea of owning my own gallery and displaying my own works still made my heart quicken with delight. And yet I couldn't bring myself to paint.

Maybe I've lost my mojo?

The urge to create used to come to me as naturally as breathing. I used to take an art pad with me everywhere, just in case. The margins of my textbooks and exercise books were filled with sketches. For my birthday party in grade seven, Dad dragged the dining table outside so that Tiffany, Cameron, and I could spend the afternoon in the warm sun practising portraiture. I remember being so mad afterwards because Cameron had done a much prettier portrait of Tiffany than he'd done of me. I think mum kept those sketches somewhere. I'd have to dig them up one day; perhaps when I became a famous artist. If only I could bring myself to continue to create.

The bell rang. It was time to go see Miss Daniels where I'd be prodded and probed and asked to divulge my anxieties. My stomach constricted. I slipped my hand into my pocket and wrapped my fingers around the cool metal object inside, sighing. If only I hadn't promised Dad that I'd go.

Tiffany squeezed my bicep as we walked up the concrete path away from the art studios, arms linked together. She'd spotted Miss Daniels heading for us with a determined look in her eye. Miss Daniels was waddling a little bit, and the mismatched brown and grey layers of her singlet top and wraparound dress flapped in the wind, revealing a carefully concealed baby bump.

She pushed her oversized glasses further up the bridge of her nose.

"I was just coming to collect you from your art class," she said. "Shall we?" She nodded in the direction of her office.

I unlinked arms with Tiffany and gave her an uneasy

smile before following along behind Miss Daniels, like a prisoner headed to the gallows.

The counselling office was just as I'd last left it, with the lumpy green sofa and winged velvet armchair in the heart of the room, fluorescents glaring down from above.

"My favourite chair," I said, recalling the feeling of claustrophobia that came with sitting in the tall, winged armchair.

"Oh yes, don't you just love the deep red and how it contrasts the purple walls?" She asked, cocking her head to the side dreamily. I was fairly certain she wasn't being sarcastic.

How on earth did she get a job in an arts school?

"Mmhm," I said. It was all I could muster because I certainly wasn't going to disagree with her this early on in the session.

I sank into the armchair and tried my best not to focus on the shadows that befell my face from the chair that loomed over me.

"I read your *Looking for Alibrandi* essay," she said. "As I'm sure Mrs Patel explained to you, because it contained certain themes, the protocol is for you and me to have a little chat and just check in."

I nodded, following, waiting for the inevitable question.

"Would you like to tell me a little bit about it, in your words?"

I shrugged.

"Well, we read a book in class about sex, alcohol, and suicide and we had to write an essay about the book. So I wrote an essay about sex, alcohol, and suicide."

Miss Daniels pursed her lips, magnifying a swollen cut on the bottom.

"Hrm. I'm not sure you've entirely grasped what the book is about, Evelyn. Wouldn't you say it's more about finding freedom?"

Slouching back deep into the green lumpy couch, her baby bump became quite obvious. I glanced at her hand and noted that the engagement ring still shone unaccompanied by a wedding band. Fading bruises ran across the back of each of her hands.

That could have been me.

After I'd returned from Purlieu, I spent every visit to the toilet checking my underwear, begging my period to come. Not even Tiffany knew about the distress of those weeks. It was a sick mixture of sweet relief, in being back home, and a consuming darkness in fear of pregnancy. The day those first spots of blood appeared, I felt a happiness I'd never equated to welcoming Lady Flo before.

My stomach turned over at the memory. I would have been just like Miss Daniels: utterly trapped, her abusive fiancé imprisoning her further now that she carried his child.

I glanced back at her belly and Miss Daniels hugged her arms around herself to conceal the bump. On her tiny frame, she wouldn't be able to hide it for long.

Don't you know you deserve better?

I wanted to reach out to her, to help her leave this cruel man. Maybe the baby could be adopted? Maybe she could raise the child alone?

But what could I possibly say to her?

Miss Daniels cleared her throat and with great effort, pushed herself out of the couch. She picked up a book from her desk and returned, this time making a point to sit upright and not accentuate her stomach.

"Have you ever heard of art therapy, Evelyn?" She asked.

I searched my memory. I think I saw a news video about it one time.

"Is it that thing they do with kids after they've been in some trauma and refuse to talk? Like interpreting their drawings?"

She smiled.

"No. It's more about exploring your emotions by expressing them creatively through art. For instance, someone might use some dark-coloured ink to draw a picture of how it felt when they didn't receive the grade they needed to get into psychology at university."

Was she talking about herself? Or suggesting the same thing could happen to me with art college?

"They can then look back on the experience with fresh eyes and the help of a trained professional to unravel what they went through at that time and find healing," she said. "You should give art therapy a go."

There it was. Yet another person telling me what to do.

She reached out to hand me the book in her hands—an art journal.

I pushed down the temptation to react and took the journal from her with a sweaty hand. The sturdy black cover and metal spiral binding were just like my old art journal— the one that matched William's perfectly.

Had he orchestrated that whole episode about bumping into each other, just to have an excuse to get to know me and win me over?

Sweat started to gather on my back. I breathed quickly to keep time with my racing heartbeat.

"That sounds dumb," I said, desperately trying to calm down and gain control.

Miss Daniels mouth bobbed opened and her brow knitted together.

"You used to—" she started. "No, I shouldn't say that."
"I used to what? Be such a nice girl?"

I couldn't take it anymore. I leapt from the chair.

"How dare you? You don't know me. You don't know what I've been through. And can't you see I'm trying? I'm trying, trying, always trying, and always failing to live up to every single person's expectations of me. Why don't you look in the mirror for a second and see your own dumb choices—like staying with your jerk of a fiancé just 'cause he got you knocked up. I'm not the only one who's failing."

I chucked the art journal at the stupid winged armchair and ran from the room, slamming the door behind me, hoping, desperately hoping she would not follow.

I didn't know where I was going but didn't care. I just wanted to get as far away from it all as I could. I couldn't stand one more minute at that school with all those judging eyes.

I rushed down the concrete path, back towards the art studios and hedged a left around the side of the building, crossing the oval. I didn't hesitate at the low metal fence, but scrambled over it and crossed the road. My feet took me along the road, over a bridge, and round the bend. The local duck park came into view and I slowed.

They won't find me here.

I set myself down on a swing and swayed creakily on it as I caught my breath, intending to tick away at the minutes until school finished for the semester.

Why did everyone have to tell me what to do? It was just like William all over again and I couldn't stand it. I just wanted to do what I wanted to do, uninhibited by the opinions of other people. Why couldn't they just mind their own business?

My creaking swing was the only sound in the whole park. Even the ducks had disappeared. A strong breeze swept through and shifted the adjacent baby swing into song with mine. A cold chill shivered through me, despite the midday sun overhead. I wrapped my school blazer tighter, grateful for the winter uniform.

It was nice to be away from all that judgement, all those people telling me what to do. To finally be alone.

I looked over my shoulder. I really was alone. There was literally no-one else in this park.

The wind sent a new shiver up my spine. Maybe this wasn't such a good idea, after all.

What if William truly had survived from that broken leg and had followed me home to Earth? What if he was watching me right now, waiting to pounce and take me back to Purlieu, just like in all my nightmares?

My heart was racing again.

No, he couldn't be. If he had followed, he would have found me months ago. And there was no way he just happened to stumble upon this duck park today. Even if he did find me, he couldn't control me on Earth—he was only the master of Purlieu. And besides, I wore my new gold chain everywhere. Going to the shops to buy it was one of the first things I did after returning from Purlieu.

My hands started to shake so I pulled the cold metal object from my pocket and held it tightly in my hand. If he laid a hand on me, I'd just blow this rape whistle, startling him by the noise, and giving me enough time to run.

I placed it to my lips.

A hand gripped my shoulder.

I jumped and jerked from William's hold, blowing the whistle. An odd high-pitched half-whistle filled the silence of the park. Heat flooded my face and my heart hurt as it pounded in my chest, quickening my breath and sending a prickly feeling across my skin.

Miss Daniels was looking at me as though I had slapped her. It wasn't William at all.

I keeled over, hands to my knees, and let the whistle drop so that I could regain regular breathing. How could I be so stupid? Of course it wasn't William. He wasn't coming for me.

I was so sick of this debilitating fear as I waited for him at every turn.

I looked up at Miss Daniels and her bruised hands.

I would never let anything like that happen to me again. And I would never let William scare me again.

But if that was going to be the case, I needed to do something different, because everything I was doing wasn't working.

I think I needed to face my fears. To return to where it all started.

I knocked my shoes together, ticking over the seconds,

waiting for Dad to arrive so that Principal Terrell Torres could determine my future. I was surely going to be expelled.

The waiting room outside his office was narrow and filled with paintings, awards, and newspaper articles of past students. I'd never make the cut now.

The school bell rang for the end of semester one, just as the door at the end of the hall opened. It was Dad looking flustered and concerned.

"Hey Dad," I said with a wave and a weak smile.

"Hey, sweetheart."

Mr Torres must have been listening out, because he promptly arrived at the frame of his office door.

"Mr O'Shea," he said, reaching out to shake hands.

Dad obliged and we followed him inside. Mr Torres sat behind his desk, clasped his hands across his rotund stomach, and sighed at us as we sat opposite him. The black spiral-bound art journal lay on his desk between us.

"I'm going to cut to the chase. Due to her grades," Mr Torres said, listing each item off on his fingers, "your financial situation, attacking Mr Vân Vũ, the themes of her English essay, and now abusing the school counsellor and wagging the afternoon, Evelyn is on very, very thin ice, I'm afraid."

"Yes, but her mother's passing—it's been a difficult time," Dad said. "We're trying our hardest."

"I'm afraid it's not good enough, Mr O'Shea. We've made many accommodations for your daughter over the past eighteen months, but I fear it's been to her detriment and has actually encouraged her acting out.

"Having said that, we're willing to look the other way just one last time."

He leaned forward and turned his attention towards me for the first time, raising his finger.

"Everything needs to be perfect for the rest of the year—your grades need to improve and you need to behave yourself with the other students and the staff too."

Dad cleared his throat and also leant forward, bringing Mr Torres's attention back to him.

"Evelyn will behave herself if the other students do too," Dad said.

Mr Torres raised an eyebrow in confusion.

"Instead of demonising my daughter, this school should be investigating the causes of their students' misdemeanours." He looked at me as if asking for permission to continue. I nodded and he went on. "For instance, Evelyn wouldn't have had to defend herself if Vân had not been spreading a rumour about her."

"What kind of rumour is that?" Mr Torres asked.

"That they engaged in coitus," Dad responded.

Mr Torres's mouth parted a little and his eyes grew wide. He avoided my gaze.

"Yes, well," he said. "I can assure you that we have a comprehensive anti-bullying policy regarding behaviour that threatens the safety or wellbeing of a student."

He'd clearly used that line before.

Dad eyeballed him, maintaining his forward posture and crossed his arms across his chest.

Mr Torres glanced in my direction. "Is what your father saying true?"

I nodded.

"And is it a false accusation?"

"You've got to be kidding me," Dad said.

Mr Torres cleared his throat again and sat up a little straighter. "I'm just trying to get the facts straight," he said. "We've come to learn it best to believe young women when they come forward with such accusations. For instance the situation from last year ..." he trailed off, letting Dad simmer a moment.

"Do you want to go forward with this formally?" Mr Torres asked me.

Dad turned and looked into my eyes. He'd been an absolute warrior so far and I knew he had my back no matter what. But now it was my turn to be brave.

"What would that mean?" I asked.

"It means you'd need to put the claim in writing. And we will investigate the facts further."

"What would happen to Vân?"

Perhaps I wouldn't have to deal with his smug presence at school anymore? And with him gone, and publicly proven to be a liar, the rumours might die down?

"For Mr Vũ, it could mean suspension, maybe jeopardise his scholarship, expulsion. Depending on the extent of what is uncovered."

Vân wouldn't just get away with it—and I wouldn't have to see him at school anymore. I let out a breath I didn't realise I was holding.

I reached into my school bag and took out my phone, pulling up the post Vân had made. I glanced at Dad and then passed my phone over to Mr Torres.

"He tried to make a move on me in aikido but I wasn't interested, so I left. He posted this the next day."

Mr Torres's face dropped, for the first time softening, yet maintaining every composure of seriousness.

"I am so sorry," he said, looking grim. "On behalf of the school, I am sorry.

"We will endeavour to look into things further and Mr Vũ will be appropriately dealt with."

I nodded and made to get up.

"We're not done yet, though, Miss O'Shea."

I promptly sat down, nerves washing over me.

"Despite Mr Vũ's behaviour, there still needs to be consequences for your own behaviour. So, from the beginning of term three, you're suspended from school for two weeks."

My stomach plummeted. A suspension. I was officially one of the bad kids. The troublemakers. The dropkicks on an educational trajectory to nowhere. It seemed entirely consistent with my persona because once again, I had screwed everything up for myself.

On our way home, the silence in the car was tense. Despite all that Dad had done in defending me before Mr Torres, it didn't change the fact that I'd still done all that stuff and surely Dad was thinking up the best way to punish me for it. No internet for the entire holidays, a side of all the cooking and cleaning, and perhaps throw in a dash of curfew? After all, despite all the hard work he'd been doing to keep me at Mianjin Arts Academy financially, I put the entire thing at risk. Again.

We reached the edge of town.

"I think we both need a break from things," he finally said. "You know, this case I'm working on is really pushing my limits, and Year Twelve, it's tough. I'll take the school holidays off. Let's go somewhere tomorrow."

What kind of punishment was this?

"Let's go for a bushwalk," he finished.

Was this some kind of reverse psychology? A post-modern parenting experiment? Couldn't he just yell and get it over and done with? Not that yelling was ever really his style.

And a bushwalk, of all things? In this cold weather? Just the two of us?

I chewed on my bottom lip. Me with my warrior dad.

"Okay," I said. "But I get to pick the place."

2

THE OLD SEDAN rattled in resistance as we moved onto the highway, early morning sunlight shining in our eyes.

"Are you sure we're going the right way? All the bush trails are up the mountains," Dad said as I directed him towards the city.

"I'm sure," I said, shielding my eyes as I focused on our destination.

"So, where are we off to then?"

"It's a surprise," I said. "I'll tell you which way to go. It'll be an adventure."

"Let's not get too adventurous, now. Work has been tough on me, Evelyn. I can't take too much heart-pounding stuff these days."

I looked at him and raised an eyebrow.

"I'm serious," he said. "That case last Saturday night—it's serial. Scary stuff. You wouldn't want to know."

"Oh, but I do."

"Let me rephrase: I wouldn't want to tell you."

"So cruel. You get me all interested and then close the book on me."

"Maybe when you're older."

"I don't think you get it, Dad. I will never be as old as you."

He smirked, "Now you get it: you'll always be my little girl."

I shook my head and watched him. He did look awfully tired. The lines in his forehead had become more pronounced, even over the past few months alone.

I directed him off the highway and through a couple of one-way streets until the art gallery appeared ahead.

"Evelyn. I did mean a physical bushwalk, not a figurative one. Looking at paintings of trees and bushes and dirt is not the same as trudging among them yourself."

"Trust me, Dad. You'll get your real, live trees and bushes and dirt."

After parking in the underground car park and walking upstairs, Dad made to move towards the art gallery.

"Dad. We're not going on some figurative bushwalk. This way."

He gave me a toothy grin and I led him away from the art gallery, turning right onto the stony path of the tree tunnel. Cold wind rushed at us, flapping my windbreaker, and bringing a strong fragrance of eucalyptus to my nostrils. It was just like I remembered.

Now that we were here, I wasn't so sure I could go through with it. My heart pounded in my chest and the cold whistle in my pocket wasn't providing the sense of reassurance that it usually did. What if we ran into William?

"Why did you bring us here?" he asked.

Neither of us had been back to the cultural precinct since I'd run away.

"I don't know. It seemed like a good idea."

"We could have gone to Canungra or Samford Valley or even just Mt Coot-tha."

I avoided his eyes, heart still pounding.

"I just—I haven't been back here since. And I just needed to see it again," I said.

"See what?"

Mum's gold locket was dangling around his neck. I touched the gold chain around my own neck and looked up into his concerned face. I could face this—face William, with Dad by my side.

"Where he took me."

Dad's eyes grew wide. He gulped.

"You really thought it was a good idea to go for a little trip down memory lane?" His voice was strained, rising.

"I'm just sick of being so afraid all the time. I thought if maybe I went back and saw it with fresh eyes—with you—that it might help."

"Oh, sweetheart."

He reached out and pulled me into a quick bear hug.

"Will he be there?" He asked, releasing me.

I bit my lip.

"I don't know."

He nodded.

"Am I bigger than him?" Dad asked.

I grimaced and nodded.

"Am I stronger than him?"

He tensed his broad shoulders. I nodded again.

"Well then, we have nothing to worry about. If this is what you want, then let's go."

He pulled me into another bear hug and planted a kiss on my head.

"He won't ever hurt you again, sweetheart."

I let out a shuddering breath and we broke apart, continuing down the path.

"I had always thought he'd just picked you up from the gallery that day and driven off someplace. They didn't really search for you beyond the cultural centre precinct."

I let his words hang.

"So that whole time, you were here, in the bush?" He asked. "No, wait. I'm sorry. I promised you when you came back that I wouldn't ask any questions."

I let out a breath of relief and we continued in silence.

Battling the wind, I turned back every so often to

measure our distance, remembering how obscure the path into the bush had been. The end of the path behind us was now just a dot of light, so I started looking about to the right for a small opening, half-expecting not to find one. Part of me doubted the path—and the Hidden Grove—even existed. Maybe I was insane and had concocted the whole episode in my own sick imagination? Maybe William had drugged me, and my memories of Purlieu were just a drug trip?

But there it was, a break in the scrub just wide enough for one person to navigate through at a time. I took a deep breath. I could do this.

"Okay, Dad. Are you ready for some real adventure?"

"Is it time to get our feet dirty?"

We looked at each other apprehensively.

"Yes Dad, it's time." I gave him a weak smile.

"I am serious, though. Before today is done, I promise you, I will take my shoes off and stick my feet in the dirt."

A giggle escaped my lips. He smiled too, breaking the tension.

I stepped off the stony path and headed into the bushland. The well-worn trail revealed the way with each step. The overgrowth was just as I remembered it: trees tumbling into one another with branches overlapping and roots weaving together. There was just enough light filtering through the canopy to guide our way.

A whipbird sounded overhead, cutting through the sound of breaking twigs and crunching leaves as we trudged along.

"Pew-pew!" Dad said, " I love the laser bird. It's my favourite."

"It's a whipbird, Dad."

"Sounds more like a laser to me."

The whipbird sounded again.

"Pewwww-pew! If we'd had laser guns at work instead of Tasers, that serial perp never would have gotten away."

I stopped on the path to turn and look at him.

"What do you mean?"

He scratched the back of his head, looking sheepish.

"Sorry. I promised myself I wouldn't bring it up."

"Come on, Dad. If you're gonna help me with my thing, I'm gonna help you with your thing. We're here to let off steam, right?"

He thought for a moment and sighed, his shoulders relaxing.

"It's this serial sex offender. We found another victim—another girl your age, almost looked like you—on Wednesday night as he was fleeing the scene. He'd set the building alight." He looked off into the bush, lost in thought.

"The smell of the burning building is still too fresh in my memory."

His jaw tensed and he reached out to steady himself on a nearby branch.

"I never used to believe in capital punishment but this guy is a sicko."

The branch snapped in his grip and he returned his attention to me like I'd never even been there. It was really out of character for him, forever the forgiving type. It made me uneasy.

"Evelyn, please be careful."

I raised my eyebrows. I was being careful—I'd brought him along for this trip after all.

"You are beautiful. And these guys only see the beauty on the outside. They only want one thing."

I laughed, "Dad, I'm eighteen. I've heard it all before."

"Yes, but you haven't heard it from me."

"I don't need to hear it from you. I see it in movies and on the internet and every year they send a sex-ed person to speak to us."

"On the internet? You're not looking at pornography, are you?"

"Gross, Dad. Porn is lame."

Despite the cool breeze through the bush, my face was

hot and sweaty. So was his.

"Well, just be careful, okay? Believe their actions, not their words."

"Okay," I said, turning back and continuing on the path, desperate to hide my face from this conversation.

"Because you could have any guy you wanted. You're beautiful."

"You have to say that, you're my dad."

"I'm serious," he said. "Don't settle."

We carried on in uncomfortable silence for a long while. Finally, Dad broke it.

"I had no idea this bush ran so deep, and so close to the city. It seems so unlikely."

"I know. It's almost ethereal."

He started to whistle the Robin Song.

It helped ease my growing nerves of what lay ahead.

Sure enough, in the distance the path opened out to reveal two old trees intertwined with one another, forming an arch. My heart skipped a beat. I wasn't insane after all. Dad's whistling stopped abruptly.

"Hey—look at that!" he said.

I took a deep breath and kept walking, straight through the arch, head held high. A veil lifted from my eyes to reveal perfect rows of towering trees, each with their little quirks—the one directly in front seemed frail, the next one along spartan. The Hidden Grove, with its hidden powers.

I heard Dad's footsteps following behind me into the Hidden Grove. He sucked in a breath.

"Impossible!" he said.

I didn't have a chance to explain the magic to him or how the trees led as portals to other worlds. All of my senses heightened as I focused my attention on the grove for any sign of William. I hurried along in the direction of the Purlieu tree with Dad scrambling behind.

I passed the tree leading to the world flooded by rain where Tiffany and I had been stuck in the mud while being pursued by William. Then there was the world with the warehouse on the beach followed by the tree to Celoso with its impenetrable wall. We turned right and passed a tree with low-hanging grey tendrils of old man's beard, signifying the Bayartai tree where the wild natives had tried to burn me alive. I'd only seen these strange and terrifying worlds because William had lied about which was the Earth tree, the tree that led back home. All the same, I was grateful for it—that pursuit by him had revealed one key piece of information that without it, I would have been all the more haunted these past months: William's power ceased at the border of his world.

There in front on the left was the Purlieu tree. I stopped and stared at the white lichen and the worn branches and let out a shaky breath. William's power did not exist here in the Hidden Grove of Earth.

I don't know what I'd expected to find. Perhaps that it had shrivelled up like some of the other trees where the master had used too much power. But there it was, just as it had been three months ago, standing proudly, beckoning.

"This is just incredible," Dad said, catching up. "They're all the same."

He wandered on past me, looking up in awe.

"Wow, except for this one here," his voice echoed through the stillness.

I followed him and found him standing by the Earth tree. It was wider, grander than the rest of the trees. But I knew that if I were to climb it right now, I wouldn't find a portal at the top because we were already on Earth. After all, you can't walk through a doorway the same way twice.

The Earth tree started to shake. I looked up just in time to see a shadow cast over me and a young man falling from the lowest branch, knocking me down, thrusting my head into the grass. William had come to get me. What was I thinking, coming back to the Hidden Grove? He'd been here, biding his time, just waiting to take me back to Purlieu. I was doomed.

I blinked the grass away from my eyes and rolled over.

He was dressed in a sleeveless mustard tunic, his skin stark white and sickly like candle wax, a shock of platinum blonde hair tied back into a ponytail. It wasn't William at all.

The young man's blue eyes were wide with surprise. He turned to survey Dad and those eyes locked on the locket dangling from Dad's neck. He sprang to his feet and yanked the gold locket from around Dad's neck.

"Hey!" Dad yelled.

Dad lurched out to grab him but the young man smashed a ceramic vial against the base of the tree. Thick, grey smoke erupted and filled the space between us. He turned and disappeared, headed away from the Earth tree.

Dad helped me to my feet.

"Are you alright?" he asked.

I broke through the paralysis, annoyed I'd shut down when faced with what I thought was my fears.

"Yes."

"He took your mother's locket," he said.

Tears welled in his eyes. He hesitated, turned on the spot, and raced after the thief.

Through the clearing smoke and the bouncing branches above, I spotted the young man scampering up a tree several over. Dad had spotted him too and was making his way up the tree. My stomach sank.

"Give it back!" he yelled.

"No, Dad. Stop!"

What if that tree led to a world on different time? Like when I'd gone to Bayartai for not even twenty-four hours and returned to Purlieu only to find that weeks had passed.

There was no way I was going to wait around for Dad to return—who knew how long that could be? I'd much rather be stuck in a world with an unfavourable time difference and be gone from Earth forever, but with Dad, than to be on Earth indefinitely without him.

I pushed my resisting body into a quick sprint across the grass to the tree. Ignoring all my previous fears of heights, I began the climb, a long way behind them both.

Up, up, up I scampered, clinging to the branches and then launching myself onto the next one above, desperate to close the gap between us.

The young man had reached the top of the tree and Dad had caught up to him. Just as he was about to grab him, the young man disappeared and Dad toppled forward after him, disappearing too.

Even though I knew they'd both gone through the portal, the sight was still disconcerting enough to make my stomach drop. I sucked in a deep breath and continued up the tree after them.

It felt like an age that I was alone in the grove, struggling to make quick work of reaching the bough of the tree. I tried not to meditate upon the potential time difference or that I could be stepping into mortal peril or a trap. Finally, body shaking, I stood on the bough of the tree, a flat space only a few paces wide. I stepped across the centre of the bough and through the invisible portal. Lightning on pause filled my vision and disappeared as quickly as it came as I planted my foot on the other side.

I never thought I'd have to do this again.

3

DOWN THE OTHER side of the tree and on the grassy grid of the Hidden Grove, I turned about in all directions. Dad was nowhere to be seen. Were those few minutes between when we'd each crossed the portal into this world enough to separate us for forever?

"Dad?" I called out with a shaky voice.

I moved into a run in the direction of the archway, panic rising, tightening my chest.

I could hear pounding feet and heavy breathing. There, between two trees at the end of the row, flashed the thief, followed closely by Dad. Relief washed over me—the master of this world clearly didn't use much power because there was next to no time delay.

I swung around the last tree and was met with blinding light shining through the archway ahead. My eyes strained to focus and I couldn't even tell if Dad had gone through but I ploughed on anyway, sprinting through the archway to the unknown world beyond.

Like an ominous golden eye in the sky, the sun beat down on the surface of a stony ochre desert. The plain ran into the horizon in all directions, bouncing the light onto me, scorching my skin from all angles, and sucking the moisture from my lips. I shielded my eyes and squinted desperately through the cloud of disturbed yellow-brown dust that surrounded me as I pounded forward.

"Dad?" I called.

The land was entirely barren, apart from some scattered rocks, and it seemed to stretch on forever. There was no sign of life. Maybe there weren't any locals. Surely no-one could possibly survive this heat for long.

If only I'd taken the time to tell him about the Hidden Grove and what would happen if he were to climb one of the trees. Then he wouldn't have chased the young man, he would have just let mum's locket go and we'd be on our way back home again by now.

There, directly ahead, through the clearing dust, Dad was standing, stock-still, looking about in confusion. I ran to meet him.

"I don't understand," he said. "Where are we?"

"I can explain everything," I said.

The dust cleared some more and the thief darted around and disappeared behind a large boulder ahead.

"He has your mother's locket. It's all I have left of her."

Dad sped off again after the thief.

"No, Dad. Wait!" I called, running after him.

He disappeared behind the boulder as the thief had done.

A moment later I reached the boulder too. Behind it was a hidden fissure in the surface of the desert with steps carved out of the rock below in varying shades of light yellow-brown like turmeric. It was a secret tunnel—just like the one that led down to William's lair. I sucked in a deep breath in fear but pushed on, stepping down and down and down into the cool darkness below. Blood pounded in my ears and breathing became hard—really hard. I stifled a sob and clutched at the hand-carved tunnels for support.

I couldn't let it get to me. It was a different tunnel, on an entirely different world, and Dad was just ahead of me. William was not here and I would make it out, eventually. I could do this. For Dad's sake.

Finally, I touched down on the last step and the tunnel levelled out. Ahead I could see a bend where the thief was about to round. There was light, and a dull roar, which increased in volume with my every step—like thousands of footsteps and inaudible chatter. My nostrils were invaded by the smell of incense, sweaty bodies, and dirt. I could hear a commotion of angry voices in a foreign tongue—maybe something European? Scandinavian? Perhaps Icelandic?

I rounded the bend a moment after Dad and the path opened on an underground citadel.

To my right and left were towering walls of limestone. The wall on the right had a gate at the end, and standing before the gate were red-haired and blonde-haired men in matching ochre hooded capes, like uniforms, batons bobbing from their hips. They were pointing and yelling down the slope at Dad. One turned and saw me, and like a chain reaction, each of his buddies turned and started yelling at me too. It appeared we were not welcome in this world.

Trembling for what might happen if they were to catch us, I sprinted past them and ran down the slope after Dad. I could hear the men armed with batons move into action behind me, giving chase, just as I chased Dad and Dad chased the thief.

The towering wall corridor ended and the cavern opened up to show a full view of the citadel. Stone-carved houses were neatly arranged row by row down the slope either side of a central road, leading into a bustling city centre. Thousands of red-haired and blonde-haired people dressed in shades of ochre with sickly white skin glowed all about the streets.

We reached halfway down the slope, where the buildings grew in size and shabbiness. Ahead was a junction with a footbridge separating the opposing directions of foot traffic, opening up to two immense buildings, and beyond that, a central marketplace, more city buildings, and smaller houses continuing down into the depths of the cavern.

The thief slipped through the throng of people who had crossed the bridge, heading away from the marketplace. They jumped aside with shock when Dad and then I pushed in past them. The gaunt, frail bodies that didn't move in time tumbled like bowling pins. The crowd only thickened as I forced my way through, desperate to close the gap between Dad and me and grow the gap between me and the men armed with batons giving chase, but with every call of the men, the crowd parted and made us more exposed.

The thief led us up onto the overpass bridge but a man armed with a baton appeared at the other end of the bridge, blocking our path. He yelled and pointed at the thief and as I broke through the crowd, finally within reach of Dad, the man looked at me instead.

"Stans!" he yelled at me in his thick foreign tongue.

I continued after Dad. The man on the bridge looked frustrated and now turned to Dad, who was about to close in on the thief, and yelled in his direction instead, *"STANS!"*

Dad froze on the spot.

The thief didn't hesitate—he climbed over the railing and jumped down into the path below of men wheeling carts half-filled with produce. I caught up to Dad, who was still suspended in mid-action.

That man armed with a baton wasn't just any man. He was the master of this world. He had used his power to force Dad to stop moving.

I quickly removed my gold chain and flung it around Dad's neck. Like magic, Dad became unstuck and turned to me.

"Evelyn—we can't let him get away!"

He moved one leg over the railing.

"More importantly, we can't let them catch us!" I said.

I pointed at the men armed with batons that were closing in on us. Dad stopped and looked over his shoulder. It seemed to be the first time he had registered we were being chased.

"Why are they chasing us?"

"Because we're not welcome here," I said. "Dad, we gotta jump!"

The men were mere metres away and the crowd had parted and thinned, making way for them.

Dad helped me swing my legs over to join him, ready to jump after the thief, but his pant-leg was caught on the railing. I fumbled, frantically trying to get it loose for him. The men closed in.

Dad pushed me off the bridge.

I landed on all fours, taking an elderly man down with me, and scraping both knees in the process.

"Go, Evelyn! Run!" he cried.

I rolled over, forcing my aching body to look up to the bridge for Dad.

"No, Dad!"

The men had enveloped him, cutting him loose from the railing. They hauled him back onto their side. A hessian sack went over his head and they tied his wrists together. All the while he writhed and kicked and yelled, but it was one man against five.

"Run!" he gave a muffled yell as they dragged him away.

I got to my feet, but I couldn't just leave him.

Hands were grabbing at me from behind. Finally, William had come forward to reveal himself—he had waited until the moment I was without gold and now he would take me to his new lair.

No. I couldn't let him. I wouldn't let him.

I turned myself around, ready to take him on, but it was just the crowd of pale-skinned locals bumping into me, eyes set on their destinations; I was in their way.

The men on the bridge were yelling and pointing about, trying to organise themselves to capture me next.

I scrambled through the crowd, away from the bustling path to the city buildings, and entered a side alley between two rickety shop houses with washing hanging between them. I ventured beyond the washing for added cover, pulling a woollen bed sheet aside as I sucked in air.

There, keeled over and gathering his breath, was the thief.

I rushed forward and pushed him up against the wall, getting a good look at him for the first time. His smooth milky face was slim with a pointed nose and chin. Despite the look of surprise on his face, a glimmer of a joke hid behind his eyes. I softened at his gaze, heat rising up my neck to my ears.

I would not be influenced. I tightened my grip and he yelped in pain.

"YOU! Because of you, my father has been captured by—by—by—" I yelled.

He pulled a hand free and shoved it over my mouth, stifling my accusations.

The sound of yelling—like that of the men armed with batons—came closer to the alley, along with heavy running footsteps. The yelling and the footsteps passed the alley and became distant. The thief let out a breath and released the hold on my mouth.

"Home. Leave. Go home," he said in clunky English.

He was sending me away? He had no right. It was his fault I was here and that Dad was captured. And there was no way I was going anywhere until I had Dad back. And I swear this thief was going to help me.

I stepped aside and pulled his arm, pivoting him until I'd pinned him to the ground. Knee to chest, I searched about his tunic pockets until my fingers wrapped around mum's locket.

"Hallo!" he yelled, "Erm—give it back!"

He squirmed under my joint lock, attempting to reach for the locket. I pulled my whistle out and put it to my lips.

"I'll use it. I swear, I'll use it," I said, mouth wrapped around the whistle. I didn't actually intend to call the attention of the men with batons, but the thief didn't know that.

He stopped moving immediately and stared, the glimmer of a joke vanishing from his eyes.

"Please. There is no need for weapons," he said. "I will stop."

A weapon? Maybe they didn't have whistles in this place. I raised the locket above his head.

"You want it?" I asked. "You can have it if you help me. Starting with explaining what the heck kind of situation I've walked into with this world and ending with getting my father back."

His eyes darted between the gleaming gold of the locket and the whistle between my teeth.

"If you try to take it from me prematurely, I will use this." I tapped the whistle.

"*Oke*," he said.

I let go and moved out of arm's reach from him. Face screwed up in pain, he rubbed his chest where my knee had been. He looked me up and down, for the first time taking me and my hiking gear in.

"You stand out too much," he said, getting to his feet and reaching for the washing line, grabbing a tunic like his own plus a scarf, and tossing them to me.

"Dress," he said. "*Portforbud.* Erm, street ban. Erm, curfew. Is looming. You dress, then we go to the *spill-ehal.*"

He turned around and slipped to the other side of the washing line.

I adjusted the scarf around my head as we walked along through the city, trying to mirror a woman ahead and how she fashioned it. I wondered how much pigment you'd need to get that particular shade of ochre she wore. Probably just a nick of blue and red in yellow.

I tripped on the tunic. It was too long for me, but I was grateful it kept my neon joggers from view.

I had no idea what a '*spill-ehal*' was or whether I could trust that the thief wasn't taking me to the men armed with batons. I could only hope that the promise of the gold locket was enough to keep me out of trouble until I got my bearings in this place.

He kept glancing at the gold locket that now hung around my neck. I instinctively wrapped my hand around it, anxious that he might attempt to steal it again.

He frowned, looked about, waiting for a decent gap in the crowd, and hissed, "*Skjule* … erm … hide, you must hide it."

I slipped the locket beneath the tunic, enjoying the coolness of the metal on my skin. Despite the depth we'd travelled below the surface of the desert and the breathy, sleeveless tunic I'd inherited, my back was completely soaked with sweat. This world was hot and dry in a way that I just wasn't used to after growing up with humid Queensland summers my whole life.

After crossing the main thoroughfare and entering another stone city block, the buildings thinned and became unkempt with worn signage, a thick layer of dust on every surface, and rusting door hinges.

The city streets were almost empty now and those that were left moved with a greater sense of urgency. The clothing in varying shades of ochre made them almost blend into the buildings.

The thief glanced over his shoulder and approached one of the multistorey buildings but rounded the corner of it and opened a hidden metal door. I followed closely behind.

A dull babel met my ears. In the dank room, men were huddled around tables throwing down small stone objects. An elderly fellow beamed and did a jig of celebration at the table nearest us. Apparently, '*spill-ehal*' meant 'gambling den'.

The thief directed me to a table in the back and went to order drinks.

The men were absorbed by their games, bent at the back in concentration, the plaited beards of the older ones resting on the tables. It looked like some kind of odd-shaped dice game.

The thief approached with stone mugs, one carrying a

mead of sorts and the other a translucent glistening red liquid. He passed the latter to me and our fingers brushed. Goosebumps popped up across the back of my hand and ran up my arm. We locked eyes. He let go of the mug, cleared his throat, and took a seat on the opposite stone bench. I sat back a little in my chair and eyed the drink suspiciously. The red liquid looked like a cross between raspberry lemonade and the syrupy thickness of blood.

"It is good. Comforting drink," he said.

I bit my lip that was still chapped from the desert above. I was tired and thirsty.

I leant forward and sipped tentatively. Sweetness filled my mouth and a sensation of relief washed down through my body as I swallowed. I took another sip. The wounds on my knees and the scar on my weak hand started to itch. I took another sip. My scar tingled.

"I'm sorry," he said. "I didn't mean it to happen. Your *vater* wasn't meant to follow. And then he *verhaftet* ... erm, got arrested."

He bowed his head. He seemed sincere.

"When I saw the *gull* ... erm, gold ... I didn't think."

"But you've already got gold of your own," I said, nodding to the delicate chain links that flashed in the gap of his collar every so often.

"Why do you need it? And what's going to happen to my dad now? What will they do to him? Why aren't we welcome here?" I asked. I didn't know where to start, which question was most important.

"For my kin," he said. "And he will surely be sacrificed. There's nothing that can be done."

I had lifted the mug to take another sip of the delightful drink, but it dribbled down my chin instead as my jaw hung loose.

"Sacrificed?"

"When someone is *verhaftet*—arrested—they do not get released, unless the gods say otherwise. Your *vater* will be hung during the Ofre Arstid. It begins in a few days. They don't like visitors here. That's why they chased you. If you're not careful, they will get you too. You need to leave."

I wiped my mouth and shook my head in defiance.

"I'm not leaving my dad. And you promised to help me get him out. Then I'll leave—with him."

He shifted in his seat and looked at where the locket was hiding beneath my tunic.

"Surely there's something we can do," I said.

"They like prison breaks as much as visitors."

"Do you even want the gold back?" I asked. He wasn't even trying.

He focused on the mead in front of him and took a long, slow mouthful before setting it down again and looking back at me.

"I will try help. It just may not be possible."

"It has to be possible. I'm not leaving without him."

He shrugged his shoulders and sighed. A blaring horn sounded and echoed outside.

"What was that?"

"Curfew has fallen. We can't be seen outside again until daybreak."

It was night-time?

"We're stuck here?"

"Not necessarily."

"So, we can still try to get Dad back tonight?"

"They'll have him in a holding cell overnight at Rådhus, which is full of *hlif*. When they transfer him to Fengsel at curfew break, that is best opportunity."

I was finding his broken English hard to follow.

"Hang on—what? Where?"

He dipped a finger in his mead and drew a rough map on the dusty table—two large rectangles with lines between them and beside them. He pointed to a spot above the right-hand rectangle.

"We are here—*spill-ehal*."

He pointed to the left-hand rectangle.

"Rådhus, erm how do you say in English? Law services?

They have many holding cell. Many *hlif*."

"What are *hlif*?"

"Erm, ones that chased us."

"Oh, the men with the batons? Like guards?"

He nodded, and then pointed to the right-hand rectangle.

"Fengsel here. Erm, like prison."

The door to the gambling den opened and two men in hooded cloaks with batons in hand entered. I froze. The thief turned to see what had caught my eye and quickly wiped out his drawing on the table.

The *hlif* approached the bartender, removing their hoods, and exchanged a few words. One was tall and thin, the other broad. The bartender nodded and they turned and started approaching each table. Nobody in the room seemed to take any notice of their presence until they interrupted their game. A murmur of disgruntled patrons echoed from each table they approached. They edged closer and closer to our table. I clutched at my mug to steady my hands.

The thief pre-empted their approach and waved them over to our table, smiling broadly and greeting them in his language. The *hlif* looked apprehensive as they wandered over. The broad one stopped beside me and leant against the table, his fat fingers gripping his baton. His hands looked like they could crush my neck. The thief spoke to them jovially, smiling and finishing with a laugh. The tall one asked him a question and the thief shrugged his shoulders, giving a short answer with another laugh. The tall one frowned and turned to me and asked what sounded like the same question.

I didn't know what to do or say.

The thief cut in but the tall one slapped him silent and turned promptly back to me. The broad one reached out and grabbed my wrist, pulling at me.

"No!" I yelled.

The grip on my wrist tightened and the *hlif* yanked at my arm. I shouldn't have spoken in English. They were going to arrest me. I would end up in prison alongside my dad and there'd be no-one to rescue either of us then.

Still clutching my drink, I swung my arm around and smashed him over the head. The stone mug cracked and fell. The *hlif* let go of me and moved back, dropping his baton. He held his head and stepped about in a dazed stupor.

The thief threw his mug at the tall *hlif*, cracking him square in the eye. He collapsed and writhed about in agony.

The thief pulled the scarf from my head and wrapped it around the wrists of the broad one, tugging his arms behind his back, like handcuffs. He made a strong knot and pushed the *hlif* to the ground on his face.

What kind of world is this?

Despite the moans and frustrated groans of the *hlif*, it was disturbingly quiet. The gamblers had stopped mid-game and were staring. The bartender clicked his tongue.

The thief threw down a ceramic vial and smoke erupted throughout the room. I couldn't see anything. A hand wrapped around mine and tugged.

"Come," said the thief.

I couldn't move. He tugged a little harder and finally my feet stumbled forward through the smoke, tripping on the *hlif* on the floor as I went. The smoke cleared in front of me just as the bartender opened a cupboard behind the counter; it was a trap door, and the thief ferried me through it down into a narrow passage cut from stone. The door swung closed behind us, taking the light with it, and the dulled sound of resumed games met my ears.

The thief unwrapped his fingers from mine and lit a lantern hanging by the door. He turned back to me, light dancing off the side of his face.

"You okay?" he whispered.

He'd saved us—both of us.

I couldn't help but be a little impressed—terrified, yes, but mostly impressed—by how he'd handled himself back there, despite his thin stature. He was clever and resourceful and cheeky, with no hesitation, no mercy. It was life or death. Fight or flight. And he was every part capable of getting the job done. He was definitely a good ally to have to get Dad back.

"I don't even know your name," I said.

He smiled wryly and extended his hand. "Eirik Eik," he said.

We moved down the tunnel. I hitched up the tunic and breathed in and out as steadily as I could, determined not to let the memories of the secret tunnel to William's lair get the better of me. My breath shuddered out.

"Don't be afraid. The tunnels are the safest place in *Verja*. The *hlif* do not know of it, though they suspect."

Verja? That's what this place was called, then?

"Eirik, why did the bartender help us escape?"

Eirik stopped and looked at me.

"Very dire, if they had caught us. Bard cover for us. He always does."

"What do you mean?"

"Well, we aren't the first to bring *hlif* into the *spill-ehal*," he chuckled and kept walking.

"But why would he help?"

"The *spill-ehal* is like a safe house for the Uppreisn. It started with this tunnel system beneath the city, a hideout for lawbreakers and the homeless, but it's more than that now."

"The Uppreisn?"

"*Já*, the rebellion movement. They want to overthrow the government. They're responsible for the Rådhus explosion, the *ómagi* mercy killings, and the Thor's Day riots."

"They sound delightful," I said.

"But that was all child's play. They have much bigger plans in motion and the *hlif* still haven't been able to find them."

He stopped once more and held the lantern up to where

the wall met the roof. There was a gap where the corner should have been and at intervals, a mirror angled down into the tunnel like a series of rectangular periscopes. The reflection running across the mirrors showed the empty city streets above.

"What I don't understand is why we can't just negotiate my dad's release. You know, can't you just tell them that it was an honest mistake that we ended up here and we would leave right away and never return?"

"It's not that simple."

We walked on for a while.

"They really don't like visitors here. The Gothi, erm, the chief master, is very protective. He doesn't want our secrets leaked to the outside world. I've personally seen the reception a foreigner was given by him. There is no negotiation."

We reached a bend.

"I have to leave the light here," he said, placing it on a hook at head height.

We followed the bend around into the dark. As my eyes adjusted, the mirrors above reflected enough light to guide our path ahead. Eirik put his finger to his lips and edged slowly, cautiously along now, gazing up at the mirrors as he went. He stopped and peered closely, and I joined him—as best as my shorter stature would allow. Above the tunnel was an open area with a looming dark building some twenty metres away. Off to the left was another immense building. These were the buildings by the marketplace I'd seen earlier and must be what Eirik referred to as Fengsel and Rådhus. *Hlif* marched in pairs around the prison building every couple of minutes. My skin prickled with goosebumps.

Eirik waved me on and we went back around the bend the way we'd come.

"We wait until curfew breaks and intercept the prisoner transfer from Rådhus—erm, law services—to Fengsel—erm … prison. If they get him in Fengsel, there is no hope."

"What's the transfer gonna look like?"

"Two *hlif* will take him, shackled, from Rådhus just after curfew breaks. When they reach Fengsel, one holds him while the other unlocks Fengsel. Then they lock him inside."

"So, we have to take on two full-grown men."

"Plus the *hlif* on duty circling Fengsel."

Four men, minimum. It was ambitious, but what other option did we have? And if Eirik was right, this was the only and best chance we'd have of freeing Dad. Plus, Eirik had literally just outsmarted two *hlif* in the gambling den without breaking a sweat.

Eirik reached into one of his many pockets and handed me two ceramic gas vials.

"Fela. They're made by the Uppreisn. Masters can't control you if they can't see you."

He gave a cheeky grin. My stomach dropped.

That little fact would have been really helpful when I was trying to escape William. I let it settle for a moment, racking my brain over my time with William to see if it rang true. The ice maidens hadn't attacked me when I'd returned from the mountains, but what about when I'd found that trap door? I'd felt compelled to finish the sweeping instead of open it and escape—and William had been nowhere in sight.

"Okay, so how do we get close enough to gas the place if there's no protection around the building?"

"The market square is right above us—they put the prison across from it so that everyone would always have to look at it and be reminded what would happen if they step out of line. We take cover there and when the *hlif* get close to Fengsel, lob the vials of gas and cross the gap while they are confused. You grab your *vater*. I get keys. We come back here before they know what's happened."

It seemed simple enough, but my stomach churned. We had one chance to make this work.

He sat down in the tunnel and leant his head against the wall.

"Now we wait."

I sat down too.

"Your English is getting better."

He shrugged. "Just a little rusty."

I wanted to ask how he knew English if they didn't like visitors in this world but I didn't really care—in a few hours I'd have Dad back with me and we'd be on our way home. I didn't need to get involved in the politics of this place.

Eirik shook my shoulder.

"Don't touch me," I said, flinching. The feeling of muscular hands gripping my shoulder sent my mind back to memories of William clutching at me. I shuddered and turned my eyes upon Eirik, forcing myself to remember where I was and what I was doing.

I'd drifted in and out of fitful sleep for a few hours at least, afraid I'd sleep through curfew and lose our chance of saving Dad. Now I had a crick in my neck.

"Curfew will break soon."

He motioned towards the bend in the tunnel. Soft light was spilling from it.

Eirik put the lamp out and led me once more around the bend. There was a staircase halfway down the corridor that I hadn't noticed before. We watched in the mirror until the *hlíf* circled behind the prison block. Eirik motioned to the stairs and led the way up and through another trapdoor. This one was concealed on the other side by a woven rug in the heart of a root vegetable stall. We replaced the trapdoor behind us and slipped through the market stalls until we were directly opposite the padlocked entrance to the prison, taking up a vantage point behind a wheeled cart next to a stall with varying sizes of stone pots. Eirik was right—the prison had been designed with three stone walls and one wall of floor-to-ceiling bars so that you could see directly into it from the marketplace. The far-right corner was shrouded in shadow where light didn't reach and I could just make out the silhouettes of sleeping prisoners.

Scattering the landscape surrounding us were large mirrors on stilts the size of soccer goals. They'd cleverly angled them in the citadel cavern so that as the sun rose on the desert above, it bounced off the mirrors and filled the whole cavity with indirect daylight.

Rådhus was the only building in the city made of limestone and it shone gleaming white in the light of day, compared to the dull yellows and browns of the stone and mud buildings beside it. It had grand pillars lining the front, breaking in the middle to leave a gap for a staircase that led to a pair of wooden double doors.

A road passed between Rådhus and Fengsel to the bridge that Dad had been captured on. I stared at it, replaying the moment when I looked up to see the *hlif* put the bag on his head. I couldn't take back that moment, but I could try to make things right.

The deep rumble of a horn echoed through the chamber. Eirik looked at me and raised his eyebrows. Curfew had lifted.

Like clockwork, the door to the building—Rådhus— opened. Four ochre-clad bodies with a fifth body hidden in the middle exited Rådhus. It was four *hlif* leading my father, not just the two we'd anticipated.

He didn't look like my father anymore though. I caught glimpses of him between the bobbing hooded heads of the *hlif* as he walked barefoot to the prison. His face was bruised and bloody and his legs wobbled with each step. They'd shaved his head, covered his skin in a white powder, and removed my gold chain from around his neck. His wrists were shackled with a chain and padlock running between them over the top of a long-sleeved starched white jumpsuit.

A sob escaped my mouth. They'd beaten him senseless—my father the cop, the man that could tower over you in height and power. The strongest, bravest person I knew, now weak and defeated. How could they?

I gripped at the cart we'd hidden behind to hold myself together, but it shifted under my weight and started to roll precariously away from the markets, pulling me along with it. I took hold of it tighter and drove it forward at the group as they made their way towards the prison. They scattered about as it came crashing towards them and I finally let go, sending it through the middle, the *hlif* holding Dad jumping to one side, two *hlif* jumping to the other, and running over the last one with a sickening crunch.

Eirik scrambled up behind me and launched himself at the *hlif* with the keys. I went the other way and helped Dad to his feet. He was dizzy and disoriented.

"Evelyn!" Eirik called, throwing the keys to me.

I caught them with my strong hand but didn't even get a chance to fumble to find the right key to Dad's shackles because the *hlif* had recovered and was now grabbing me from behind while another was wrestling Dad to the ground. Dad was too weak to fend him off and I could do nothing to help him because the *hlif* had wrapped his arm around my neck. I grabbed his wrist, elbowed him in the stomach, and tried to twist around until I had him in a shoulder lock but it didn't work. He slipped out of my grip and easily overthrew me, pulling me back into a headlock. I choked and coughed as his grip tightened and my head became lighter. He snatched the keys from my hand. His baton swayed precariously at his waist. I pulled at it, but it was attached and wouldn't come loose. I bucked and thrashed, and swung the baton about at his body, connecting with his groin. His cry filled my ear as he pulled me down with him, falling and shrinking into a ball in pain.

I gasped for breath and rolled off him, looking frantically for Eirik. Dad was pinned down by the other *hlif*. The two that were on guard duty rounded the corner of the prison and rushed to his aid, retrieving the keys from the *hlif* groaning by my side. They promptly took Dad, still struggling, over to the prison and locked him inside.

Hooded *hlif* started streaming from Rådhus in pairs and,

shocked by the sight, came running. Locals were exiting their homes to see what all the commotion was.

"Evelyn, it's no use. We have to go!" Eirik called.

A couple of the *hlif* coming from Rådhus started yelling commandingly at us.

I ran up beside Eirik who had a *hlif* at his feet with his head stuck in a pot.

The group of *hlif* across the compound continued to yell commands. The ground began to rumble. Rock formations sprung up in a circle around us, blocking us from the prison and trapping us with both of the guard duty *hlif* who had lunged forward at us.

"Run, Evelyn. Run!" Dad yelled with a slur.

But I couldn't—we were trapped.

The *hlif* looked at us, equally surprised by the rock prison that had suddenly erected. Eirik took a *fela* from his pocket and smashed it between the *hlif* and us. Thick grey smoke flooded the space and Eirik tugged on the back of my tunic, pulling me over one side of the rock formation with him. We ran the length of the prison, rounded its side, and then went into the city streets beyond.

Eirik skidded into a side alley. I tried to keep pace as he led me through another hidden entrance and into the silence of the secret tunnels below.

4

I SLID DOWN the wall of the tunnel and collapsed, holding my head in my hands. We'd failed. We'd been so close, but now Dad was in prison.

Eirik looked just as defeated as I felt.

"I'm sorry we couldn't save him," he said.

"You don't have to feel guilty."

"But I do."

"It's all my fault. I should have followed the plan. I, I, I—" I faltered. "It's always my fault."

"Hey, don't be so hard on yourself."

I looked at him with exasperation. I'd just blown our best chance. Couldn't he see what a major screw-up I was? How I brought things on myself? With Cameron, with William and Purlieu, with Vân, and now with my dad and this place.

"I mean it," Eirik said. "You were brave to fight the *hlif*."

"Ignorant and stupid, don't you mean?" I said. "I heard them—it was more than one voice that used the power of the master to erect that rock prison. How can there be more than one master?"

Sounds of yelling and running filled the streets above. The *hlif* were clearly very angry we'd escaped—twice now.

"Keep it down," he whispered, looking at the nearest rectangular periscope. "Let's go somewhere else."

He led the way down the tunnel, back where we came from.

"During the festival of Mánis—erm—the Moon Festival, we have this ceremony called the Conferring where the masters share their power. They say it's to dilute it, to keep their power in check. But I think they just want to grow their ability to control the nation, because they can be in more places at once. That's how they keep everyone in line."

We rounded a bend in the passage, and he stopped walking.

"They have a rotation roster where a quarter of the masters are on duty at all times, but no-one knows which *hlif* pairings they're in. Just another way to make us fear them and play by their rules. And of course, they don't share their power with just anyone. They share it only with their sons."

I felt numb as my voice rasped, "How many masters are there?"

"Nineteen. And there will be another one tomorrow."

I leant against the wall to steady myself.

"So, you have the Gothi, the main master?" I asked. "And then all these other ones too? His children?"

"His brothers and nephews, and soon his son, *já*."

"And they all share the power?"

"*Já*. It gets a little weaker, the more they spread it out. That's why the *fela* work on them."

But not on William.

Eirik ran his fingers through his hair and massaged his temples.

"We need to get some proper sleep and regroup. I'm taking you home."

What kind of home would a young man like him—a thief, a gambler—have?

"Wait a minute. I'm not going to just give up and go have a nice long nap. That's exactly what they'd expect us to do— to shrink away and hide. We have to try something else, while they're not expecting it."

"No. The streets are deadly to us right now. The *hlif* will be very vigilant and out in force. And besides, there are people who can help us, but not right now. We need rest."

My eyes were itchy, my body aching. The idea of rest did sound nice. I nodded along.

"But we can't have anyone clue in that you speak English—that you're a foreigner."

Eirik went silent for a few minutes. I closed my eyes and allowed my racing heart to slow down.

"There is a group of people called the *ómagi*, 'the damaged'," he said. "They take on menial roles but the Epli helps to make their lives more bearable."

I opened my eyes and raised a brow.

"Epli?"

"The drink at the *spill-ehal*, remember?"

"The red one?"

He nodded. "It's one of the reasons the Gothi doesn't like visitors—one of the secrets he's trying to keep. The Epli is a powder from ground rocks, rocks found only in the lowermost caverns. It has special healing properties that have helped us to live underground for so many years and make the damaged seem, well, not quite so damaged."

I looked at the scar across my weak hand. Did he mean to say that it could be permanently healed?

William's face flashed through my mind—how he'd flinched when my scar had returned. He didn't love me as I was. He had only wanted to change me. But the scar, my weak hand, was a part of me.

If it had the ability to physically heal, there was no way I would ever drink Epli again.

"They say we are gods, because only the gods have access to the Elixir of Idun and man perishes upon consuming her golden apples."

He rolled his eyes and got serious again.

"Anyway, my kin would only let you stay if they thought you were a maid I'd won at the *spill-ehal*. One of the damaged."

He had a family. A wife maybe? A baby?

He reached over and took my weak hand, turning it over, gazing at my mangled skin. His face was curious, soft.

Goosebumps ran across my skin again. I yanked my hand back.

"The scar will help to convince them. But your disability will be that you are a mute." He smiled cheekily. "Get it? Because then they won't know that you're not from here—because they won't hear you speak!"

I sighed, shaking my head, and reluctantly smiled. "Not to mention that I would have no-one to talk to anyway—because you're the only person here who seems to know English."

"So, you'll agree?"

I nodded. I could be a mute maid for a day if it meant a shower and bed.

He reached over and pushed a stray hair from my face.

"Braid your hair tightly and I'll get you a *kápa* to wear. You need to look like you're used to hard labour."

After heading downslope through the maze of tunnels for long enough to get bored of the sound of crunching dirt against rock, we reached a dead-end and exited through a small door into a chicken coop. It was the backyard of a mud shack in what appeared to be their version of suburbia. The one-storey houses were crammed together in a sea of flat roofs down the slope. Eirik rifled through a pile of dirty clothes that lay by the backdoor and threw an ochre singlet and coverall at me.

"Roll the sleeves and cuff the legs," he said, pulling a yellow tunic out for himself.

I turned around and changed as quickly as I could, tying the coverall up around my waist and turning back to Eirik as I fixed the sleeves and pants as he'd said. He was busying himself with picking invisible lint from his new tunic.

A row of enclosed leather shoes lay beside the door. He selected a smaller pair and handed them to me too. I hid my joggers in a corner of the backyard and slid my bright blue ankle socks into the leather shoes, which were slightly too big.

"These people aren't going to mind that we're taking their things?" I asked.

"Anyone who houses an entrance to the tunnel system is part of the Uppreisn, so no."

I nodded, unconvinced.

Out in the street, the crowds of locals swelled, people moving up the slope to start a new day of labour. We slipped amongst them but headed in the opposite direction. The further from the city and deeper into suburbia, the more dilapidated and spread out the mud shacks became and the number of people joining the throng decreased. Rusted metal bins with incense sticks poking out of them lined the streets and gaudy statues of bronze gods littered the front entry of each of the homes.

Away from the anxiety, adrenaline, and focus of trying to get Dad back, my mind finally started to relax and tick over at a normal pace. I looked at Eirik properly—his thin frame, stark white skin, and ponytail swishing as he walked.

Like déjà vu, a memory nagged at me.

"You look really familiar," I said.

He smiled a crooked smile and nodded to those walking towards us and said under his breath, "Haven't you noticed? Everyone in Verja looks similar. That's what happens when migration is illegal."

He veered off the path towards one of the houses. It was indistinguishable from the houses around it, except for the pair of effeminate statues out front, which were exceptionally gaudy. The big eyes and tilted expressions unnerved me. I hung back and let him enter the house by himself.

Through the open door, I watched as a girl, maybe high-school age, flew into his arms. She had straight platinum hair to her waist and a scrawny figure. He pulled back from her and they exchanged a few happy words but as he looked up, he was silenced by another figure in the room. A woman's angry voice reverberated out the front door.

There was a break in the yelling. Eirik was saying something and laughed awkwardly. More yelling. He scratched his head and put his hands up defensively. He was lying to her.

He turned and looked out the front door right at me and waved me to come inside.

I swallowed, reminded myself to keep my mouth shut, and walked head high through the door into the main room of the house to stand beside Eirik. The room was minimally furnished and neatly kept, though a thin film of dust lay on every surface. Stone benches with cushions lined two walls and a stoneware coffee table and a woven straw rug centred the room. On the other wall was a stone altar that held a collection of effigies and candles and half-finished incense sticks. A hall led away from the entrance in one direction and a dining room sat off to the left through an archway in the stonewall.

The woman who had done all the yelling was frail, with puffed-up red cheeks, ashy hair, and had frown lines in her frown lines. She was brandishing a broom. She had to be Eirik's mother. I looked to the girl, who narrowed her eyes at me—she must be his little sister, then.

Eirik started speaking again in his native tongue. It looked and sounded like he was introducing me. He pointed to my scarred hand. They nodded slowly along. Eirik looked at me now and pointed to each of the women in turn, addressing his mother as 'Mama' and the girl as 'Ta'.

The girl ran off down the hall and Eirik followed after her. Mama looked supremely annoyed about the situation but started talking at me anyway in a brusque way, motioning for me to follow her through the house.

She toured me from room to room. Down the hall through the first door was a bathroom of sorts, then Eirik's room, then Elisabeta's, where Eirik was sitting on the bed coaxing his sister, followed by Mama's. Back through the sitting room and main entrance we passed the dining room and headed into the kitchen, which featured a stone stove and fireplace. Off to the side of the kitchen, she opened a door to a cupboard-sized room. Disturbed dust flew through the air and made me cough. It clearly hadn't been opened in some time. Beyond the cloud of dust, a bed had been jammed into the room. There was barely space to get in and out of it.

Mama looked at me pointedly. I supposed this was for me.

She removed the dirty woollen sheets, kicking up more dust, and made to exit through another door off the kitchen that led outside.

There was a knock at the front door. Mama stopped and looked at me, motioning for me to go and answer it.

I made my way back through the kitchen and dining to the front entrance and opened the door. It was a young girl, probably around the same age as Elisabeta. Her long blonde hair was almost golden, and she had one of those rosy, innocent smiles that made her eyes sparkle. She was holding a basket in her hands with a felt tea towel over the contents. Her smile dropped and was replaced by curiosity at my sight.

Mama swept me aside and greeted the girl with a wide smile. The girl poked her head inside, beamed, and waved to Eirik who had just entered the sitting room. His cheeks flushed pink.

I stifled a laugh. The girl was clearly smitten by him, even though he was at least six or seven years older than her.

Mama took the basket and the girl courteously left. She shoved the basket into my arms and left the room, I assumed to return to my bedsheets.

"Let's go prepare breakfast so that we can eat and get some sleep," Eirik said.

It was a meagre meal of a mashed root vegetable that looked similar to potato, served in bone broth with sliced yellow-tinged freshly baked bread from the basket the girl had delivered. Eirik set three portions on the dining room table as Mama returned inside. I started to dish up the fourth portion, but she took it from my hands and returned half the portion of mash to the pot over the coal fire, grumbling under her breath, and then slopped it down in front of me on the kitchen bench.

Leaning against a wall in the kitchen and wolfing down the food, I listened to the family in the room beyond. They recited a chant of sorts and were silent for a few moments. Cutlery and bowls scraped, and they started to eat.

Eirik and Elisabeta chattered playfully. She clearly idolised her big brother, laughing loudly at his antics. Mama interrupted them in her cold tone, and they finished the meal in silence.

My stomach grumbled. The food had not been nearly enough to satiate after the exhaustion of the last twelve hours. I licked the bowl dry and glanced at the pot of remaining mash.

It was frustrating that my bodily needs were getting in the way of hatching a plan to get Dad out. Every moment we delayed was a moment longer he had to stay a prisoner. What if his wounds became infected? What if they starved him to death before the Sacrifice Season even started? I didn't want to worry about playing a good maid while I could be putting my energies into making him a free man.

My stomach grumbled again. Eirik was right—I would be useless to Dad if I didn't take care of myself first.

I returned my gaze to the pot of mash, but before I could sneak an extra helping, Mama entered the kitchen carrying the empty bowls from the dining room. She ordered me to follow her out the back to do the washing up in a pail and then left me to it.

As I returned to the kitchen with the clean bowls, Eirik was waiting for me, bread roll in hand. He offered it to me, yawning.

"Mama and Elisabeta are out and won't be back for a few hours," he said. "And sorry about Mama."

I reached out to take the bread gratefully and our fingers brushed again. I flinched.

"What's up with her?" I asked, shoving the bread roll gratefully into my mouth. It tasted like semolina.

"Well, I've been spending a lot of time these last months in the Hidden Grove. I tell them my extended absences are because I've been at the *spill-ehal* and this time that I won you in a game," he said, smiling cheekily.

I raised an eyebrow.

"Such a gentleman."

His cheeks flushed pink.

"What have you been doing in the Hidden Grove anyway?"

He looked at me discerningly and thought for a moment. "I want to get them out of Verja," he confessed. "I just don't know where to take them."

"Who?"

"My kin."

"Why do you want to leave?"

"Same reason you do. This place is like a graveyard. We're already buried underground, we just haven't died yet. But I want my kin to know life without rules and restrictions; without having to count the bread parcels and ration everything out; without constant, imminent fear of being sacrificed."

I nodded in understanding. I wouldn't want to live here either if I were him.

"Can you tell me more about it?" My voice shook a little. "About the sacrifice."

He started clearing up from the meal, putting the

remaining bread back in the basket and returning the lid onto the pot of mash.

"The Gothi tells us that the blood of the sacrifices keeps the Epli running," he said. "They are sacrificed by hanging in a public ceremony. Everyone is expected to be there—even the masters. They only come out en masse for the Conferring and the Ofre Arstid—the Sacrifice Season. Over the course of the year, those who have broken laws are sent to Fengsel and make up the ones to be sacrificed. The season goes for as many days as there are sacrifices—one per day, beginning on the winter solstice."

"And this begins when, again?"

"In two days."

A pit dropped in my stomach.

"But your *vater* would be last in line, as he was the last imprisoned. So, it could be many days still."

"How many others are there?"

He shook his head. "Erm, *fimtán* or *sextán*?"

"How many?"

"Erm, I don't know how to say those numbers in English."

He held up two hands and then one hand.

"Fifteen or sixteen?" I asked.

He shrugged. "I think?"

"We need to find out exactly how much time we have to work with," I said.

"Can you tell me about where you're from?" he asked.

I didn't appreciate the change in subject. My dad's life was on the line, after all.

"Uhm, it's called Earth and it's full of rules and regulations. Lots of people go hungry all the time. Oh, and there are lots of wild, dangerous animals," the words tumbled out of my mouth quickly. The sooner I answered his question, the sooner we could keep talking about Dad.

"Have you been to any other worlds? Please—I only have a few more worlds left to search, and I was on my way to them when I met you and your *vater*. I'm running out of time. Please tell me about them."

He was running out of time? What about me and my dad?

"Well, you should have thought about that before you stole the locket."

He hung his head.

"I am really sorry," he said.

I pursed my lips.

"I know," I said. "I'll tell you what I know. Later. But now we need to figure out how to get my dad out. Where should we start? Perhaps the Gothi can be persuaded? I could just go back home and get something of value to him as a trade."

Eirik shook his head.

"It's been tried before, unsuccessfully. The Gothi values order and control and doesn't want for anything. There's nothing you could offer him," he said. "I'll take you to people who can help, but like you said, let's find out how long we have. Let's go count the sacrifices."

"Okay," I said, rubbing my eyes and standing up, mustering as much energy as I could.

Eirik looked to me, yawning again.

"Perhaps after that nap I promised," he said.

I nodded.

He went down the hall while I opened the door to the tiny maid's quarters. I slipped the shoes and my socks off and shoved them under the sheetless bed before flopping down onto it and quickly falling asleep.

Feeling a little more alert after a few hours on the hard straw mattress, a cold bath, another bread roll, and a pair of Mama's shoes that fit much better without the need for my blue ankle socks, Eirik and I headed back up the slope to the city centre.

Passing the shophouses that led to the marketplace, hand-drawn posters had been plastered across each of the buildings. I veered away from Eirik to take a closer look. One was an old man in a coat with a thick gold chain around his neck, the second a young man with hair in a ponytail, and the third was a redheaded girl in khaki clothes and a windbreaker. My heart skipped a beat. The second and third pictures were Eirik and me.

Beneath the images was scrawling writing that I couldn't read.

"Intruder alert."

I jumped. Eirik had sidled up behind me and was whispering over my shoulder.

"Citizens, it is your duty to report," he continued, reading the poster.

"It's us," I said.

"*Já.* But so long as no-one hears you speak, dressed like that they have no reason to look at you twice."

He took my arm at the elbow and tugged me along as we blended back into the crowd entering the marketplace. Past spice vendors, racks of barbequed chickens, and bickering salesmen, we weaved through to the other side of the marketplace to the edge preceding the prison precinct where the crowd gave a wide berth. It wasn't far from where we'd perched ourselves that morning but the mess we'd left behind was now cleaned up as though it had never happened.

The prisoners themselves were sitting around inside the prison looking mildly content. With daylight, I could now see that they each had matching bald heads and white jumpsuits. Nearby the locked entrance, one of the prisoners' faces was particularly swollen and bruised.

I sucked in a breath.

It was Dad. He looked even worse than before.

Eirik took me under the elbow again and dragged me on, hissing between his teeth, "They're watching, Evelyn. Always watching. Blend in."

He dumped me at a stone table with a view of the prison and went off to speak to a vendor selling beverages.

I stole glances across to Dad but he didn't notice me. He was sitting, looking at his hands, forlornly.

If only I could let him know I was here, comfort him a little, tell him that everything was going to be okay because I hadn't given up on him. But I was meant to be a mute, so I could hardly call over to him, let alone yell out in English that I was here to save him.

But I could whistle.

I took a deep breath and began to whistle the Robin Song.

He snapped his head up and locked eyes with me, wide-eyed as I finished the first verse. Eirik rushed to my side, sloshing two drinks onto the table and hushing me with his eyes. He ducked down to my height.

"Stop! People don't really do music here outside of the festivals."

Sure enough, as I looked about I noticed that several people around the marketplace had stopped their shopping to stare suspiciously. An elderly woman with a hunched back had her head cocked to the side in confusion. She shook it and carried on through the marketplace.

Eirik took the seat opposite me and I chanced one more look at my father. I gave him a weak smile and turned my attention to the cup before me. It was filled with the glinting red liquid of the Epli.

"I can't count the prisoners because they keep shifting in and out of the shadows in the corner," I whispered.

Eirik lent forward over his cup too, sighing into it, "We could come back during mealtime to count the number of trays being brought in by the *ómagi*."

He downed his drink.

"Come on, there are a few things I need to get anyway."

I peeked over at Dad again; he turned the corners of his mouth into a discreet smile and nodded encouragingly.

I left the Epli behind and followed after Eirik to a tin stall. As he picked his way through cake moulds, I took in the people bustling about. Many of their clothes were tattered and faded and their eyes were distant, slightly unfocused. They were impoverished, or perhaps just oppressed. Either way, there was a sense of hopelessness in the air and they seemed to have come to accept it.

But not Eirik. There was life in him. Determination. He was not sitting idly by awaiting the capture of his spirit. It was admirable the way he was fighting for more for himself and his family.

He avoided my eye as he finally selected and paid for a mould with multiple concentric circles, quickly stuffing it into a hessian bag given by the attendant.

I followed him down several rows and out of the marketplace into an alley. There was no foot traffic here. We entered a cluttered, dusty shop of craft supplies and he went straight to the counter. The woman was frail and slow to even notice our presence, looking straight through us. Her skin was tinged yellow and so thin her bones almost poked right through.

When Eirik finally got her attention, he purchased some sort of metal medallion and a length of purple ribbon. She had trouble counting the coins and never really met Eirik's eye the whole time.

Back out in the alley, angry words burst from me: "Why don't they do something?"

"What do you mean?"

"They're obviously really poor. Why don't they leave or get the government to do something?"

"Evelyn, people have tried to do something and ended up in Fengsel." He looked down the alley to the marketplace and back again.

"But there is a revolution brewing."

"You mean the Uppreisn, the rebellion?"

"Not just a rebellion but a revolution."

"Oh. Why don't you do that instead of running away?"

Eirik was taken aback. I didn't mean to sound so harsh, but it was true. He could help fix things, be a part of the solution.

"Because it's too far gone. They will fail. And the amount of bloodshed it would require …" he trailed off.

It must have been pretty bad if he was willing to leave his whole life behind. But if going to Purlieu with William had taught me anything, running away from your problems never worked. Yes, it was admirable that he was doing something by leaving, but if there was a possibility to fix things, shouldn't he stay and try?

"So, this revolution, what are they planning on doing exactly, and when?"

"I don't know, but I want to find out. It would be messy—the perfect cover to get my kin out. And when the revolution fails, the Gothi will likely clamp down on security and we may never get out, so I really do need to know, to time everything right."

I hoped they weren't planning on it anytime soon—I needed Eirik's full attention.

"There is a meeting happening today. A secret one, run by the Uppreisn," he continued. "They were the ones I was thinking we could see about getting your dad out. I was planning on going anyway."

Angry voices echoed down the alley from the marketplace. A woman screamed. Clanging and smashing ceramic followed. More screams. Before I'd really registered the sound of chaos, Eirik dashed away and stuck his head around the wall of the alleyway. He pulled back and looked at me, his eyes wide with panic.

"*Hlif*," he said.

I ran up beside him and looked out. *Hlif* were swarming the marketplace, pulling on people's collars to get a close look at them before shoving them away and moving onto the next person, toppling stalls as they went.

"It's just like last time. They're doing a flash raid. I think they're looking for us," Eirik said.

I sunk my hand into my pocket and wrapped my fingers around the whistle inside, taking deep, slow breaths.

"This way," he said.

Eirik wrapped his arm around my shoulder and tugged me along with him, out of the cover of the alley and into the marketplace. We crossed through it, zigzagging past people in a panic and dodging the carts of produce. Root vegetables spilled across our path as a middle-aged man fell to the ground, a *hlif* hovering over him in interrogation. Eirik pulled me sideways and out of the line of sight. We carouselled around stakes of dried fish and exited the marketplace on the other side, stepping through the tinkling glass doorway of a trinket shop.

I stood frozen just beyond the entrance.

Eirik poked his head behind the counter and into each of the towering rows of stock before returning to me. The shop was deserted—no customers or attendants. He pulled me away from the door, took me by the shoulders, and stared at me hard.

"Everything will be fine. They're not going to recognise you, Evelyn. Just act normal."

I slowly released my grip of the whistle and steadied my breathing. He was right. Dressed up in the ochre coverall with my unruly red hair, pale skin, and spindly figure, I fit right in here.

He let me go and started pacing.

"I'm coming with you to the Uppreisn meeting," I said.

"You're so feisty," he said with a smile. "But you know you won't be able to understand anything they say?"

He went over to one of the windows and looked out.

"I know."

"Okay. If you insist."

The sound of chaos was still coming from the marketplace.

"We should stay put for a while until things settle down outside. They're just trying to scare us. They'll keep doing these random raids just to scare us."

He resumed his pacing. Standing and watching him was making me anxious, so I weaved into one of the rows of trinkets to take a closer look. They were religious artefacts—

bronze and stone statues and lucky charms and purple flags fashioned into imagery of gods and goddesses. I fingered an angry figurine holding a sword.

Eirik had given up on his pacing and followed me into the aisle.

"Frey—god of peace."

"He doesn't look so at peace."

"Well, he did go on to be beheaded, so I guess I don't blame him. The stories about him gave me nightmares as a child." He gave me a grim smile.

"Mama used to tell the stories of the gods at bedtime. They were terrifying."

"What? Like Thor and Odin and stuff? You believe in them?"

"It's not easy to."

He picked his way through the figurines, turning each of them face down.

"When you look at the life we live—celebrating the festival of Manis, yet never laying our eyes upon it, going to greet Porri, yet it never being there to be greeted. Our ancestors before us—before Verja—lived in a very different world where I'm sure their beliefs came as naturally as breathing. Here, it just doesn't make so much sense. But people believe and are ruled by their superstitions and devotions. The Gothi encourages it. After what I've seen through the Hidden Grove, I'm not so easily convinced."

"Where did your ancestors come from? How did they find Verja?"

I started turning the figurines face down too. His eyes met mine and he gave me a cheeky grin. I liked it when he did that.

"It was the old wars that drove them here. The Hidden Grove rose to meet them in their hour of need. Raganhar Áki led the people of his village, which was under siege, through the Hidden Grove and into the desert above."

"And the cavern?"

"At first, they lived in the Hidden Grove itself, but they

couldn't grow food there, so they ventured out to the desert during winter and eventually dug their way down to create the caverns. With each new child, they dug a little further."

A door at the back of the shop opened and closed but there were no footsteps, rather a *click, click, click* of rickety wheels turning. Eirik fell silent and exited the aisle. I followed a beat behind him.

A girl with a shock of red hair wheeled into the shop from out the back in a decrepit wheelchair of sorts.

"Hilda!" Eirik said with affection in his voice.

She smiled back at him and then looked past him to me.

Eirik approached her, waving for me to follow him. When I held back, he spoke slowly to me in his language and made hand signals, highlighting my muteness to the girl. I rolled my eyes and signalled back at him to say that I was mute, not deaf. Hilda laughed. Eirik blushed.

The door tinkled open behind me. A lanky young man with short-cropped auburn hair entered the shop flushed red and breathing hard. A vein protruded over his left temple and his eyes were bloodshot in panic. He looked straight past me with surprise at seeing Eirik. He rushed up to Eirik and exchanged hushed but tense words. Eirik was clearly taken aback by being greeted in this way. The girl wheeled forward and tried to interject but the young man dismissed her. She looked dejected and wheeled herself to behind the front counter. The argument became progressively louder and tenser. The young man finally acknowledged my presence by pointing at me furiously. Eirik swiped the hand away and said something off-handed. He passed the young man, ending the conversation abruptly.

Eirik waved for me to follow again as he headed for the door. He paused to look through the window, let out a breath, and stepped outside. I followed along behind.

"What the heck was that all about?" I hissed in his ear.

The marketplace was deserted now; eerily so. Carts were overturned, produce was scattered across the ground, red liquid was dripping from a stone jug to my left.

"Valki—he's my best friend. He heard about the intruders into Verja and knew I had to have been involved, with my jaunts into the Hidden Grove and all. He was not exactly impressed that I'd jeopardised the revolution for a bit of gold."

"What do you mean? Is he part of the revolution?"

"He *is* the revolution, Evelyn. Well, he started it all anyway. The meeting is in the basement of his house, the shop."

I made to ask another question, but he hushed me. The *hlif* had moved on, the raid was over, and people were starting to return to the marketplace, albeit looking a little ruffled and worse for wear.

He cocked his head to the side asking me to follow him and we zigzagged once more through the marketplace, this time to a dingy corner of roughly constructed metal shacks. Eirik entered the third one along of its kind. Clanging and metallic scraping noises were coming from inside that sent a shudder up my back. I cupped my ears and followed him inside.

The walls and ceiling were pockmarked with smears of black ash above several coal fire pits. Sparks were flying in the centre of the room as a boy was pedalling a stone wheel, grinding the side of a metal knife. Nearest the door a man with his plaited beard flung over his shoulder was alternating between firing a block of red-hot metal and banging down on it on an anvil.

Eirik got the man's attention. He put the block back in the fire and approached us as Eirik pulled a pair of rusty brown scissors from one of his pockets. There were engravings and moulded shapes across the handles of the scissors, obscured by the rust. Eirik passed them to the man who tried to pry the scissors open without success. He gave a grin and after a few moments of what seemed to be bartering the price of repair, we left the smithy without the scissors.

"Time for lunch," Eirik said.

Back through the marketplace, we made a beeline for where we'd started the day. As we passed by the prison, a line of people with different ailments—from clubbed limbs to disfigured faces to droopy expressions—were walking dutifully towards the prison bearing trays of food. The *ómagi*. I counted seventeen, bearing seventeen trays. Which meant we had sixteen days to free my dad once the Sacrifice Season started. The question was when was this revolution going down, and would it impact our plans to break my dad out of jail?

That afternoon, we made our way back to the trinket shop. Hilda was as we'd left her, propped behind the cashier counter on her rickety wheelchair. She gave us a nod as we entered and silently directed us out the back to a room of multiple doors and down a ramp into a large derelict basement filled with broken and old merchandise. In small huddles around boxes and canisters were men and women quiet, yet buzzing, their eyes alight with hope. There was even a young girl—short, with an upturned nose and a hood covering her hair—sitting at the foot of the ramp, rubbing her hands in anticipation. There were probably forty people among them all.

Valki was in the centre of the room and noted our arrival with a reluctant grin and roll of his eyes. He approached us and gripped Eirik's hands briefly, whispering something into his ear before returning to the centre of the room.

We shuffled over to a nearby corner, far enough away from everyone else so that Eirik could whisper to me about what was going on.

"Apparently there's some secret guest coming that will be a game-changer in their bid to overthrow the government."

Eirik scanned the scattered groups in the basement and nudged me.

"We all have something in common," he said, pulling back one of his sleeves to reveal a thin red line running around his wrist. "We've all had a loved one sacrificed."

I looked around the room and sure enough, each person had matching tattoo-like marks on their wrists.

"When someone is sacrificed, *hlif* come to the home of their immediate blood relatives the next day with a year's supply of Epli and mark them like this. It's so that the *hlif* know to look out for us as potential resistance."

They were branded and judged for the actions of another as though it was hereditary. What was up with this sick and twisted world?

The silence in the room took on new heights as Valki stood up on a table. Hands flew into the air and were waved like inaudible applause. He began to speak strongly and passionately just above a whisper. It was clear that everyone knew this was risky.

"Congregating for purposes other than kin or government celebrations is forbidden," Eirik whispered in my ear. He continued to whisper every so often, summarising Valki's speech: "He's talking about the years of oppression, from Raganhar Áki's sons … He's naming incidents from the last ten cycles—the supposed Rán drownings, the great mine collapse, the maiden reaping, the marking of the kin … He's saying that we deserve our freedom and will no longer be oppressed by the Gothi."

Finally, Valki leapt from the table and turned to draw attention to a man that had just entered the basement. The man gave a wide smile, a glint of gold replacing his right canine. He was wrapped in an ochre cloak, his greying beard plaited.

My stomach dropped. Disguises aside, there was no denying it—it was Mr Cuthbert.

The man who had pretended to be my friend but had really been manipulating me. The man who had worked with William to trap me in Purlieu. The man who had posed as a merchant but was nothing more than a selfish, merciless mercenary.

There was a new buzz in the room. Eirik's jaw had dropped along with mine, as though this was not his first encounter with Mr Cuthbert.

Mr Cuthbert's steely eyes had lost none of their shrewdness as he contemplated the room before him, daring someone to oppose him. He strode over to the table and hoisted himself up with a vigour I wasn't expecting.

Quiet shouts came from a gaunt, fiery woman in her thirties nearest the table and the crowd murmured support. Valki waved his hands to quell them and spoke reassuringly.

The smooth tones of Mr Cuthbert's voice sent a silence over the crowd. He spoke the local tongue with such clear fluency that if I hadn't known he wasn't from here, I wouldn't be able to tell the difference.

After gathering himself, with furrowed brow, Eirik resumed his translation for me, "He's saying he's spent the last few cycles in Verja, learning our ways and getting to know the people from the shadows. He's reassuring everyone that he is trustworthy and that he has a plan. He knows what we need and will do all in his power to give it to us. The government is corrupt"—a new murmur of disgruntled agreement went across the crowd—"and the only way to overthrow them is to become one of them."

The hooded girl by the ramp trembled.

The woman near the front asked a question and Mr Cuthbert responded without missing a beat. Eirik went stiff. I nudged him to continue. He swallowed and looked at me apologetically.

"She asked what kind of a timeline they're working towards and he said it will happen during the ceremony of the last sacrifice of the season."

You mean, my father's sacrifice?

A pit was forming in my stomach. Eirik and I would be working towards the same deadline after all.

The woman was asking more questions, going back and forth between her and Mr Cuthbert. Eirik was grappling to keep up.

"She's asking about the logistics. He said something about the signal being the breaking of one of the mirrors and the stage with the masters will collapse ... from a tunnel to the gallows. After the signal, there will be rioting to distract the *hlif* and the inner circle will take care of the rest."

There was a nodding of consensus amongst the crowd. Mr Cuthbert swung down from the table. Valki smiled, clearing his throat, and took back the reins of the meeting, holding up a piece of parchment paper.

"He wants to create a roster for shovelling the tunnel and the pit. They'll need up to five volunteers for three-hour stints around the clock to make it in time."

Valki put the paper down on the table and slunk back through the crowd to the ramp with Mr Cuthbert as people moved forward to sign on.

They seriously bought that crap?

I couldn't believe how little it had taken to convince them that Mr Cuthbert was trustworthy and his plan was going to work.

Hilda rolled steadily down the ramp and to Valki's side. She looked concerned. He bent down and she whispered in his ear. Valki's face remained neutral, but he turned immediately to Mr Cuthbert. A moment later Mr Cuthbert was moving stealthily back up the ramp.

Something was wrong. Why were they just letting him get away like that? After everything he'd ever done?

Valki moved forward again and was trying to get everyone's attention.

I flitted from our corner and up the ramp, moving quickly to close the gap. There was a rapping at the door of the shop, but Mr Cuthbert was making his way through one of the side doors. I skidded to a halt at the top of the ramp and turned to run after him through the door and into the side alley. A blur of yellow knocked me aside and I fell, grazing my hands with a sting. Slightly dazed, I gathered myself up off the dirt and ignored the blood that oozed from my palms.

The hooded girl was ahead in the alley with Mr Cuthbert and they were exchanging words quickly as though they knew each other well. But the girl's hood had fallen, and it was not a girl after all, but a boy with long neat auburn hair and desperately wide eyes.

Eirik scrambled up beside me just as a loud smash came from the shop followed by shouting and footsteps.

The crowd from the meeting flooded out of the side door behind us, pushing me to the ground again. Dust and feet clouded my vision. I coughed and coughed, shielding my head from the stampede of sandaled feet as Eirik grappled with my arm, attempting to haul me back upright.

"It's another raid. The *hlif* are coming," Eirik said. "Quickly!"

The Uppreisers ran for the main street and Eirik and I followed on behind them in the opposite direction from Mr Cuthbert and the boy.

What would happen if we were caught? What would happen to the revolution if the Uppreisers were caught?

I looked back just as *hlif* exited the side door of the shop, splitting to chase after the boy who was now alone at the other end of the alleyway and to chase us and the Uppreisers.

Eirik yanked at me to keep pace with him as we turned out into the main street which was a mess of a crowd moving in all directions, *hlif* grabbing at bodies whether they were innocent or guilty.

Eirik pulled me into the next shop over, ignoring the disgruntled cries of the owner, and behind a tattered tapestry and low stone trapdoor in the wall into the maze of tunnels. He put his finger to his lips as we took silent gulps of air, staring at one another with wide eyes as we strained our ears for signs of being followed.

Had anyone seen us enter the shop? Go through the trapdoor?

My stomach tightened as I strained to hear what was

going on beyond the trapdoor in the shop and the street beyond. There was screaming and yelling, both in fear and indignance. Cutting through the cries came the sound of thumping and moaning as though the *hlif* were trying to subdue a captive woman.

The shop door opened, and two sets of heavy footsteps entered. The repeated disgruntled cry of the owner resounded through the shop. The gruff voice of a *hlif* responded, followed by a guttural one. Their footsteps moved throughout the shop, objects clattering to the ground in their wake. Both pairs of footsteps stopped on the other side of the tapestry. The gruff voice grunted a string of incomprehensible words. I felt for sure that the sound of my heart thudding against my chest was about to give us away. I placed my hands over my heart and pressed tightly against it in a desperate bid to quell the sound. Eirik had watched my movement and reprimanded me with his eyes, frozen with his finger still pressed to his lips.

The footsteps moved away from the tapestry, knocking a few more metal items to the ground. The door opened and closed once more.

My shoulders slackened and I closed my eyes as I exhaled.

The noise outside slowly died down. My heart rate slowed. I looked at Eirik once more.

"Do you think they all got away okay?" I asked.

"I hope so."

"What will they do to them, if they were captured?"

"Fengsel. They'll be put in Fengsel."

I quivered.

Eirik took my hand and together we ran down the tunnels back to his home.

In the kitchen corner, I gazed at the dried blood that lined my hands. I let the silence fill the room and waited for Eirik to emerge from the shock written all over his face.

"I hope Valki's okay," he said finally. "The last thing I said to him was that he was a fool. We might not see eye-to-eye on things anymore, but I still care about what happens to him; if he were put in Fengsel. If he were to die—" He stopped.

"It didn't sound like anyone had been caught. Everyone ran away pretty quickly," I offered.

"But that was Valki and Hilda's home. He could hardly pretend that they weren't present at an illegal gathering that happened in their own basement."

"Maybe they'll go into hiding? In the tunnels? Maybe they'll find another spot to dig the passage from?"

Eirik grimaced.

"Let's hope so."

Silence clung to the air and I cast my mind back on what had unfolded in the last two hours, wracking my brain to recall the new revelations and questions that had been forgotten in the haste and panic of the raid.

How did Eirik know Mr Cuthbert? Who did he know that had been sacrificed? And how on earth was I going to get my dad free in just over two weeks when Eirik was going to be distracted with his own escape plans—assuming the Uppreisers had all escaped and their plans to revolt would still be going ahead.

"I thought I'd have more time," he said, clearly thinking back on the meeting as I had been. "I thought for sure any plans they were hatching would take months, maybe even years."

He finally looked to me, eyes returning some of their usual glint, and surveyed my hands. He stood up so suddenly that his chair toppled over. Ears burning red, he clumsily put it upright and scrambled around the kitchen for a pitcher of water, a bowl, a felt towel, and a little metal medical kit. He returned to the table and wrung the towel out in the bowl.

"I need more time than that to get the gold and figure out where to take them," he said.

He took one of my hands in his, sending a wave of goosebumps up my arm. Trickling water over my hand and into the bowl, he began to wipe it clean, stinging my palm. I bit back pitiful cries of pain and focused on the conversation.

"What exactly do you need the gold for?"

"A piece per kin, to get past the guards on rotation at the uppermost caverns and to protect them from whatever lies beyond the Hidden Grove. I can't leave anything to chance."

Even though he had stolen the locket and was the reason my dad was in prison, he'd done it for his family. I couldn't help but feel that there was something honourable in that. He must really care about them. It was a rare trait.

"Because they always keep one master on duty in the guard rotations at the upper caverns," he continued. "To keep Bornholm safe and to prevent people from exiting and entering Verja."

"Bornholm?"

"It's where the masters and their kin live—up at the towering walls where we entered Verja from. Through the gate."

"Wait—so if you hold up your end of the bargain and help me get my dad free, you're gonna have my locket. So, how are my dad and I supposed to get past the masters then?"

Eirik concentrated on cleaning up the palm of my hand, his forehead screwed up.

"I do have an idea," he said after a few moments. "But I don't know if you'll like it."

"I'm willing to try anything at this point."

"Okay. We could go back to the blacksmith," he said slowly, "and get him to melt the locket down and make rings out of it—enough for your kin and mine."

"Would that work?" I still didn't really understand how gold stopped the commands of the masters.

"I don't see why not—how do you think it was made in

the first place?"

"So, melting it and refashioning it won't affect its ability to stop the commands?"

"No," he said. "So, what do you think? After I help you get your *vater* out, we make rings out of the locket?"

"Okay," I said. It was win-win, after all.

He smiled. I smiled back.

"You've got a good head on those shoulders," I said.

His smile turned to a grin.

"My *vater* did always say that I didn't have to be a big man, but I could be a smart man."

A red tinge grew across his cheeks and he turned his attention back to my hand.

"Okay, so that solves that dilemma," I said. "But we've got a few more problems yet."

Eirik rinsed the towel in the bowl, dried my hand off with a clean corner, and rummaged through the medical kit for a reel of cloth that he wound around my hand. He took my other hand and repeated the process, being extra delicate across the pre-existing scars on my palm.

"You said that the Uppreisn could help us get my dad out. How exactly? Assuming they haven't all been rounded up and thrown in the prison."

"I thought there was a chance they were going to run raids on Fengsel—that that might have been their plan. But if they survived today, they'll be consumed with digging up until the day of the last sacrifice."

"So what good are they to us now? What are we going to do?"

"Relax, Evelyn. Did you not hear me? They said that the revolution would take place during the last sacrifice of the season—not after. It sounds like they just need to get all the masters assembled in the one place to pull it off and they need as much time to prepare as possible, so there's no reason they'd wait the few extra minutes until after your *vater*'s sacrifice. They could just as easily do it before the proceedings."

My shoulders slackened.

"Oh."

Assuming they dug the tunnel in time and the revolution went ahead, maybe dad wouldn't be sacrificed?

"And I have another idea too," he said. He glanced at me quickly then back to my hand, "Mr Cuthbert."

My jaw dropped.

"So, you do know him?" I asked.

Eirik nodded slowly.

"And you do too?" he asked.

I nodded back.

"I met him," he said. "The first time I was in the Hidden Grove, toying with the idea of finding a place to take my kin. We became friends."

My stomach turned over. Mr Cuthbert wasn't capable of real friendship.

"That's how I learnt English," he continued. "We taught our language to each other. He wanted to come here and meet the people and he thought that maybe there was something we needed that he could offer, something he could trade with us."

He wiped his hands dry on his pant legs and wrapped my weak hand with the cloth, thumbing lightly across the back of my hand. Our eyes met again but I pulled my hand back and looked away hastily.

"I told him everything," Eirik said, putting the supplies away. "And he did try to meet with the Gothi but it didn't go so well, and Mr Cuthbert barely made it out alive. That's why his poster is still everywhere in the marketplace and I haven't seen him since."

I could see it now, his resemblance in the posters, in my mind's eye.

"Anyway, he told me about the perfect place to take my kin but I've never been able to find it. And I wonder—you know Mr Cuthbert too, so perhaps you might know the place?"

He leapt from the table and dashed from the room,

reappearing a moment later with a scroll of thin cloth. He unravelled it on the table. Rows and rows of circles littered the page. Most had scrawled writing in the circles and large crosses through them.

"It's the Hidden Grove," he said. "I've crossed out the ones that are too old that Mr Cuthbert warned me against—where the master used too much power—as well as the ones that I've checked and aren't the right ones. These ones here," he pointed to a few that were crossed out but also underlined, "are what I can tell are decent options but not the perfect one that Mr Cuthbert described."

He pointed to a circle near the centre.

"This is the tree to Verja."

There was a circle nearby that was not crossed out. He noticed my gaze.

"That's where you're from, isn't it? The bigger tree."

"Earth," I said.

"I was on my way to explore it, when," he trailed off and his cheeks turned pink again.

I didn't much fancy the idea of this thief coming to my world and feeling obliged to babysit him as he and his family adjusted to the shock of life in Mianjin.

He was looking at me expectantly.

"Like I said earlier today. You wouldn't like Earth. I mean, it's aboveground with heaps of room to roam and we don't do capital punishment—I mean, 'sacrifice'. But at the same time, people are always telling you what to do and how to feel and where to go and there's never any peace.

"And people die by spider bites, jellyfish stings, and being eaten by sharks," I added for good measure.

Eirik shook his head.

"That doesn't sound anything like what Mr Cuthbert described," he said. "You sure you want to go back there?"

I nodded. "It's still home."

Eirik put a cross through the Earth tree on his map.

"Where else have you been?"

I cast my mind back on each of the horrible worlds I'd

encountered.

"Well, there was Celoso. I think it was in this region here," I said, pointing off to one side, "they don't like visitors, just like Verja. They've erected a wall around the Hidden Grove so no-one can go in or out."

"I haven't seen that one. It must be this one here," he said, pointing to a lone unmarked circle in the mid-left section. He scribbled inside the circle and crossed it out.

"Okay, then there was Bayartai. The Hidden Grove came out on a jungle atop a mountain."

"Oh, I know this one—Mr Cuthbert said not to bother with it," he motioned to a circle already crossed out. "The young queen is very oppressive?"

I nodded.

"Have you ever come across a world that is perpetually raining?" I asked.

"Per-pechewlly?"

"Uhm, it means 'never stops'. At least, it was raining pretty persistently when I went there."

"Oh *já*. This one here."

"And what about one on a beach with a building on the dunes?"

"What is a 'beetch'?"

"Uhm ... it's sandy. It's where the sand meets the ocean—the sea—a wide expanse of water."

To someone who knew only caverns and dirt his whole life, was this making any sense to him?

He slowly started to nod.

"Oh, you mean the strand. Yes, where Raganhar Áki came from, they had beaches too," he said. "You're saying this one had a building, by the water?"

I nodded.

"Mr Cuthbert told me of this one too. It is one of my backup options. The master of this world, he said, she is rather obliging."

He pointed to a circle in the same region as Celoso.

It dawned on me that it wasn't just the same world I had

visited when Tiffany and I were trying to escape but also the one Mr Cuthbert had told me about the morning after I'd first met him. What had he said? That it was his homeworld? With the master who changed her name to, what was it, "Queenie Queen"? No, that wasn't right.

Did Eirik know that he was considering taking his family to the world that Mr Cuthbert was from? Would he care?

There was just one world left for me to describe to him. But I really didn't want to get into it. I searched the map for where the Purlieu tree would likely be. There it was, a few rows over from the Earth tree. Again, he caught my gaze and pointed to the Purlieu tree, which was already crossed out.

"Oh, that world is no good. I tried it but the master accused me of trespassing, said that I was not welcome in his world. And then had his dog chase me back to the Hidden Grove."

Eirik lifted the ankle of his pant legs and revealed a scar the shape of a bite mark wrapped around his calf, the perfect fit for the jawline of Bodie the fox. He smiled grimly.

So, I had seen Eirik before, and even watched the very altercation he was describing.

If only he knew I had a matching scar.

I nodded along. He didn't need to know that I'd been to Purlieu or what else happened while I was there.

"That's all I know," I said.

His smile faltered, returning to the scroll. There were still three worlds that were unknown, all surrounding the Verja tree.

"Why didn't you start at Verja and work your way out?"

He looked at the map and shrugged.

"I wanted to get as far away from Verja as possible, just in case. So, I started from the edges and worked my way in."

I nodded.

"I have the best part of two weeks to visit these three worlds. And get your *vater* out of Fengsel."

He drummed the table, thinking.

"If I can set things into motion with your *vater* tomorrow, then that should leave me some time to duck away to the Hidden Grove for a night."

My heart rate quickened, and heat prickled over my skin.

"You want to just leave me here—by myself?"

"Well, *já*. There's no reason for you to come with me."

"But you're the only person I can actually speak with here, who knows English."

"It will only be for one night. You'll be asleep the whole time."

"Yeah, but what if it isn't just one night? What if you get caught up in those worlds you're exploring or the time difference is wrong? I could be totally stranded here. By myself. As a mute maid."

What if he found gold while he was gone? He'd have no reason to help me anymore.

"No. I refuse to let you go," I said.

"Then come with me."

"Eirik, no. We're running out of time to get my dad out. And you promised to help me. If you go, the locket is off the table."

His mouth dropped open and his forehead crinkled.

"But, Evelyn—"

"No. It's out of the question. You can go and explore those worlds after we get him out."

There was a bit of added incentive for him.

He pursed his lips. I folded my arms and held his angry gaze. He softened and gave me an amorous smile, shaking his head.

"How do you do that?" he asked.

I unfolded my arms and looked away, feeling the heat creep up my neck. Even though it was getting in the way of my plans, I couldn't help but admire his singular focus on his family and wanting to get them out. It was like how Dad was with me, always sacrificing for my sake. It was honourable. Eirik was honourable.

"Now, what could you possibly do to 'set things in

motion' tomorrow that would help get my dad out?"

He drummed his fingers on the table again and let out a breath. He looked about the room seeming to collect himself.

"Well, I was thinking," he began. "If the revolution is going to happen during the last sacrifice, if I can get Valki to guarantee two things, all we have to do is just make sure that the revolution happens and succeeds and your *vater* will be a free man."

"And what are those two things?"

"That the revolution starts before he gets sacrificed, during the formalities. And that when they overthrow the Gothi and the other masters that Mr Cuthbert and Valki—or whoever will be running things after they win—promise to set your *vater* free."

"But you don't believe it's actually possible for them to win."

"Okay, well, you could both escape during the chaos of it all."

"That's a lot of 'ifs'."

"At very least, it makes a good contingency."

He tried to give a cheeky smile, but it fell flat.

"There has to be another way. A way that doesn't involve waiting until the last possible moment to get him out," I said.

"I agree. We need more room for error. But this is a starting point at least. And breaking someone from Fengsel is way easier said than done, Evelyn."

His back had stiffened, and I had the distinct impression that he'd just chided me. His eyes had gone distant and it took a few moments of awkward silence before he relaxed his shoulders and really looked at me again.

"Okay. Then we go to Valki tomorrow to get his assurances and then set to work digging those tunnels while we think of an alternative," I said. "Assuming that Valki's alright and the revolution is still happening."

It would give me time to think about all the different

prison break movies, TV shows, and stories I'd heard over the years.

"Yes. But after the Conferring."

"That's tomorrow?"

"*Já*. It's the Moon Festival. And then the next day the Sacrifice Season will begin."

I opened my mouth just as Elisabeta walked into the kitchen.

Her petite figure drew up to its full height as she slitted her eyes and set them on Eirik.

She looked angry and confused and had clearly overheard us speaking in English. She started yelling at Eirik and pointed furiously from him to me. She picked up a stone jug and held it above her head threateningly. She was going to smash it. Mama would come running. The con would be up before it even really began.

Her eyes started to tear up. Eirik held his hands up defensively and started speaking really quickly. He looked desperate, strained, and tried to step towards her but she stepped back and gave me dagger eyes behind her tears.

"Please Ta. Please don't tell anyone," I said. "I promise I'll be out of your life before you know it."

Eirik looked at me like I was crazy.

"She already knows that I'm not from here, Eirik. Just tell her what I said."

He shrugged his shoulders and turned to Elisabeta. Her eyes smouldered over with suspicion as he spoke but with some coaxing her face began to relax until she finally, slowly, put the jug down.

She started pacing, speaking feverishly to herself, throwing her hands up in the air every so often. Eirik strode forward and enveloped her, picking her up into him. She kicked about in protest but then went limp and cried into his chest. He rocked her back and forth like a babe, soothing her.

Elisabeta calmed with a shudder and whispered something to Eirik. He glanced at me. She nudged him. He gulped.

"What?" I asked.

Her eyes fell on me with such seriousness that I felt awkward under her gaze, despite that Eirik was still holding her in his arms.

"She said," Eirik translated, "if you ever do anything to harm my kin, I will tell everyone."

She tumbled out of his arms, spat at my feet, and ran for her bedroom. As the pitter-patter of her feet disappeared, silence fell between Eirik and me.

That could have been worse. That could have been the end of our charade. Who knows what Mama would have done? Kicked me out, surely? And where else would I have to go if she did that? The trinket shop? The *spill-ehal*? I'd need to be careful not to upset Elisabeta. I'd need to be careful not to get caught by anyone else. I needed the security and the concealment of Eirik's home in order to survive in Verja until it was time to leave with Dad.

Eirik gave me an apologetic smile.

I took stock in the fact that Elisabeta loved her brother very deeply and wouldn't want to incriminate him just to take me down. Hopefully.

5

MAMA THRUST AN arm around the bathroom door, holding a simple yellow dress. I suppose that was her way of asking me to wear it.

I flattened the dress down, grateful to be out of the hot and restrictive coverall for once, and stepped out into the living room. Eirik was sitting, waiting, in a clean pair of slacks and a shorter tunic.

Back down the hall, Mama was yelling at Elisabeta and chasing her into the bathroom. This must have been a usual occurrence because Eirik didn't seem to take any notice. He was gazing at me instead, mouth ajar.

"Mama made me wear it," I said.

He nodded and shut his mouth.

There was a knock at the door, sending him to his feet in a hurry. He made to leave the room as I went to answer the door. It was the bread girl.

I reached out to take the basket from her, but she stepped around me and poked her head into the house, forcing me backwards. She caught sight of Eirik leaving the room. He looked over his shoulder and she gave a little wave, blushing. He reluctantly stopped and waved back at her.

Flustered, yet beaming, Mama came running up the hall, sweeping past Eirik into the living room to take the basket from the girl. She looked to be apologising. The girl gave a most polite smile back at Mama.

A horn blew in the distance. Mama jumped.

The girl excused herself and left the house. The moment the door shut, Mama's face dropped, and she shoved the basket into my arms, hurrying back past Eirik down the hall to the bathroom.

I raised a questioning eyebrow to Eirik, but he avoided my eye, ruffling his hair and mumbling as he walked away.

Elisabeta came running past him, now fully clothed in a similar dress to mine, and flopped into a chair in the living room, crossing her arms. She gave me an evil glare, the feelings of the previous night clearly having not faded.

I left her to her distaste and took the basket to the kitchen. Removing the felt tea towel, I grabbed up two bread rolls and slipped them beneath my pillow in the maid's quarters for later on when Mama would no doubt give me only a half serving of lunch.

Moments later, we were all finally out the door, making our way up the slope, filtering into the throng of people moving towards the city centre. Eirik was keeping his distance but kept glancing over to me. Elisabeta gave me dagger eyes again, so I turned my attention to the surroundings instead.

Large purple flags with yellow circles had been erected everywhere and the people looked a little cleaner than usual. At intervals, lining the path leading up to the prison building, were lit lanterns with *hlif* out in force in front of each lantern. Apparently, this festival was a big deal.

The crowd had slowed and were shuffling into place around a large stage that I'd not noticed off behind the prison block. The stage was lined with chairs across the back of it and a large spinning wheel like you'd see at a carnival. And there, front and centre of the stage by the wheel, were the gallows.

My stomach dropped. These people were for real.

Public executions always seemed like something that only happened in stories, not in real life. I was naïve, I know. But in my little sheltered neck of the woods in Mianjin, life was a whole lot more innocent and safer. If I were to ever draw a scene like this, people would just assume I was mimicking some medieval painter. I wouldn't blame them for thinking it was fiction.

We settled into a spot around a hundred metres from the stage, too far away to really see or hear anything, to my equal relief and panic. As much as I didn't want to witness the creation of another master today, I wanted to acquaint myself with the mechanics of the ceremonies of this world to glean any bit of information that could help me free my dad.

As the dull roar of the restless crowd filled my ears, I noticed that the people around us weren't actually facing the stage. They were facing the large sun mirrors that lined the area and the mirrors had been angled down and sideways, engineered to project the reflected image of the stage.

A deafening horn blast sent a wave of excited movement through the crowd and Eirik used the distraction to sidle over to me. My heart skipped a beat.

Men in regal purple cloaks and short-cropped hair processed into the precinct and up onto the stage, taking a chair each. Their plaited beards ran in shades of auburn and hovered above their laps at varying lengths. Some looked haughty, others bored. The one on the farthest end, who looked to be the oldest, started digging in his ear the moment he sat down. The one next to him had plaited his whiskers into cornrows and was looking around with contempt at the crowd. His neighbour on the other side had a gleam in his eyes, watching the podium in earnest. He was nudged by a beefy one next to him and they shared a chuckle.

Just one chair remained empty.

With another horn blast, *hlif* came to stand on stools beneath each of the mirrors. With another, a middle-aged man with bulging eyes and droopy ears dressed to the hilt in shimmering purple garments stepped up to a podium just in front and to the side of the stage. His auburn beard was thick and wiry, plaited tightly together and slicked with oil. He began to speak but I had no hope of hearing more than muffled noise from this far away.

"That's the Gothi," Eirik said in my ear.

An echo reverberated from the crowd and a moment later the *hlif* beneath the nearest mirror spoke. He was repeating the words of the Gothi, passing the message to the crowd, just as the one at the mirror before him had.

"He's talking about his son, Heidelbert, who is next in line to be made a master. He had his Overgangsrite yesterday."

"What's an 'Over-gangs-right'?"

"Erm. Like a rite of passage. He became a man."

I watched the mirror as a boy with an upturned nose stepped onto the stage. He was nervous, reluctant; his desperately wide eyes fastened on his father.

It was the same boy I'd seen the previous day at the Uppreisn meeting, but his hair had now been shorn short. I looked at Eirik and raised an eyebrow. He looked at me. He clearly recognised the boy too.

The Gothi moved from the podium to the stage and with the other masters began a charade of movements with incense and chanting around the boy.

What had this boy—Heidelbert—really been up to yesterday at the Uppreisn meeting? Was he a spy for the Gothi or a sympathiser? And how did he know Mr Cuthbert?

The masters were now circling him, touching his eyes, his mouth, his hands, speaking in unison. They were making him into a master by their words.

The Gothi returned to his podium and the other masters filed back in a line by their chairs, leaving the boy alone in the centre of the stage. All eyes on him, the crowd held a collective breath. The Gothi nodded encouragingly, expectantly, assertively. Heidelbert hesitated, shaking, and the Gothi stared fiercely at him, disapprovingly. Heidelbert stepped forward and turned his attention upon the nearest *hlif* standing guard by the stage staircase. He pointed to the *hlif* and made a command. The *hlif* began to jump up and down in a comical fashion. The crowd snickered and laughed. He spoke again and the *hlif* stopped. The Gothi barked menacingly at the crowd and silence fell. He didn't seem impressed with the command. Heidelbert went white. Both he and the *hlif* were shaking now.

Heidelbert pointed at the *hlif* again and spoke another command. The *hlif* strode mechanically over to the path leading into the grounds and stuck his hand into the flame of one of the lanterns.

I shuddered remembering the queen of Bayartai and how she'd ordered one of her people to their fiery death over the pit.

Robotically, the crowd started to clap and the Gothi nodded approvingly. Heidelbert spoke to the *hlif* and the *hlif* removed his hand from the flame and immediately gave a blood-curdling scream, nursing his melted and blackened third-degree burnt hand. Another *hlif* ushered him away, still screaming. The clapping died down.

The Gothi motioned to his son, inviting him to take a seat with the other masters. He was one of them now. My stomach turned over, sickened at the image before me—twenty Williams sitting side by side, controlling these poor, defenceless people.

The Gothi spoke once more, his message echoing down the line of *hlif* criers. Again, there was a robotic clapping.

"He's thanking everyone for coming and is looking forward to seeing us again at noon tomorrow for the first sacrifice of the season," Eirik said. "Happy Moon Festival."

Moving to stand, the masters were dismissed at the horn blow. When they'd cleared the prison precinct, the crowd buzzed with joy, shouting, singing, and dancing as they threw purple streamers about.

My face felt cold, my head light. Tomorrow was the first sacrifice.

Oh please let Eirik be right that Dad is last in line.

An arm wrapped around my shoulder.

"It will be okay," Eirik said. "We've still got *fimtán* days."

His touch was warm and comforting. I leant into it.

We were ripped apart. Elisabeta had shoved her way between and took Eirik by the hand. He looked at me apologetically. She swung their hands as they walked ahead towards the path back down to the family home. At the path, Eirik gently let go of her and parted with his family, saying something to his mother while pointing at me. Together, Eirik and I headed through the city streets to the trinket shop.

Hilda was not behind the counter when we arrived. The door was smashed in and trinkets were littered on the floor.

"Maybe they're still out celebrating?" I suggested, avoiding the broken glass.

"Unlikely."

Or maybe they were all rounded up after the Uppreisn meeting.

Eirik led us out the back and down the ramp into the basement. The smell of freshly unearthed dirt mixed with incense reached my nostrils. More trinkets were scattered across the ground and a storage shelf lay on its side.

"Valki?" Eirik called out.

A few moments passed and an overloaded shelving unit at the back of the room shifted on casters, opening to reveal Valki standing in an open doorway, his skin covered in a thin layer of dirt dust.

Eirik and Valki looked relieved to see one another, embracing in a rough, brief hug. They exchanged a few words and Valki motioned for me to follow them through the hidden doorway—careful to replace the shelving unit and close the door behind us—into a room with four doors, one for each wall. He nodded me through the one opposite, which opened onto a space the size of the maid's quarters at Eirik's house. Hilda was instructing three men as they dug away at the furthest wall of the space creating the start of a new tunnel.

Enough of them had escaped capture in the raid, then.

A thin layer of dirt dust covered each of them as though they'd been at it for many hours. One of the men sat down wearily. He was the oldest of the group, malnourished, greying, and wrinkled. Hilda pursed her lips and said something snarky. She huffed when he waved her away.

Valki took him up and ushered him out of the room, Eirik following along with them. The girl grabbed the shovel, looked me up and down, and shoved it in my hands. She may have been young and wheelchair-bound, but there was something special about her. She had a powerful, yet graceful jawline that I traced with my mind, imagining how the charcoal shading would gather under her chin on a piece of pastel paper. Perhaps it was the way she held herself with a straight posture and her head held high? I couldn't help but be a little impressed.

Sixteen hours since the Uppreisn meeting and this little dugout was all they had to show for it? If this was going to be my contingency, they were going to need all the help they could get.

I thrust the shovel into the ground and hauled the dirt over my shoulder into a wheelbarrow. It felt good to drive my shoulder behind each shovel load, throwing the frustrations and disappointments of the past few days into it.

My hands quickly became raw, burning as I gripped the shaft and drove the shovel again and again into the ground. Sweat gathered on my back, mingling with the dirt dust and turning my dress slowly brown. Mama wasn't going to like that.

But I continued on, digging and digging and digging,

moving to the beat of my fellow workers, keeping pace with their unwavering strength. Together we could do this. Together we could build this tunnel. We had to.

The wheelbarrow filled and emptied and I lost track of time, listening to the collective breath and sound of metal shovels scraping the dirt, until Hilda spoke up and the men put their shovels down, peering over at me as I continued.

They left the room, but I kept on shovelling.

Maybe we didn't have to shovel all the way over to the gallows? Why not dig a line straight to the prison compound and have Dad slip out of the prison into the tunnels below, *Great Escape*-style?

The idea hit me so quickly that my hand slipped on the shovel and I brought it down on my foot, slicing through the top layers of skin.

"Crap! Ouch! Oh, I'm such an idiot!" I cried out, falling.

I reached out to caress my foot and survey the damage but realised I wasn't alone in the room—the girl had never left with the other men. She was staring at me, wide-eyed with surprise, shocked into immobility.

Blood was spilling from the cut. I looked about for something, anything to wrap it in.

Hilda finally moved, reaching for her scarf and tossing it to me. I wrapped it quickly, pulling it firmly around the wound.

"So you *are* the one they're looking for!" She said slowly, clumsily. "Are you okay?"

I stopped wrapping my foot to look at her, my heart quickening.

"You know English too?"

She nodded and swiftly manoeuvred herself from her chair onto the ground at my foot, unwrapping then rewrapping my foot in a practised criss-cross pattern.

"My brother and I were going to go with Eirik, originally. So we learnt English from him."

She wasn't Valki's maid, she was his sister.

"What? Why didn't Eirik tell me he wasn't the only one

who knew English?"

"Well, Valki doesn't agree with Eirik that we should leave when there is another option—to stand and fight. He's ashamed of ever having learnt English. Maybe Eirik wanted to spare him that?"

The fact that I was speaking to someone other than Eirik for the first time in two days sunk in and I realised how much I'd missed having a girl to talk with, even if she was a few years younger than me.

"What changed his mind?"

"When we realised how hard it would be for me to physically leave Verja and climb the Hidden Grove trees, Valki had the idea that it would be better to stay and fight for a future here."

"But you guys have a shop. You must be doing okay."

"There's no future for me as an *ómagi*. The way things are now, I can never marry or amount to anything other than a shopkeeper to my parents' old shop."

Yet she was clearly sound of mind and capable of ordering grown men about. What was wrong with this place?

"What happened to them?"

"My parents? They tried the political route of making a change for me and were sacrificed for it."

She pulled up the sleeve of her tunic to reveal that thin red tattoo line. Just like all the other Uppreisers.

"I'm really sorry," I said.

She drew her lips together tightly, acting a whole lot older than she probably was.

"I'm Evelyn, by the way."

"Hilda."

So, her parents had been in the prison at one point too. Who knew what she might know to help get my dad out? I relished the opportunity and decided to get as much information out of her as I could.

"Eirik filled me in about the revolution," I began.

"Yeah—why are you helping? Why don't you just

leave?"

I was taken aback by her abruptness but there was no malice in her eyes.

"My father and I …" I hesitated. "… accidentally came to Verja and he was captured and put in Fengsel. I managed to escape. Eirik is speaking to Valki right now about the possibility of moving the revolution slightly forward to before my dad's sacrifice because if the revolution is successful, we'll be able to leave together afterwards."

"When it is successful, you mean."

"Yes, that's what I meant."

It had to be successful.

"I did notice you were digging with a particular fervour."

We shared a smile.

"I don't like your chances, though," she said.

"Of what?"

"Getting my brother to move the revolution forward. We need as much time as possible to dig this out and just yesterday one of our people were captured during the raid."

"Oh. Yeah, we wondered about that. I saw the mess outside."

"We hardly even have time to clean it up. But we're lucky they didn't find anything and Valki managed to convince them we were unaware our basement was being used for an illicit meeting."

"How'd he manage that?"

She smirked.

"I may have had a thing or two to do with it."

Her smile disappeared. "But anyway, your vater is no longer the last one in line. And as much as I'm sad that Yvette was caught, because she was always kind to me—fiery, but kind, that extra day is really going to make a difference."

My heart sunk.

"But why do you have to do it at the sacrifice?" My voice was high and hollow.

"Because the masters won't gather like this again for

another whole cycle. And every day we wait is another day we're under their oppression."

"Is there anything else I can do, then? Dad and I just want to leave—we never meant anyone any harm."

Hilda tapped her hand on her knee.

"What about the *ómagi*?" I asked. "The ones that bring the meals for the sacrifices—are you able to get me onto the roster or something?"

"Those *ómagi* are specially chosen. It's a great honour to serve as they do. It's not the kind of thing that you just put your hand up for. And it's not the kind of thing that I'd ever get nominated for."

She looked at her stiff legs sprawled across the ground.

"The Epli didn't help?"

She shook her head.

"We tried when I was younger. But after my parents died, I stopped taking it."

"But didn't you get, like, a year's supply?"

She grimaced.

"We sold it. Most people do. It just doesn't seem right. Like blood money."

I nodded. It could hardly replace the loss of their loved one. Loved ones in the case of Hilda and Valki.

"So, do you know any of them personally, the *ómagi*?" I asked, getting back on track. "Could one of them get a message to my dad? A note maybe?"

Hilda looked doubtful.

"Please. He's all alone in there."

She pursed her lips but nodded. My shoulders relaxed.

The door opened and three fresh-faced men entered the small tunnel cavity, sending Hilda's face red. Eirik and Valki followed along behind the men and immediately noticed my bandaged-up foot. Valki gave Hilda a stern look that made her scramble back onto her chair and he exchanged words with Eirik.

Eirik leant down and helped me to my feet. It hurt, but I could walk.

Upstairs at the back of the house in their washroom, I bathed fully clothed to rinse the dress of the dirt that had accumulated, sending brown liquid down the drain. The water was a comfort to my aching muscles and raw hands. Eirik sat on a stool by the bath, looking at me without really looking at me. His face was grim.

"I had an idea," I said. "What if we dug a tunnel straight to the prison compound? My dad could slip down into it without the *hlif* even noticing he was gone."

Eirik sighed.

"Believe me, it's been tried before. The whole prison block is built upon bedrock. You'd need some serious tools to cut through it and that kind of noise wouldn't go undetected."

"Oh."

"Valki confirmed they'll be starting the revolution during the formalities part of the sacrifice. They just need the masters gathered and nothing would be gained by waiting a few extra minutes. He also said that the sacrifices would stop under his leadership so he would ensure your *vater*'s release," Eirik said, waiting as I wrung the dress of excess water. He tossed a felt towel.

Valki would be the leader if the revolution were successful? But what about Mr Cuthbert and this Heidelbert character? What if they had other plans?

"Hilda told me that my dad is no longer last in line to be sacrificed—that someone was captured during the raid yesterday, which means the revolution is meaningless to me."

Eirik looked sheepish.

"Yes, I found out that she could speak English too. Thanks for the heads-up, by the way. Is there anyone else that I should know about?"

"Just her and Valki."

I re-braided my hair and held Eirik's gaze, looking for a lie, but found none.

"So where does Mr Cuthbert fit into all of this?" I asked.

"Valki seems to think he genuinely just wants to help. Apparently, he knows how to stop the transfer of the masters' power."

"I don't trust him," I said.

"Mr Cuthbert? Something tells me that neither should I. The way Valki talks about him, it reminds me of how things used to be between Mr Cuthbert and me. It's making me uneasy for Valki's sake."

"But even still, he has access to the masters through Heidelbert. Maybe there's a way there? Maybe Heidelbert could use his power to free my dad? Can you arrange a meet-up with Mr Cuthbert through Valki?"

"I can try. He might make me work for it because I'm not exactly in his good books at the moment."

"You're his best friend."

"And he's still pissed off with me."

I grimaced, thinking of Tiffany and how things hadn't always been smooth sailing with her. I got it.

"You'll have to go home though," he said. "Valki said you're a hindrance." He motioned to the cut on my foot. Heat flooded my cheeks.

6

THE CROWD WAS buzzing with anticipation, filling the space behind the prison block facing the stage and gallows. With Mama and Elisabeta either side of me, we were in a similar spot to the previous day and I was grateful that the sounds of death would not be heard from this distance.

Mama was looking anxiously for Eirik who hadn't come home after going back to speak with Valki. She glanced at me and clicked her tongue at the stains spattered across the dress where I'd been unsuccessful in washing the dirt out. With Eirik away, I'd had no way of explaining to her how they had gotten there or why the fabric was crumpled from wringing it out.

I forced my attention away from her disapproval to the gallows.

My stomach turned over and over as the cruelty of the Bayartai queen ran circles in my mind. The look of the man who had carried me as she commanded him to burn himself alive over the pit: blood draining from his face, his eyes wide with sheer terror, but obediently turning and climbing the human spit roast; the smell of burning hair and unseasoned meat that clung to my olfactories in an unmovable, unshakable way.

I shuddered. How brutal was this sacrifice likely to be?

Weaving through the crowd, Eirik emerged, just as the horn blew for the crowd to settle down. I smiled. Mama caught sight of him and relaxed her shoulders, her forehead unknotting to be replaced by sombreness and grief. She quickly fixed a fake smile and her eyes glazed over. Eirik and Elisabeta shared a grim look, setting their faces as their mother's. He sidled in between Mama and me and faced the nearest mirror. We were tightly squashed together in the throng. He discreetly wrapped his hand around mine and gave a quick squeeze of reassurance before letting go again. My heart skipped a beat.

"Valki will set up an audience with Mr Cuthbert," he whispered.

That was something, at least.

The horn blew again, and the masters filed onto the stage taking their places, the final chair occupied by Heidelbert. The old man on the far side started digging in his ear again. The horn blew for a third time, the *hlif* taking their place, and after a final blast, the Gothi stood at his podium and turned to the prison building to watch as a prisoner was processed down and up onto the platform by the spinning wheel.

Looking at the mirror to the right, it presented a different angle on the proceedings. Two women and several children were closest to the stage, tears streaming down their faces, at odds with the hungry looks of everyone else around them. It must be the prisoner's family.

The Gothi began to address the crowd, his *hlif* beneath each of the mirrors parroting along.

"The charges against him are freethinking. His fate is left in the hands of the gods," Eirik said.

At this, the prisoner stepped forward and spun the wheel.

"There are five possibilities on the Norns. See how the segment colours go from white to shades of grey, to black?

They increase in severity. White is to be set free; the grey ones progressively are: someone takes his place, return him to confinement until the next season, or send him down the river; and black is hanging. It's their way of ensuring the gods have the final say in the matter."

Eirik had never mentioned any of this. I thought there was only one outcome—to the gallows, no questions asked. It changed everything. I looked at him, bewildered. There was a four out of five chance that Dad wouldn't be hanged.

"It almost always falls on hanging," he whispered, reading me.

But what if we could rig the wheel?

The wheel clicked over and finally stopped on the black segment.

"Hanging," Eirik whispered.

One of the women from the family collapsed. *Hlif* moved forward to surround her, lifting her up and bringing her onto the stage by the man, placing a noose around each of their necks. I could just make out the sound of her wailing. Elisabeta started shifting beside me.

"That's his maid. The maid always goes with them."

A pair of *hlif* moved about behind them with incense in a procession of ceremony, chanting. They removed the incense and one moved to a handlebar on the gallows frame.

"Don't look away," Eirik whispered.

Everyone else was fixated upon the pair, even the family in the front row. Heidelbert was the only exception. His eyes kept darting away as he wrung his hands in his lap.

Eirik wrapped his hand around mine again but this time didn't let go, giving it a hard squeeze.

A trapdoor opened from beneath each of them and they fell with a bungee spring just a ruler length down. Enough for their feet to hang loose as they writhed about.

Eirik's hand was calloused and dirty, rough across the upper pad of his palm, just like mine. Valki certainly must have made him work for it.

I glanced across at him, eyes still glazed over, lips twisted into a thin smile, face fixed on the gallows. Large bags hung from beneath his eyes. Had he worked through the night? He certainly was dependable—one who followed through on his promises, one who fought for what he believed in. I couldn't help but respect him for that.

I don't know how long it went on for, but my feet were sore and my eyes dry from staring as I locked my body into place, not allowing myself the luxury of shaking with fury or fear or distress. But the writhing finally stopped. It took the man far longer than the woman.

The Gothi turned back to the crowd from his podium with a wide smile. The *hlif* at the stool nearest us mirrored his smile and gave the echo of his speech.

"He's talking about cooperating with the government and ridding the community of bad eggs," Eirik whispered. "He's encouraging widespread celebration of the sacrifice."

The prisoner and his maid were left hanging as the Gothi and masters began to process out to the rhythm of horn bellows.

The celebration began with a murmur, growing into a cacophony of cheers and whistling and laughter. As we shuffled onto the downward slope to the family home, bonfires were lit in metal bins and objects were ceremoniously thrown in with great intention and joy.

This was what my father was in for? And the people were invited to party?

By the time we reached the house, I couldn't contain the shaking any longer and it seemed I wasn't the only one. As Eirik, Mama, and Elisabeta each entered the house, their smiles dropped. The mood was sombre, and Mama went straight to her room. Elisabeta waited a moment and then followed Mama down the hall.

Eirik collapsed into a chair in the living room and rubbed his face. I slid down the wall and hugged myself. We stayed like this for some time.

"Are you okay?" I asked.

"Mmm," he said.

"Your family were in a fantastic mood today," I said.

He cracked a quick smile into his lap.

"But seriously, you can't just leave me hanging for twenty-four hours," I said. "What if something had happened to you? I'd have never known."

He looked up, eyes bloodshot.

"I'm sorry," he said, holding up his dirty hands. "Valki made me do a few shifts."

"Why?"

"He wanted me to prove I wasn't undermining their efforts," he said. "I think he also wanted to take advantage of the opportunity to try to convince me to join their fight."

"Why? Why can't he just let you go?"

"Because he believes in what he's doing and he can't imagine someone thinking otherwise," he paused, thinking. "He's always been a bit altruistic, Valki. I think he got it from his parents."

"But you're looking out for your family just like he is. You just have different ideas on how to do that."

"Yeah, but with Valki, it's like if you're not *for him* you're *against him*. It's just how he is," he said. "He really is a good man. Helped me out of some tight spots over the years and was there for me when no-one else was. But we've just grown apart a bit. Don't see eye-to-eye like we used to. End up fighting most days. It was easier when we were children. The idea of leaving him when I leave here still hurts though."

I stood and moved over to him, placing my hand on his shoulder comfortingly. He placed his hand over mine and gave it a squeeze.

"So anyway, did he manage to sway you?" I said with a cheeky smile.

Eirik grimaced up at me.

"The cultural shift from dictatorship and oppression to freedom will not be as straightforward as Valki would like to think. I'd prefer to start afresh without the baggage."

It sounded rehearsed. Or perhaps that he'd had to repeat

it multiple times to his best friend who failed to hear him. It was nice that they could be so honest with one another, though.

Tiffany flashed across my mind. Perhaps we were honest with one another in a different way: an honest agreement to not be so honest. Sometimes it hurt too much to be vulnerable.

I stepped back from him to my place against the opposite wall again.

"Anyway, the meeting with Mr Cuthbert is set for tonight," he said. "After dinner."

My stomach dropped.

"Why didn't you lead with that?" I said. "What on earth am I going to say?"

Mama emerged mid-afternoon to boss me around the kitchen and dining room, cleaning and cooking up a feast, including an extravagant cake using the concentric circles mould Eirik had bought. She was incessantly frustrated that I didn't seem to get her instructions and took a lot of it out on Eirik. Eventually, she gave up and drove him from the kitchen to make himself more presentable.

Mama herself was bathing when a knock came at the door. It was the bread girl and what appeared to be her parents. I turned to Eirik and Elisabeta in the living room where they were sitting dutifully.

No-one had told me we were expecting dinner guests. Was this all part of the celebrations of the first sacrifice of the season?

Mama came up the hall with a beaming smile on her face, going over the top to welcome the guests into the house. Eirik and Elisabeta got to their feet and greeted them after Mama, and they all made their way into the dining room. The bread girl hung back to walk beside Eirik, her ears shining red as she looked out from under her eyelids with a demure smile. Eirik shoved his hands deep into his pockets and took a seat on the other side of the table.

I served up the meal—roast chicken with crispy starchy root vegetables and thickened gravy—and waited on them by the stern instruction of Mama's eyes. It was the first time I'd seen them actually eat together, including the ritual of chanting before the meal followed by a moment of silence whilst staring at the effigy in the middle of the table.

As the meal progressed, Eirik started to relax and crack jokes like his usual self, making the bread girl swoon. She barely looked at anything other than her plate and him the entire time. Eirik, rather, directed his attentions between the father and Elisabeta, in a rhythm of formal, serious conversation, and idle clowning around. Every so often he threw a quick glance in my direction.

With each glance, my heart did a double-beat and I started waiting for the next moment his eyes might pierce me. I distracted myself by turning my mind upon escape plans.

If digging beneath the prison was a no-go, along with the likelihood of being able to get close to the prison disguised as one of the *ómagi* who delivers food, what, other than bargaining with Mr Cuthbert, were my options?

There was the idea of rigging the spinning wheel. Where did they keep the wheel between sacrifices and how would one even rig a spinning wheel to stop on a particular section without making people suspicious? I'd have to bring that one up with Eirik later.

I continued to mull the options, varying from downright risky like stealing the keys to the prison, to half-baked like posing as prison guards, to audacious like blowing a hole in the building.

Rigging the spinning wheel was certainly less hands-on but it also left it to the last possible moment to rescue Dad. Perhaps that could be one of our contingencies?

It would be really great if I didn't need any contingencies—if only Eirik would step in and fix it for me. Maybe he would come up with something so brilliant that I wouldn't have to do any of this heavy lifting? And perhaps once he's freed my dad, we'll all leave together, back to Earth?

Chairs started scraping. The two families got up from the table and made their way to the living room, Mama bringing the extravagant cake with her. Things felt awkward—tense, even.

I cleared the table, moving between the dining room and kitchen, glancing through the dining room opening into the living room to see what was happening. Mama and the father were having a heated discussion while everyone else tried not to look too interested in the outcome.

With the table cleared and the dishes washed, I stood at the entrance to the living room, giving Mama plenty of room to either shoo me away or call for me should she need more service. The last thing I wanted was to be in her bad books. She may have been a pain in the arse, but she was still Eirik's mother and I needed somewhere to stay, a cover while I laid plans to get Dad back.

Sure enough, she motioned for drink refills. I moved forward with a pitcher of their precious Epli to offer top-ups.

If Eirik were to come with me to Earth, would he have to bring his mum and Elisabeta with him?

I tripped on the floor rug and fell to the ground, the clay pitcher smashing, red liquid soaking steadily through the rug.

Eyes wide and livid, Mama scolded me with loud, angry words. I slowly got onto my hands and knees, gathering the broken pieces, and darted a look at Eirik. He sat by his mother, wordless, detached, avoiding my eyes for the first time that afternoon. Why didn't he defend me? Why didn't he help me clean up this mess? Why couldn't he even look at me?

Mama hastily rolled up the rug, pushing me from it, and shoved it into my arms, directing me out of the room to dispose of it all and clean up my mess.

I walked, dazed, into the kitchen.

Lying on the bed in the maid's quarters, hours after the guests had left and the house was winding down for the night, I went over the note I'd written Dad one last time: I apologised for getting him sucked into this mess, reassured him that I was doing everything I could to get him out, and promised that I was doing fine—that the one who stole Mum's locket was actually helping me. Then I explained the mechanics of the Hidden Grove and how he had ended up imprisoned in Verja.

It was as much as I could fit on the scrap of baker's paper I'd found in the bottom of the breadbasket. And writing with a lump of coal I'd nicked from the cold fireplace was a challenge in and of itself.

I wiped the black residue from my fingers and folded and tucked the parchment into my pocket. I'd be seeing Hilda tonight.

The beauty of it was that if the note ever went astray, no-one would be able to read it.

The door creaked open and Eirik poked his head inside. My heart did a double-beat.

"Hey," he said.

"Hey."

I should have been mad at him. Mostly I was just confused.

He slumped down on the bed at my feet and I scrambled back to make room for him. He sighed and turned to hold my gaze. His eyes were glassy and a little red. Had he been crying?

He forced his mouth into a smile that just made him look worried.

"The first day of the Sacrifice Season is always the hardest," he said.

He was tracing the tattooed red line around his wrist.

"My *vater*, he was a good man, really. The mine collapse was a complete accident. But it killed many people, so they put him in the prison for manslaughter. It happened just before the end of the Sacrifice Season of that year. And when he spun the Norns it landed on 'return to confinement until the next season'. The Gothi was particularly smug about the justice of the gods that day."

A whole year of waiting for his probable death?

"That's horrible," I said, reaching over and placing my hand on his.

He stopped tracing the tattoo and relaxed a little.

"He didn't deserve it and neither did Sunna, our family maid," he said, shifting his body to face me. "Elisabeta was very close to her. That's why she hasn't been particularly warm to you—or to anyone else for that matter. I think she thinks that she can't handle pain like that again so she chooses to just not love in the first place. It's why she's so overprotective of me."

"A year is a long time. I can't even imagine," I trailed off.

"It all became too much about halfway through. So—" he grimaced a little and shook his head. "I attempted to break him out by posing as a *hlif* and stealing the keys."

My stomach sank. He'd already tried—and failed—two of my riskier ideas.

"Instead of ending up on death row, because I was underage, they gave me a public punishment instead."

"Public punishment?"

He nodded but also seemed to notice a change in me. He took my hands and held them tenderly, his face turning soft in earnest.

"Oh, but it's okay. It will be different this time. We've got allies and the tunnels, and who knows what Mr Cuthbert is really up to. We can do this. We can get your *vater* out."

His words hung in the air. I searched his eyes for deception, but he really believed it was possible.

He glanced at my lips and then down at our hands.

My heart thudded. Was he about to kiss me?

A comfortable silence filled the space between us for a beat and then two.

He looked at me, his eyes conflicted, then looked away again, taking his hands back, and moving off the bed.

"It's probably time we went to see Mr Cuthbert," he said.

Entering the trinket shop, the glass now cleared, the doorframe empty, a weary-looking Valki greeted Eirik but chose to ignore me. He waved us to follow him out the back and stopped at the top of the ramp. Valki said something and Eirik looked exasperatedly back at him. I watched, waiting.

"I'm sick of playing translator. She knows about your English, Valki—Hilda told her," Eirik said. "You can tell her yourself."

Valki's face sapped of the little colour remaining and looked at me nervously, almost like he was afraid of me, or rather, afraid he couldn't communicate with me.

He looked back at Eirik but Eirik just folded his arms.

"Erm …" Valki started.

He scratched the ground with his shoe and let the words tumble out of his mouth: "Yvette, she dies. Your *vater* is last sacrifice again."

Eirik cleared his throat.

"He means the one that got caught at the meeting." Eirik stepped in. "Apparently she was in pretty bad shape from the arrest. She died in Fengsel today. They've got to speed up the digging again to finish in time."

Dad was last in line again? So, if the revolution went ahead, he could be set free?

Valki led us down the ramp, past the overflowing shelving that had now been put back upright, and through to the secret room of doors. Hilda was there, checking over the digging roster. She looked up as we entered and gave me a friendly smile, dodging Valki's eyes. Valki barely hesitated, taking us through the door to the left. I dug my hand into my pocket and slipped Hilda the letter as I passed by. She nodded.

Through the door, there was a secret passage that sloped upwards immediately. Silently we followed Valki up it and into another shophouse, through a back alley, and into another basement.

I hoped the letter would reach Dad and provide some clarity to his situation. He must be so confused—just like Tiffany had been—in this strange world, that he wouldn't even understand how he'd reached, immediately locked up with no way of getting back home. Treated like a criminal just for being there.

Through a hidden door in the basement, we entered a compact office with dimmed lights and a study desk across the middle. Behind the desk, with crossed arms and a smug smile, sat Mr Cuthbert. He raised an eyebrow at both Eirik and me as we emerged through the door.

There were those beady eyes that didn't think twice before inflicting pain. The thief, the mercenary, the murderer. I shook a little but stood my ground and gritted my teeth. He was going to repay me for all the harm he'd caused.

"I thought it was you," he said to me. "I had to see for myself."

I felt everyone's eyes on me and heat prickled across my neck. Mr Cuthbert stood and made his way to the other side of his desk, leaned up against it, and crossed his legs. His pant leg rode up to reveal a jagged scar around the ankle.

"I must admit, I thought you were done for," he said.

My hands clenched and opened. I wanted to slap the smugness off his treacherous face.

"No thanks to you."

"So, what happened?"

I was painfully aware that both Eirik and Valki were listening in. They didn't need to hear any of this and neither did Mr Cuthbert for that matter. It was none of their business and I had no desire to share.

"I got out."

"I am impressed."

I shifted on the spot.

"You know, out of all the girls, you were my best trade. It could have been good for all three of us, if only you had leant into it. Shame it did not work out."

My stomach constricted. I reached into my pocket and wrapped my hand around the whistle.

"And now I cannot return to Purlieu," he said.

He pursed his lips in annoyance. My hand gripped the whistle hard, the cold metal biting into my skin.

I'm not a victim.

I took a deep breath and released the whistle.

"So, what's your big plan, then?" I asked, taking the reins.

A smile curled at the corners of his mouth. He made his way back behind his desk but didn't sit down.

"Big plan?"

"Surely you're not just helping these people out of the goodness of your heart," I said.

He chuckled.

"Oh, Miss Evelyn. My, you have changed."

"Because Valki tells us that he's going to be in charge around here once all the masters are gone. But I'd hedge a bet that you've got other things in mind."

Mr Cuthbert scratched at his chin and shot a look at Valki.

"Yes, that is the plan—right, Mr Unfrid?"

Valki tightened his jaw and nodded stiffly.

"Then what of Heidelbert?" I asked. "He's a master. Are you going to kill him too?"

Again he smiled, and then began to pace slowly behind his desk.

"Master Heidelbert will be our backup plan to overthrow the other masters; he knows this. And he is wilfully onboard. He sees the potential in the Epli that his father does not."

"What do you mean?"

"It is a clever little powder. The Gothi fails to see the trade opportunity, however."

"And the *hlif* are just going to fall into line under Valki's leadership when one of their beloved masters still lives?"

"The *hlif* know me well. I frequent their quarter when going to visit Master Heidelbert. They think I am one of them. They will listen to me."

He stopped pacing and looked at me squarely.

"Now Miss Evelyn, why should you care so deeply about the success or failure of my ventures?"

"Valki promised that the revolution could begin just before the last sacrifice and that after the revolution there would be no more sacrificing."

"He did now?" Mr Cuthbert glanced at Valki. "I do not believe that it was his to promise."

My heartbeat quickened.

"What do you mean?"

"Well, Master Heidelbert might be concerned about appeasing the gods," he said, staring at Valki now.

"But I thought that Valki would be in charge."

"Fortunately for Mr Unfrid, Master Heidelbert also wishes for the sacrifices to stop. But why do you really care, Evelyn?"

"Because."

My lip quivered. I steadied myself.

"Because my dad is in Fengsel. He is the last sacrifice."

Mr Cuthbert tsked.

"And I know you have access to Heidelbert so you could do something about it."

"But it sounds like you have got everything sorted—you need only wait until the last day of sacrifice for the revolution and he will be released," said Mr Cuthbert.

"That's too risky."

"You do not believe in the success of the revolution?"

He whistled through his teeth, glancing at Valki again, and shook his head mockingly.

I gritted my teeth. "How about a trade, then?" I asked.

Eirik cleared his throat. I ignored him.

"I'll do anything you want in exchange for something

that I want," I said.

"Evelyn—" Eirik began.

"Intriguing," Mr Cuthbert said. "Go on."

"I want you to get Heidelbert to use his powers—or even just his authority—to free my dad."

Mr Cuthbert twisted his mouth, considering.

"I suppose I could relay a message to him and see what he comes back with."

"No," said Eirik. "Evelyn, you can't trust him."

"And what about you, Mr Eik?" Mr Cuthbert asked, finally acknowledging him.

"I didn't break any promises," Eirik said. "I told you everything you needed to know and warned you about the Gothi. You just didn't listen. And then I never saw you again. What was I supposed to do?"

The room was still and tense.

"You gave me false information," Mr Cuthbert said.

"So did you, apparently," retorted Eirik. "Where is this supposed perfect world you told me about, huh? I've looked almost everywhere and can't find it."

"It exists. Keep looking."

"Why can't you just tell me where it is?"

"I can. But you have nothing I want to trade the information for."

Eirik scoffed and shook his head in distaste. "What happened to you?" he asked. "We used to be friends."

"That is what I wanted you to believe. What you needed to believe. But you have outlived your usefulness I am afraid, Mr Eik."

"Evelyn, please," Eirik said, turning to me. "You can't trust him. He'll just say that Heidelbert said 'no' without even asking. You have to go with him."

Eirik was right. I needed to hear it from Heidelbert for myself. To plead my case if necessary.

"And I'm coming too," he added. "To make sure he translates correctly."

"I do not believe I am making a deal with you but with

Miss Evelyn," Mr Cuthbert gave Eirik a stern look.

"Those are my terms," I chimed in. "We're both going with you. But Eirik will behave himself." I said the last part with gritted teeth.

Mr Cuthbert glanced at each of us, his smile returning.

"Very well. I will take you to see Master Heidelbert and you can ask him yourself. In exchange, you will be retrieving the black daggers for me." He looked at me knowingly and nodded his head.

The black daggers? As in the ones in Purlieu?

"They are the only thing that can stop the transmission of the power," he said.

"What black daggers?" Eirik asked.

Mr Cuthbert pulled back his ochre cloak and unsheathed a dagger at his waist. The sheen of the stingray skin handle and night-black blade glinted in the dim lighting.

"This is not the first time that I have rid a nation of their masters. But this is the only dagger I have on my person and more are needed for the pit beneath the stage. I have a stash elsewhere, but I won't be giving that location away to you. Miss Evelyn, you know where the other ones are."

He looked at me. He wanted me to return to Purlieu. Was it a trick to get back into William's good books by presenting me on a platter to him again?

My heart started pounding.

"Why can't you go get them yourself?"

"I do not wish to be found out by the masters prematurely. I have been meaning to send someone to retrieve them and what better person than you, Miss Evelyn, someone who already knows their exact location?"

I could feel Eirik's eyes on me.

Even if it was a trap and William was there waiting for me, if I could get those daggers back and return to Verja, Mr Cuthbert would have no choice but to get me that meeting with Heidelbert.

"Deal," I said. "But I'm taking your dagger with me.

Mr Cuthbert laughed.

"No, you are not."

I bit my lip.

"It's okay, Evelyn," Eirik said. "I'll go with you."

"Okay," I said. "And when we return with the daggers, Mr Cuthbert, you're going to have that meeting with Heidelbert all ready to go."

Mr Cuthbert nodded, moved from behind his desk, and opened the door to signal it was time for us to leave.

As we exited the room into the basement and went back out into the back alley, I could feel Valki's brooding silence.

"Evelyn, where is this place exactly? Is it on Earth?" Eirik asked.

"No," I said.

"So, where is it? And what was he talking about at the start?"

We found the door into the other shophouse and I dodged Eirik's questions, rounding on Valki instead.

"What did Mr Cuthbert mean about the daggers being the only thing to stop the transmission of power?" I asked.

"He says it prevents blood inheritance of power," Valki mumbled.

"How?"

"When you kill them with that blade, they can't pass power on," he said, kicking at loose gravel on the ground.

So that was his plan—kill the masters with the black daggers so that no-one could inherit the power, so that there would be no more masters in Verja. Just like he did in the castle in Purlieu.

Valki's face was screwed up and sour-looking.

"What's wrong, Valki?" I asked.

He kicked at the ground again.

"Mr Cuthbert, he … erm …" Valki stuttered, "… undermined my authority."

I nodded.

"It did sound as though he thought he was in charge," I

said.

Valki booted open the door into the secret passage.

"What are you going to do about it?" I asked.

"I will make him let me come to see Master Heidelbert. And Master Heidelbert will see my importance and keep me on as leader after revolution," he said. "For Hilda."

Silence hung in the air again, intensified by the cramped tunnel.

He really did care about his sister, putting himself on the line for her sake. Not like a blanket commitment to altruism for the sake of all of Verja like I had assumed, but an intense love for Hilda. Eirik was right, he was a good man. Hilda was lucky to have him. Eirik was lucky to have him.

"I'm sorry I was insensitive," Eirik said. "About the outcome of the revolution. I really do hope it works."

Valki snorted.

"If you really believe it would, then you would stay, fight," Valki said, raising his voice.

"I don't have to stay and fight just to prove that. Besides, it's not the revolution itself that I'm concerned about—it's the fallout afterwards. You think that everyone is just going to fall into line behind you? It's not going to be that easy."

"Of course not easy, but doesn't mean we should just give up."

"Eirik, Valki, don't do this. You love each other. Just agree to disagree," I said, knowing Eirik would regret his words later, another fight to add to their tally.

"I'm not giving up—I'm creating my own opportunity," Eirik said under his breath, ignoring me.

We had reached the door into Valki's basement. Valki glanced at me and then back at Eirik.

"That much is clear," Valki said.

What did that mean?

Eirik glared straight past me to Valki. Valki shrugged his shoulders and went through the door, not caring to wait for us.

Eirik avoided my eye and slipped past me, carving the

path back down to his house in silence.

7

ARMING OURSELVES WITH gold around our necks, multiple *fela* vials in our pockets, and a rucksack slung over Eirik's shoulder with bread, water, his Hidden Grove map, and little medical kit, leaving enough space for the dozen or so daggers, we journeyed out into the shadows of the streets under curfew. Eirik led the way to the nearest entrance to the secret tunnels and we travelled through the maze of them until we ran out of tunnels on this side of the main thoroughfare and then took to a well-worn track of back alleys. *Hlif* marched in pairs on the main streets, giving us plenty of space to zigzag our way up the cavern.

The city buildings thinned and were replaced by mud flats like Eirik's. We avoided the main thoroughfare and instead slipped beside the houses and through their backyards, darting across the street and doing the same thing all over again.

The towering limestone walls loomed ahead. We edged back towards the main thoroughfare that led up to them, diagonally opposite the gate to Bornholm, and waited in a backyard with a restless chicken coop. Two *hlif* passed by and two others by the towering walls looked the other way. We slipped around a strategically placed mud fence and then squeezed through a fissure just large enough for one person at a time.

"The staircase is back between the limestone walls. Where are we going, Eirik?"

"To the desert above, of course."

He continued through the tight crevice. Turning side-on, I sucked in my tummy, stretched my arms out beside me, and followed along behind him.

"I don't understand," I said.

Eirik disappeared around a bend in the fissure. My heart started pounding. It was incredibly cramped.

"Eirik?" I whispered.

I emerged around the bend and exited the fissure onto a stairwell beside Eirik. He put his finger to his lips and nodded for us to continue up the stairs.

Up and up I climbed behind him until finally, the tunnel opened out onto the Verja night sky behind the large boulder. I had gotten so used to the smell of sweat, incense, and disturbed dirt in Verja that I'd almost forgotten it was there and what it was like to breathe clean air. Without it, here in the open sky, oppression lifted from my senses. The sun was just beyond the horizon, casting light on the wind-carved desert, making strange shadows that looked like waves on the ocean. Heat smacked my skin, so we pushed on to the tree arch and through to the Hidden Grove.

I clutched at my chest and stopped to catch my breath, taking in the calming sight of green foliage and soft grass at my feet.

"I don't understand," I said between breaths. Eirik had stopped a few paces ahead. "I thought you needed the gold to get your family out of Verja. That wasn't so bad."

"It's easier with two people," he said. "But my real concern about the gold is protecting them from what lies beyond Verja. They're my kin. I'm not leaving anything to chance."

"Why didn't you go that way when you were running away from my dad?" I asked.

"Because your vater is fast," he said with a wry smile.

Eirik pulled out his map and handed it to me.

"Lead the way," he said.

I stopped a beat at each tree to make sure we didn't miscount and end up in the wrong world, which was entirely unlikely. I knew this path all too well.

I took us up the third row, past the tree that led to the world in perpetual rain. A few trees on he pointed to one on his left.

"This is the one with the strand. My backup option," he said.

Mr Cuthbert's home world.

"You know, Earth isn't so bad," I said.

His brow furrowed.

"That's not what you told me last time."

"I didn't tell you everything. For one, we have forests of trees like this everywhere instead of dirt and dust and incense. And the weather is just gorgeous—in summer you can sit out on your patio and watch the storms roll in, and in winter just one warm blanket is enough to keep you cosy all night long. Oh, and the food in winter—apple strudel, wine poached pears, orange spiced braid …" I trailed off, remembering each like they were licking my tastebuds.

To think that I was just a few minutes' walk from the tree home to Earth and if I were to climb it, I would be free of this whole escapade. But I wouldn't really be free. I couldn't return home without Dad.

And he wouldn't have gone home without me either. Like the time I'd gotten locked in the bathroom at the Saturday markets on a wet and cold winter morning. Mum had stayed home sick that day and I'd wandered off just before pack-up time. The door had jammed shut, swollen from all the moisture in the air. After screaming for help and wrapping myself in toilet paper to keep warm on the cold tiles, an hour later he finally found me, with the markets all packed up and everyone gone home.

"And what about law? Is it governed?" Eirik asked.

"I mean, every country is different. Heck, even our states are run differently. But where I'm from we don't do sacrifices. If you do something wrong, you'll get locked up but eventually—most of the time—you'll get let out again. My dad is a policeman, actually. He helps to enforce the law and keep the people safe. So yeah, it's not so bad."

"*Já*, but it's clearly ruled by many masters, just like Verja."

"No, Earth doesn't have any masters with magical powers and stuff."

"But they rule?"

"Ah … yeah."

"Same thing," he said. "And I want a place without masters."

My heart sank a little.

"Oh. Does that even exist?"

We turned right at the Celoso tree, the Purlieu tree just up ahead. My stomach flipped over. We were really doing this. We were really going back to that hateful place.

What if I was tricked by Mr Cuthbert yet again? And William was there, waiting? Could I fend him off? Would I be able to escape him again?

"Are you okay, Evelyn?"

Eirik was looking at me sideways, his eyebrows furrowed, eyes sincere. My face felt hot and cold at the same time. I stopped walking, steadying myself, breathing long and slow.

Light was streaming through a thicket in the tree canopy, shining in my eyes.

I could tell him. About Purlieu and William and all that had happened to me. It would be easier if he knew. It would be kind of nice if he knew.

I stepped into the shade. The words were just too hard to voice.

"What is it, Evelyn? What's wrong?"

"I'm fine. I just need a moment."

"Evelyn, I know something is going on with you. Just

tell me. I want to help," he said. "Is it about this world we're going to?"

"It's nothing. Just make sure you've got those gas vials at the ready."

Eirik pursed his lips. I handed the map back and approached the Purlieu tree.

"Oh," Eirik said, looking at the map. "The one with the dog and the angry man."

Angry didn't describe the half of it.

I averted his gaze, desperate to not relive the nightmares in my mind's eye by having to share them aloud with him. I took a deep breath and reached for the first branch. I took another breath and hoisted myself up, beginning the arduous climb to the top.

We would be okay. We had gold. And the *fela*—not that they could really stop William. But if we could reach the castle, we'd have the daggers too. And William—if he was even alive—wouldn't even know we were there. We'd stay close to the cover of the forest and head straight for the mountains. It would be okay.

I could hear Eirik bounding up effortlessly below me. He was clearly a skilled climber, his thin frame perfectly suited to the task, not to mention that he'd already climbed hundreds of trees of the Hidden Grove.

I reached the top bough and hovered on the edge waiting for him to join me. His fingers interlocked with mine as he stepped up beside me. Goosebumps ran up my arm and down my back. He gave a cheeky grin and tugged me after him across the bough. Like the flash of a camera, the image of his smiling face was replaced by blinding white light. It was gone as quick as it came as I set my foot down on the other edge of the bough.

I was in Purlieu once more.

Eirik's fingers slipped from mine as he headed down the tree. I followed suit, gripping tightly to the branches, my arms so shaky I could barely hang on.

I never thought I'd return and yet here I was willingly

entering Purlieu, putting myself back into William's sphere of power.

As my feet hit the ground, I continued to cling in my shaky fashion to the trunk of the tree. If only Dad were here like he was meant to be, like I'd planned on him being, I'd be feeling a little safer right now.

"Evelyn?"

Eirik returned to pry me from the wood.

"Evelyn, what's going on? What's up with this world? What happened here?"

Tears had welled in my eyes, but I shook them away.

"I'm fine. I'll be fine. Let's just get this done."

I looked about the unchanged Hidden Grove through the ghostly green light. It must have been sunset.

We made our way back through the Hidden Grove and the tree arch. There was the cluster of oversized mushrooms in the sparse pine forest. Little white daisies poked through the pine needle floor. Springtime.

Eirik moved forward at a confident pace. I reached out and grabbed him back.

"Steady now. This way."

If William were about, he'd have his eye trained on the forest edge nearest the Hidden Grove. Instead, I zigzagged us slowly through the forest to the left, away from the typical route, slowly bringing us closer to the clearing.

When I was satisfied that we'd travelled far enough, I slunk to the edge of the forest and looked back on the treehouse that centred the clearing.

It was barely recognisable. The treehouse prison was now an ashen mess, the glass cage in shattered pieces on the ground. Black streaks marked what remained of the tree trunk. Daisies and fresh grass shoots were growing through the blackened radius surrounding it. There was something eerie about it all.

"Whoa," Eirik said. "What happened to it?"

"Fire," I said.

On the other side, weeds overtook the cornfield, and the

farm animal pens were empty but the gates were closed.

The quiet—that's what it was.

It shouldn't be this quiet. Everything was overgrown and unkempt like nobody lived here anymore.

Had William died that day? Or simply left? Or maybe he'd abandoned the farm and was now a recluse in his cave? Or lay waiting in the shadows, the whole scene a trap set by his powers?

"The angry man must have left," Eirik said. "Which means, no master, right? Perhaps my kin could come here instead?"

The idea made me feel uneasy, but I kept my mouth shut.

We retreated into the forest and carried on towards the river, hiding in the shadows lest Eirik was wrong and William still lurked in the clearing beyond.

We reached the river but there was a slight problem with my plan. There was no tree cover for the ten paces between the forest and the embankment of the river. And William's cave overlooked the river.

"What is it?" Eirik asked.

"We need to cross that river, but we'll be exposed."

"Who's watching, Evelyn?"

"The angry man."

"How are you so sure?"

"I'm not. I just don't want to take any chances."

"Who is he? What did he do to you?"

"Nothing, okay. Can we please just stay focused?"

Eirik pursed his lips and sighed.

"Okay. Well, we could just wait for nightfall," he said.

I didn't particularly like the idea of bumbling our way about in the dark to the castle and back again or staying in Purlieu any longer than we needed to.

I bit my lip, feeling my brow furrow into the makings of a headache.

"I think we're going to have to just make a run for it," I said.

My heart was pounding. Eirik was watching me with

worry. He took my hand again and gave it a good squeeze.

"It actually makes more sense to go slowly," he said. "It's easier to notice sudden movements."

I stared at him a moment, shocked by my fear.

"I love that you know stuff like that," I said.

He released my hand and got down on his belly, legs and arms splayed out. I followed suit.

Slowly, painfully, we left the shelter of the trees and made our way across the open plain of grass. I dared not look aside for fear of catching William's eye, but stayed focused on the edge of the embankment. It crept closer, closer, closer until finally, I slid over the edge and down the embankment to the water. The river was happily churning along, lapping at the boulders that scattered across it. I crouched by Eirik as we measured up the river. Over to the right was the series of boulders close enough together to cross. Hidden by the height of the embankment, we openly skipped across the river by the rocks and then returned to our bellies, snaking our way slowly up the height of the embankment, over the top, and along the grass once more.

Finally, I stood behind the widest trunk I could find and took a deep breath. Eirik shifted around it beside me. I strained my ears for any other sounds. The wind whistled softly through the trees, branches creaked, the water continued to ripple and lap. No sign of William alerted to our presence.

Cutting through all of it, a screeching sound came from above. I jumped and turned about, looking for the source, my heart back to pounding again.

Pterodactyls were nesting in the trees above us. Their metallic feathers shone in the light of the dying green sunset as they huddled together, a rolling sea above of emerald and burgundy. The forest seemed to be full of them.

Eirik made a strangled noise in his throat. He was looking up at them, transfixed.

"They're harmless to humans," I said.

"They don't look harmless."

"Come on, the sun is setting."

Hidden by the trees, we continued on foot through the forest beneath the vast colony of pterodactyls until we reached the base of the first rugged mountain. Memories streamed back of that terrible night I'd spent trapped in the mountainside cave, hurting from William's betrayal and then pinned down by the tree that had fallen in the avalanche. That moment of utter hopelessness, sure I was going to die there. But I didn't.

The mountain wasn't cloaked in snow this time but the cave was still covered by the tree, which was now dead; many of its pine needles were brown and dry as a blanket on the mountainside.

We rounded the mountain, following the river, which was rushing and wild in this part.

There, cast in shadow by the mountain, was the fire-ridden village and the castle beyond.

"More fire?" Eirik asked.

"Yep."

"Were you here when it happened? And how did Mr Cuthbert know you knew about this place? How do you even know him?"

Where would I begin? What was the shortest version? How could I possibly share any of what I knew without having to unravel the entire narrative? And what good would talking about it do, anyway?

I felt my mouth bob open, numb and powerless, words unable to form.

I couldn't talk about it. I wouldn't.

"I—I—I—" I tried. "I just know, okay?"

I know I sounded annoyed and short and it definitely wasn't the impression I wanted to give Eirik. Really, I just wanted to reach out and touch his hand again. But there wasn't any other way to put a stop to all his questions. And now I had to live with the consequences of driving a wedge between us.

I stepped out of the green light and joined the village in

the shadow of the mountain, just like in the darkness where my secrets could stay hidden.

Eirik kept pace with me but I avoided his gaze and surveyed the crumbling village instead. As we walked past the tragedy of death, I held my breath, hoping he would remain silent too.

We went into the drive via the open wrought-iron gate, the turreted sandstone castle towering over us. My eyes set on the gunmetal door with the sun-shaped pattern in the bricks surrounding it. The door was wide open. Did I leave it that way? I couldn't remember.

"So, where are they?" Eirik asked.

"The daggers? Just at the end of the entrance hall."

We walked through the open door into the great hall, but in the shadow of the mountain with nightfall coming, it was too dark to see anything inside. It had been morning the last time I'd set foot in the castle and light hadn't been a problem.

As my eyes adjusted a little to the darkness, the immediate entrance area became clearer. An oil lantern sat either side of the door at the height of the doorframe, embedded in the sandstone work.

"I don't suppose you have a lighter in that little box of goodies, do you—something to make a fire?" I asked.

Eirik fumbled around in the rucksack and pulled out the medical kit, producing a tallow candle the size of a pencil, a small piece of steel, and flint. He struck the flint with the steel and lit the candle. When the flame held, he reached up to the first oil lantern. The wick caught, and then with a *whoosh*, the flame spread across the sandstone ledge and continued its way around each of the four walls until the flame returned and lit the lantern on our other side. Light filled the entire chamber, flame licking the walls, removing any memory of shadow.

The lavishly dressed skeletons lining the walls beneath the flames remained unchanged from my last visit. Eirik gasped at the sight.

I set my eyes upon the dead king and his royals at the end of the hall and moved towards them, my footsteps echoing off the high walls.

A beat behind me, Eirik followed, now two pairs of echoes bouncing off each other.

There must have been thirty skeletons or so on either side of us. It was a long hall, but I was eager to leave Purlieu, so I picked up the pace.

"What's through here?" Eirik asked.

There was a door that led off the hall to the left that I hadn't noticed last time in my hunger and exhaustion. He diverted from the path and went over to open it.

"Eirik, please. I just want to get out of this creepy place. Can't we just grab the daggers and go?"

"I'll just be a second," he called back, moving through the doorway.

I felt naked in the hall by myself, so I followed in behind him.

It was a circular room, a study of sorts. Topographical maps and tattered books lined the walls and sat in piles. On the table in the centre of the room, a stack of parchment lay unfurled. The one on top appeared to be Purlieu's lay of the land with the Hidden Grove clearly marked with nothing between it and the mountains. Other than the village and castle, the rest of the map was labelled with patches of flora and fauna, the pterodactyls but a blip in the forest by the first mountain. It must have been a much smaller colony in those days.

Eirik shuffled through the maps.

"They're not just of this world. Look here, it's the one with the strand and the building by the beach."

He was right. The warehouse by the water was undeniable.

Eirik gathered the scrolls up in one roll and started putting them in his bag with our supplies.

"What are you doing?"

"What? They might come in handy. Besides, these guys

have no use for them anymore."

He certainly didn't have a problem with taking things that weren't his.

"Give me the bag," I said. "I wanna get these daggers and get out of here."

He zipped it up and handed it to me.

"You go ahead. I want to look around for another minute."

I sighed and left him in the room and continued towards the throne.

There they were: seven skeletons sitting either side of the throne, each with a black dagger sticking from their eye socket. I took a deep breath and approached the first. It was a petite woman, or maybe it had been a young girl, in a voluminous green-and-silver–embroidered gown. In one quick movement, I took hold of her skull with my right hand and pulled the dagger clean with the other.

I placed each of them in the bag as I went along the row until I reached the last one. Again, it was eerily quiet, my movements the only sound echoing off the walls. Eirik should be done by now.

I wheeled around and there he was, stock-still by the door to the map room, eyes locked on the entrance to the castle. I followed his gaze.

A low growl echoed off the walls. Bodie, William's fox, was hunched at the door, rat in mouth, scars across his face and body. He dropped the rat, and his growls grew deeper. My stomach turned over.

Bodie launched forward and Eirik turned and started running down the hall towards the thrones and then passed me, headed for the smaller hall that lay beyond the chamber.

I dumped the bag and sprinted after him. My shoes pounding the sandstone, willing myself to go faster. I could hear Bodie's paws scratching at the ground behind me, gaining on me.

A door appeared at the end of the hall, ajar. If we could only reach it in time, we could close it behind us.

But I could feel Bodie too close behind me, just like with the wolves, feeling his breath almost upon me. I turned on my heel, holding the dagger out defensively. Bodie had leapt to strike, his jaws clamping down on my shoulder just as the dagger entered his belly.

Pain shot down my arm and up my neck. My screams mingled with his high-pitched whine.

Bodie released my shoulder and sprung back off the blade, crumpling in a heap. I fell backwards from the force of impact, landing on my wounded side, crying out once more. The dagger clattered beside me.

Through scrunched eyelids, I looked back to make ready for a second attack but Bodie wasn't moving. Blood seeped from his soft middle as he panted and whined, dying.

Eirik rushed back by my side but I couldn't stop staring at Bodie. Our eyes were locked as the blood continued to seep from him, staining the sandstone floor. If it hadn't been for that dagger, it would be me dying on the floor instead.

Something shifted in his amber eyes. The panting and whining stopped and though his eyes were still directed at mine, they weren't looking at me anymore. He was gone.

"Evelyn; oh, Evelyn. Are you okay?"

I shook myself out of it and looked down at my arm. It was completely drenched with my own sticky crimson blood. I ignored the searing pain and undid the wraparound of my coverall, removing the sleeve. Eirik pulled back the straps of my singlet and bra to get at the wound.

"How bad is it?" I asked.

He started wrapping my shoulder with the reel of cloth from the medic tin.

"He didn't get a good hold of you so it's not too deep."

I watched the blood trickle down my arm and drip onto the floor as he tied the cloth in place. Pain throbbed down my arm with each heartbeat. I gritted my teeth.

"Here, suck on this."

It was a powdery deep pink orb the size of a marble.

"Why? What is it?"

"Epli—in pill form."

I turned my weak hand over. The blood had gathered in the crevices of my scar.

"Oh. No, thank you."

Eirik raised an eyebrow.

"I don't want it to change who I am," I said, feeling heat gather in my face. I knew it was stupid—I should have been more concerned with getting an infection or something, but my scars were just so much a part of me now.

Comprehension dawned on his face.

"I get it," he nodded. "You know, you never told me how it happened."

I tried to formulate the words to describe it in a way he would understand. I'd never had to explain it to anyone before. William had never asked.

"How do you know I wasn't just born with it?"

He took my weak hand and rubbed his thumb over the palm, clearing the pools of my blood to trace the lines of the scar.

"Because I know what a scar like this feels like."

Did he have a hidden scar? Or perhaps it was his father from the mine collapse?

"It's a rope burn. I was trying to help a friend."

He watched me for a moment.

"You are very loyal," he said.

My cheeks flushed with heat. He placed the pill in my other hand and looked me straight in the eyes.

"The Epli, it won't affect this scar while you've got all this other healing that needs to be done. Please take it, it will help."

I could always just spit it out if I started feeling tingling in my hand.

I put it in my mouth and rolled it around, settling it by my left cheek. It was sweet and made syrup with my saliva. After a few moments, my shoulder started to tingle in a soothing way, numbing the pain, giving me a new breath of energy.

Eirik helped me to my feet. He collected the dagger as I tied the torso of my coverall around my waist.

"How do you feel?"

He searched my eyes. Pain stung at the site of the wound with each beat of my heart, but with the Epli it was bearable.

"I don't know. I think I'm okay."

"Do you think it was alone?"

Eirik looked over my shoulder to Bodie. I turned to face the dead fox. Its fur was not sleek and clean like it had once been, its face and torso mangled by scars. Had William done this? Or another predator?

"I hope so," I said, moving past its body and back down the hall.

We returned to the throne room and gathered up the bag of daggers, adding the bloody one to the lot.

In a comfortable silence and shrouded in darkness, we left the castle and continued through the village and round the mountain. Out of the shadow of the mountain, the last bit of daylight was slipping behind the horizon, giving off just enough green light to pick our way through the forest. Above, there was increasing activity in the trees, the pterodactyls shifting and clicking and screeching. Eirik kept looking up at them.

"The maps indicated that they're meant to be much farther west," he said.

"The maps are old. They don't even show the treehouse," I said. "Maybe they migrated here? Because there are a lot more of them now than before."

"Before, when?"

I clenched my jaw. I'd walked into that one. I swallowed the remainder of the Epli and cleared my throat.

"Than on the maps," I said.

It was true, though. It seemed this entire section of forest was covered in them, providing a deafening polyphony of clicks and screeches, like bats at dusk but ten times louder. Even if they were of no harm to humans, animals were unpredictable and with that many of them, they could cause a lot of harm. It made me anxious.

We finally exited the forest. It was too dark now for William to make out our silhouettes, so we walked openly out and down the river embankment.

I felt a little woozy, the tingling in my shoulder gone, replaced by a dull throbbing.

"Hey, can we stop a moment?" I said.

Eirik's stomach grumbled. "Yeah, let's take a break," he said.

He pulled out our water and bread supplies from the rucksack as I washed my arm in the river. I couldn't really see what I was doing but I could feel most of the stickiness leave as the smell of iron filled my nostrils. I wiped my hands on my pants and took a bite from a bread roll.

The screeching of the pterodactyls behind us intensified.

"Ah, you know what? I can wait," Eirik said. "Can we get out of here?"

He stuffed the items back into the rucksack.

A large mass of pterodactyls took to the sky behind us and Eirik yelped. He got up and started crossing the river by the boulders and reached the other embankment before I even had a chance to get to my feet.

"Come on, Evelyn."

I followed after him and reached the other side just as Eirik flew at me and tackled me to the ground, the sound of the pterodactyls' screams deafeningly close. My chin squelched into the mud.

"What the—" I said.

"It swooped at us, I swear."

Eirik's eyes widened. He wrapped his arms around my middle and rolled us round just as a pterodactyl plunged at us with its claws, missing by inches. My stomach constricted.

"Go, now! Let's go!" I yelled.

We scrambled to our feet and ran up the embankment, slipping from the mud. Eirik got ahead of me on the grassy meadow, running straight up the middle. I could feel the pterodactyls hot after us.

"Eirik, this way!"

I veered left to the velvet curtained cave that was William's lair, hoping against all hope that Eirik was following. I pushed past the three-layered fabric, and collapsed, gasping for air.

Eirik fell down behind me, the space filling with utter darkness as the curtains swished closed behind him. I hurriedly got to my feet.

I'd willingly brought myself into William's lair. What if he was there, in the middle of the room in his bed, waiting? What had I done?

I scrambled over to Eirik and grabbed at the rucksack still slung over his shoulder, rushing to arm myself with the steel and flint, striking it. Sparks flew, giving off a blink of light in front of me. I stepped forward quickly around the room, continuing to strike the steel to the flint, giving off barely enough light to discern my steps forward. The futon was empty and unmade, stained with dried blood. My pile of canvas paintings and art supplies were no longer stacked beside it but were strewn across the floor as though William had had a raging fit after I left. I continued striking the steel to the flint and made swiftly around the four corners of the room but no-one else was there. I went to the lantern beside the staircase entrance on the other side of the room and lit it, bringing it back with me to Eirik's side. I sat down with a heaved sigh. We were alone. Safe from William and safe from the pterodactyls.

"Eirik? You okay?"

He was still breathing heavily in a heap on the ground, the noise strangled and flurried. He grunted and got to his feet.

With the lantern's light, I could see just how much of a rage William had gone into. His study desk was upturned, drawers scattered about at odd angles, books were pulled from the shelves, and the gramophone was broken in two, the horn of it with a great dent in the metal tubing. Painted canvases had great slits through them, and feather down covered the floor like snow along with shredded pieces of my school uniform.

In this room, William kept the secrets of his attempted conquests. In this room, he had kept Tiffany prisoner. In this room, he had hidden my mother's locket so that he could control me.

I clutched at the locket around my neck, my heart pounding as the memories flooded back, this time all too vivid. Like he was in the very room with me.

"Are you okay?" Eirik asked back.

His breathing had returned to normal and he was looking at me with concern now.

"Evelyn, what is it about this place? What happened here? How did you know about this cave?"

I fixed my eyes on him to distract myself.

"I've been here before."

"And what happened?"

I tried to form words—any words—but nothing came. Despite the sincere concern in his eyes, I couldn't do it.

"Evelyn, you can trust me."

My mouth bobbed open, my forehead crinkled, my heart pounded. I sputtered. I just couldn't do it. I busied myself with putting the steel and flint back in the bag.

The pterodactyls were still making a racket outside. Eirik sighed, got up, and started poking around. I looked at the contents of the study desk strewn across the floor near me. William's box of treasures was missing. Eirik rifled through the papers on the ground—old ledgers, scraps of paper, torn pages from the hardcovers—and his hands landed on William's art journal. He started flicking through it. My stomach flipped over. Any second now he was going to see multiple sketches of my face drawn in charcoal by William's hand. I tried to think of something to say to distract him, but the page flipped over to the first sketch of me. He stared at it for a moment, confused.

"Evelyn, it's you."

"Eirik—"

"You lived here? With the angry man? What did he do to you?"

"I don't want to talk about it."

"Evelyn, I just want to—"

"If you can't respect that, you don't respect me."

"You don't trust me."

"No. It's not that."

"Then what is it, Evelyn? You know I didn't mean for your *vater* to be put in Fengsel. The guilt is tearing me to shreds. But I did apologise and yet you've continued to be suspicious of me. It doesn't seem to matter what I do to help you; you just won't let me in."

"Won't let you in? Don't trust you?!" I was yelling now, "I have put my entire trust in you, following your every suggestion and advice! I've put my dad's life in your hands. You can't say that I haven't trusted you."

But should I have trusted him? Was he manipulating me just like William had? Or did he have my best interest in mind? It wasn't like he was my only hope—I could always turn to Hilda, Valki, or Mr Cuthbert.

"If you really trusted me," Eirik yelled back, "you'd let me in!"

"I don't have to share every intimate detail about myself with someone to trust them. And besides, it's none of your business."

"I thought—"

"You thought what? That you could be all flirty and nice to me but then let your mum treat me like a dog? What is wrong with you? You're so—so—so—hot and cold."

"You don't know what's going on in my head." There was a tinge of sadness in his voice.

"Heh," I smiled mockingly. "Why not let me in?"

"Very funny."

"Look. I don't want to talk about it, okay? Can't you just leave it alone?" I said.

He huffed. "Fine."

The sound of the pterodactyls flapping wings and screeching made up for our silence. Eirik started inspecting the volumes on the shelves that had survived William's rage. He made his way down the entire length of the room before the noise outside had dulled and he spoke again.

"I'm sorry I overreacted about the birds," he mumbled. "Didn't much fancy being dinner."

"I've never seen them do that before," I said, grateful for a change in subject. "I guess they're top of the food chain now that there's nobody else here. But I always thought they ate, like, fish and eggs."

"I don't think this would make a good world to bring my family to," he said.

I smirked. He was right about that.

It was silent outside the cave as well as inside.

"Let's get out of here," I said.

I closed the art journal, blew out the lantern, and headed for the layered velvet curtains, eager to leave Purlieu behind.

Back in the Hidden Grove, we headed for the Verja tree.
"We did it," he said.
I went back into Purlieu and lived to tell the tale. Just.
"Yeah, we did."
And it really didn't take that long either. We'd probably been gone for three hours, tops. I glanced across at Eirik, his cheeky grin looking back at me. I couldn't help but smile back.

"I don't want to fight again," he said.

I didn't want to either. Couldn't we just pretend like it had never happened?

"But I was thinking," he continued. "We're already here. What's the harm in popping in and out of a few worlds? You know, just for a quick look, cross those last three trees off my list?"

I recalled our earlier argument about the matter and the hard stance I'd taken on not allowing him to deviate from his promise to me.

"Eirik, no. We have to get back. Every moment we delay is another moment my dad is trapped in that prison wondering if he'll ever get out."

"Please, Evelyn. My kin mean everything to me. I need to know where to take them. The anxiety is killing me."

He stopped walking and clasped his hands together. A thin film of tears glazed across his eyes.

"Please."

We were already in the Hidden Grove, after all. Surely it wouldn't take that long?

I bit my lip and waited a beat.

"Okay," I said.

His face lit up and his shoulders relaxed, the tears gathering in the corner of his eyes.

"Really?"

I nodded.

"So, what kind of world are you looking for, exactly? How did Mr Cuthbert describe it?"

"Erm ... It's a quaint, overcast mountainous village. The master left the world and never returned."

"How will we know when we see it? Is the village nearby the Hidden Grove entrance?"

"That, I'm not sure about. I'm hoping I'll just know when I see it."

He unrolled the map and located the first of the three trees remaining. It lay diagonally between the Verja and Earth trees. I gave him a reassuring smile as he twisted his hands together in nervous hopefulness and ignored the reason he was so keen to visit these worlds. He wrapped his hands around the lowermost branch to hoist himself up but sprung back immediately from the tree, holding his hands out.

"What is it?" I asked.

I reached to touch the tree but recoiled with a small gasp, hands smarting. The branches were ice cold.

"It's not that cold," he said, sucking on his fingers,

thinking.

I raised an eyebrow.

"If it's the right world, it will be worth it," he continued.

I reached out and touched the tree again. My fingers burned from the cold; a chill shivered up my arm. It was like gripping an ice cube.

I looked at Eirik doubtfully, but his face was set with determination as he took hold of the branch and started hoisting himself up. I'd have to make quick work with my hands and rely on the insulation from the shoes on my feet.

Down in the Hidden Grove of this new world, the general temperature was no better. A terrible chill blew at us, ripping through the light fabric of my Verja-issued coverall. I started to shiver.

Eirik moved into a run. I followed suit, welcoming the warmth as my heart pounded and breath came out deep and fast.

Reaching the tree arch, I stepped up to see beyond. There was a blizzard rushing across the featureless landscape beyond, forcing wind and snow alike across the threshold of the Hidden Grove, whipping up my hair. Cold ripped through my body like I'd never experienced before. I couldn't feel my face. Eirik went through the archway a few paces, holding his hands up to shield his eyes. His clothes flapped about; his legs spread wide to stay grounded. He looked in all directions but only lasted moments before he returned to the Hidden Grove, teeth chattering. He shook his head.

"Surely the whole world is not covered in winter," I said.

"It's overlooking an ocean of ice," he said. "Even if there are other parts of this world not in winter, it would be impossible to reach them. This can't be it."

We ran back to the Verja tree.

My whole body was shaking uncontrollably, my skin covered in goosebumps, muscles stiff despite the elevated heart rate from running. Eirik pulled his map out, crossed off the tree we'd just climbed with a shaky hand, labelling it with a few scribbles, and then pointed us on to the next one. I gritted my teeth and forced my frozen hands to grip the branches, climbing once more.

It felt an age before we finally touched down on the other side, still in shivers. Eirik's lips were blue. He pulled me into him and held me in a tight hug, shivering and shaking as one. The shared body warmth eventually kicked in, seeping into my skin, deep into my bones and down to my extremities. It felt nice to be held but when the numbness dissipated, I cleared my throat.

We really should continue now that we were in this new world, not knowing what lay ahead within it—good or bad. I pulled away from Eirik. Our eyes met briefly before he led the way once more towards the tree arch. I hurried to move into step with him while I imagined Tiffany's roasting for letting logic rule me while I'd had the perfect opportunity to continue to cosy up to a boy. I couldn't help but smile. She would have loved to tell me off and lament my prudishness. Like the time I'd talked art history with Mataia Kepu at the fish and chip shop while she'd been around the side of the building making out with his twin brother. I tried to explain that I wasn't interested in him like that, but it took her weeks to drop it.

We exited the Hidden Grove into an overflowing garden of flowers. It was like a living scene from Monet's *Water Lilies* with a limited oil palette of pastels and cadmium yellow. A carpet of lilac petaled flowers paved the way, increasing in size the further they went. In the distance, they propped up like stop signs at a school crossing. Lush green shrubbery dotted with draping silky peach blooms lined the path. Dappled light cast through to warm the last tinge of cold left within me. Everything felt soft, almost hazy around the edges, and utterly inviting.

I stepped forward, crushing lilac flowers with my feet. They emitted puffs of blue pollen that smelled like strawberry vape. It was peacefully quiet.

"This isn't the place," Eirik said.

"But it looks perfect."

"It's not natural."

"I don't think there are any masters here. Or even animals for that matter." I cracked a smile. "No oversized birds to contend with."

We were walking along the path of lilac flowers, little spritzes of blue haze erupting with each step, making pillows of clouds around our feet. My ankles started to itch.

"Look—it's just fields of flowers that go on forever. No mountains. No grey skies."

I stopped walking. The flowers were halfway up to our knees in this spot.

"You're right."

The puffs of cloud were rising up my body, now at my hands. They prickled in irritation. I looked at Eirik who was scratching at his palms. They were red raw.

"Eirik?"

He let out a grunt of discomfort, releasing his hands.

"Evelyn, I think we need to get out of here. Now."

The itchiness travelled up my arms, my fingers burning. With panicked leaps and bounds, we returned the way we came, the blue pollen flying about in the air, disturbed by our hasty movements, new bursts sent up in the air with each step.

I stumbled through the tree arch away from the floating pollen, Eirik hot on my heels, and collapsed upon the grass of the Hidden Grove. My skin felt like it was on fire and I didn't have enough hands to scratch it all at the same time. I rolled around, ignoring the sharp ache of my shoulder, the cool grass soothing my red and raw skin.

The itch eventually gave way and I lay puffing by Eirik's side, suddenly keenly aware of his presence so close by. He was looking at me.

"Are you okay?" he asked.

I thought of my exposed ankles, my arms, my neck, my

face. Yes, everything seemed to have settled down. I looked back at him, the skin from his face down his neck a gradient of pink to red. He was considering me.

"I think so. You?"

"Yeah, I think so."

He sat up and stared through the tree arch. I mirrored him.

"Too good to be true, that place," I said.

The blue mist was slowly dissipating in eerie innocence. My red raw skin was testament against the fact.

"Well, I stand by my original conclusions about the Hidden Grove. You'd have to be crazy to want to live in any of the worlds," I said.

"But Mr Cuthbert said there was a place. The perfect place."

"For your sake, I hope he's right."

I took one last look at the idyllic garden and stood to continue our campaign.

We made for the last tree left unlabelled on his map, diagonally opposite the Verja tree, and took to climbing once more. My body resisted each pull and push, damaged and weary from all the Hidden Grove had thrown at me over the last few hours. Eirik seemed distracted, lost in thought, but I was grateful for the comfortable silence between us. It gave me the ability to focus my energies entirely on forcing myself to keep pace with him up the tree.

What would we find in this final world? Would it be just as Mr Cuthbert had promised?

Knots formed in my stomach as I dreaded another world that was out to get us.

As unlikely as it was that the last place Eirik should check is the one Mr Cuthbert had told him of, surely it had to be the one? If only Mr Cuthbert had relented and told Eirik which world was the one, it would have saved the trips to two killer planets.

"I need to make a decision," Eirik said.

I paused to survey him, hugging the branch at my chest for stability. He avoided my eyes.

"I can either do the right thing, or follow my gut."

He scaled the next branch above.

"What makes you think they aren't the same thing?" I called up to him.

"They definitely aren't."

"Oh. Well, of course you should do what is right then. That's what a real man would do."

He chewed his lip, mulling. After a moment he sighed and looked down at me, something hidden behind his eyes.

"You're right. I need to be a man."

What were we talking about exactly?

On the other side of the light portal and down the tree, Eirik rubbed his hands.

"I've got a good feeling about this one," he said.

I hoped he was right.

The knots in my stomach increased. The Hidden Grove was always so peaceful, it made it hard to judge what lay ahead.

We edged towards the tree arch tentatively. Blue skies with fluffy white clouds filled the view beyond it. Our feet left the lush grass of the grove for coarse sand that crunched as we stepped onto the sandy slack of a dune.

It was certainly not a quaint, overcast mountainous village.

My stomach turned over.

Dead and dying bloody bodies in regimented blue linen with gold embroidery lay haphazardly across the plain like remnants of a recent battle.

I quivered at the sight of open wounds, the missing limbs, the entrails, the blood-smeared bayonets. A few paces away a man with a wiry brown beard and freshly injured eye was gasping for breath. He was holding his side, hand covered in blood. The smell of sweat and faeces and iron came and met me where I stood, waking me from my stupor.

The man let out a rickety breath and didn't breathe in again.

Eirik fell to his knees beside me.

"But—it can't be," he said.

His jaw dropped open as he stared across the battlefield.

"He said—he said—he said it existed," the words came out in fits as his voice cracked and he choked back tears. "No!" he sobbed.

He took his face in his hands and bent over, knees to the ground. His whole body shook, no sign of his usual joking, hope-filled exterior.

"Why would he lie? Why?" he asked, the tears spilled out and dripped from his hands, pooling on the sand.

I knelt down beside him and wrapped my arms around him, holding him tightly as he wept.

"Maybe the place he told you about is in a different season so you didn't recognise it? Or located further away from the grove?"

I already had trust issues with Mr Cuthbert as it was. So, Mr Cuthbert had lied, Eirik had misunderstood him, or the world Mr Cuthbert had told him of no longer existed— either unsafe to visit because of the time difference or completely withered and inaccessible.

"Every day my kin spends in Verja they suffer," he said. "All I ever wanted was to offer them freedom. Now I can't even offer them that."

I hugged him tighter.

"I've wasted so much time travelling from world to world."

And not one of those worlds was truly habitable.

"Time I could have spent with them. Time I'll never get back."

I wished there was something I could say, something I could do to make it better, to help him, to fix this. But I came up dry, so I just went on holding him as his body shook first with despair, then with rage.

"I will make him pay for this. I will."

He lifted his head, revealing his blotchy face. It was set with determination. Then he collapsed and began weeping again.

"I don't know what to do," he said.

His shoulders slumped, defeated. I rubbed his back and soothed him.

"We can go back to Verja," I said. "Have a big brainstorming sesh over your map of the grove."

He settled down and took to shaky breaths. I swept the stray hairs from his face and tucked them behind his ears. His eyes met mine briefly. I gave a reassuring smile.

"Don't give up," I said.

He shuddered out a great sigh and looked at me again, this time with greater strength. He uncupped his face and wrapped his arms around me, hugging me back.

"And if worst comes to worst, you could always camp out on Earth for a while," I said.

He let out a small laugh and sniffed back tears. Giving me a quick squeeze, he pulled away and wiped his face on his tunic.

"So, what do you think?" I asked.

"Worst comes to worst," he said with a small smirk.

We got to our feet and brushed the sand from our knees. Eirik pulled his map out and crossed the final world off, adding a few notes to it.

"To Verja?" I asked.

He gave a final sniff and nodded.

We returned through the tree arch, gladly leaving the smells of sweat, faeces, and iron behind. As we climbed up and then down the Verja tree, the distant smell of dirt and incense met my nose instead.

What a ridiculous array of events. From Bodie to the pterodactyls, a freezing blizzard, killer flowers, and a civil war, the grove really was out to get us. And now to return to Verja, a world that was trying to sacrifice my dad and would do the same to me if given the chance.

My feet hit the grass, Eirik following closely behind. He fell into step with me. He had calmed down now and taken to glancing at me every so often. I could feel his eyes on me, considering me, piercing me.

I glanced back at him. Amidst the blotchiness and red rawness from the cold, the poisonous flowers, then the tears mottling his milky skin, his eyes were downcast, sad.

He reached over and took my hand in his and stopped walking. My heart did a double-beat. I stopped and moved back beside him, our fingers laced.

"What is it, Eirik?"

I gripped his hand back, the warmth sending a fresh wave of electricity through my body.

His face was so close, his lips parted, inviting. He pulled me into him and brushed my lips with his. He let out a soft breath and our lips met and then our bodies intertwined in a perfect ache of euphoria. His body softening like putty into mine.

I couldn't believe this was happening; that all this time, he really did want me back. I didn't realise just how much I wanted him, and now, with his lips caressing mine, I wanted more of him.

He jerked away.

My body went stiff. I opened my eyes in surprise. He had a bruised look about him, like he was at war with himself.

"I can't do this with you, Evelyn," he said.

What do you mean?

"I need to be a man and follow through on my promise," he continued. "I need to do the right thing."

What on earth was he talking about? What was so wrong with kissing me?

He looked away. I felt cold, naked.

What was going on?

He paced for a moment, looked back at me with those broken eyes, and turned away again. Were those tears again?

I made to move after him.

"I am betrothed to another," he said.

My mouth dropped open. I stumbled back a few steps. *What?*

"I don't understand," I said.

He was taken. But he had kissed me.

I had thought he was one of the good ones. I had thought that he proved that there were good ones.

"I am bound for marriage. My *vater* set it up before he died. How was I to know I would meet you?"

Marriage? To whom? How had this never come up?

"What the heck, Eirik? How could you fail to mention something like this?" He'd been leading me on this whole time. Just like William.

"How?" I repeated. "Who? Who is she?" Did I even want to know?

"Freja. The one who brings the bread."

The bread girl? The little girl who is smitten with him? The little girl who probably hasn't even had her period yet is betrothed to him, a man?

I felt hollow inside, like the wind had been knocked out of me. This couldn't be happening.

And he wanted to choose her over me? He couldn't even talk to her, couldn't even look at her.

"She comes of age just before the last sacrifice of the season. It's when we're due to wed. And when she is mine, I can take her with my kin away from Verja."

That was why he was in such a panic to line his little ducks up in a row with the gold and finding the right world before the revolution. And he had just used me to help him search for a world where he intended to take not me but his future wife. His tiny juvenile wife.

My face flushed hot with embarrassment.

He was choosing her over me. That was what he meant by doing 'what was right'. But how could marrying a child be the right thing? And then taking her from her home and her family to some foreign world against her will?

Tears betrayed me, streaming down my face. I hastily wiped them away.

What a fool I'd been to think that he wanted me. To think that he was a good man.

I turned and started to walk away.

"Where are you going?"

I kept walking, passing the next row of trees.

"Evelyn, where are you going? The arch is the other way."

I went on, passing another row.

"Evelyn!"

I heard the stomping of Eirik's footsteps after me. His hand wrapped around my wrist and tugged. I ripped it from his touch.

"Don't," I said.

"But Evelyn, we need to get back to Verja. Your *vater*. My kin."

"You think I don't know that!?" I yelled.

Tears streamed down my face against my will.

"I wish—" he began, looking at my lips. "But we can't."

He looked away again. I pushed past him and headed for the tree arch. I couldn't believe I'd let him convince me to go looking at those other worlds. That I'd been charmed by him just like William.

"Evelyn, you can't just waltz back into Verja. We have to be careful."

Eirik fell into step beside me. I folded my arms and kept walking.

He was right. It would help no-one for us to be caught by the *hlif*. We couldn't have them boarding up the exit from the underground citadel.

I trudged through the tree arch, across the hot desert, behind the boulder and then down, down, down the tunnel, all the while trying to ignore Eirik's presence too close by my side. It made my stomach constrict and my throat tighten.

"Evelyn, we need to talk about this."

I let his words hang in the air. He could talk if he really wanted. It didn't mean that I had to.

"You don't understand," he said. "A betrothal, in Verja, it is a binding contract. To dishonour it would bring great shame on all my kin. I wouldn't be able to find a good match for Ta. We would not recover from it."

It was like he forgot that he was leaving Verja and wouldn't have to follow those rules and traditions anymore.

"You have no idea what it's been like," he continued. "How many times I wanted to reach out and ..." he trailed off.

My fists clenched, nails digging into my skin.

I needed to forget this. I needed to stay focused on what I was here to do. I needed to devote myself to Dad's rescue. If I could defeat Bodie, evade the pterodactyls, and survive killer plants, I could beat Verja and save him. I would not be distracted by a boy. Least not a boy who had chosen someone else over me.

I could do this.

We reached the part of the tunnel where it met with the fissure and our hands brushed. A wave of goosebumps swept over me.

No. I had to focus on Dad. Just like he had sacrificed so much for me, starting with getting me into art college. It had been his idea, after all.

"Evelyn, take a look at this place," Dad had said, thrusting a brochure into my hands. "It's got local and international artists for teachers and they teach pathways to exhibiting as artists in regional and state exhibitions and galleries."

He was reading the brochure bullet points over my shoulder.

"Why wait until university to start your career as an artist?"

I flipped over the brochure to the back fold, which displayed the semester fees.

"Dad, are you sure?" I'd asked.

"Don't you worry about that. Worry about *that*," he'd said, flipping back to the front and pointing to the image of a girl with a Young Archies winner's certificate.

"We have to get you into that school."

And from that moment, he'd dedicated everything to making sure it happened.

I slipped sideways into the fissure, rounding the first bend. The familiar, yet unwelcome, smell of sweat, incense, and disturbed dirt met me. I could hear Eirik's breathing behind me. Too close behind me. I moved as quickly as possible through the cramped space, desperate to create some space between us until finally, I emerged behind the cleverly placed mud wall and into the underground citadel once more.

As we neared the marketplace bustling with people moving away towards their homes, Eirik made to continue down the slope.

"Where are you going?" I asked.

"Home."

"But the daggers," I said.

Eirik's face was strained.

"Can't it wait for tomorrow? Curfew is about to fall," he said.

"No. My dad is in prison, Eirik. It can't wait."

By morning I could be on my way to see Mr Cuthbert and Heidelbert.

I grabbed the rucksack off him and marched ahead through the marketplace to the trinket shop.

8

I SLIPPED INSIDE the trinket shop through the newly replaced door, Eirik not far behind me. No-one was at the front counter, so I continued through to the room of doors at the ramp that led down to the basement, just as Hilda was making her way up it with a pulley rope. She almost rolled back down at the sight of me but quickened herself to my side.

Hilda inspected my body, her lips twisting in concern.

"I wasn't sure I was going to see you again—either of you," she said.

I raised an eyebrow, heat flooding my cheeks. Had she picked up on the attraction between Eirik and me?

"I wouldn't just leave my dad here," I said.

"You were gone a really long time," she continued.

Her eyes widened.

"You don't know?" She asked. "Evelyn, there are only two sacrifices left."

A pit dropped in my stomach.

"What do you mean there are only two sacrifices left?" I started yelling, "How can there be only two sacrifices left?!"

Valki rushed into the room and wrapped his hand around my mouth, the dirt from his dusty hand getting between my lips.

"Quiet," he whispered in my ear. "No English."

"Hey!" Eirik yelled in my defence.

The curfew horn sounded outside.

I struggled against Valki's hand, whipping around and out of the hold to face him, breath huffing out of me like a hot wild horse.

"I demand you take me to Mr Cuthbert," I said in my quietest angry voice. "I need to see Heidelbert. Now."

"Mr Cuthbert didn't think you were coming back either," Hilda whispered.

"He started making other … other—" Valki tried.

"—arrangements," Hilda finished. "He thought you ran off with the daggers. We thought maybe that you two …" she shook her head, letting her unfinished sentence hang.

"While my dad is still here, trapped? Never," I said. "Will he still honour his end of the trade?"

Valki nodded. I relaxed a little.

"Now?"

"He's not here," Valki said.

"Where is he?" My voice was rising again.

I would go back to the Hidden Grove to track him down if I had to.

Valki was tight-lipped.

"He's in Bornholm," Hilda said. "With the secret weapon."

"Fine. I'll go and find him myself then," I said.

"No." Valki filled the entire doorway to the shop. "You jeopardise everything."

I turned towards the side door instead.

"He's back tomorrow," Valki said.

I turned back and examined his face.

"Fine. Tomorrow you're taking me to see him."

"Not until you give the daggers."

I slumped the rucksack onto the floor at his feet.

"Go on then," I said.

He bent down and unzipped it, doing a quick count. He

pulled one out. It was the one covered in Bodies' blood. He raised an eyebrow.

"After we see Heidelbert," Eirik said, "I promise I'll come back and help finish the tunnel."

Another promise.

"Without revolution, Hilda will have no hope of good life," Valki said.

"I know. But you could always come with us," Eirik said.

"She cannot climb. And too big carry now. You know that," Valki said, with an edge of resentment. I couldn't tell whether it was aimed at Eirik for his insensitivity or at Hilda and her physical limitations.

"Bornholm trip better be quick," Valki said.

The tension between Eirik and Valki had returned.

"You don't have to go," Eirik said.

"I do. For Hilda. Master Heidelbert must see my leadership."

"What leadership?" Eirik said.

Valki retorted in his native tongue, quipping in a much faster, ferocious manner. Eirik yelled back just as quickly and they went back and forth for several moments, raising their voices.

I grabbed the dagger from Valki, threw it into the bag, and zipped it up. They stopped abruptly and turned to watch me. Eirik sighed. I shoved the bag into Valki's hands. He stepped backwards from the force, eyed Eirik, and then took it downstairs.

The sound of shuffling feet came from the marketplace.

"Do you hear that?" Hilda asked.

"But curfew has fallen," Eirik said.

The tension from Eirik and Valki's argument evaporated and was replaced with worry.

I went back into the shop and peered through the new glass door. My stomach turned over. Pairs of *hlif* were systematically going from house to house, looking stern, focused, dangerous.

I dashed back to Eirik and Hilda just as a rapping came

at the door to the trinket shop. I flinched.

"It's the *hlif*," I said.

Hilda's eyes widened in alarm. She made a strangled noise.

"Go tell Valki, quickly," she said.

Another rap came at the door. Eirik headed down the ramp to the basement and returned a moment later with Valki.

"Go home. Wait for me," he said to Eirik and I then turned to Hilda. "Get our papers."

Eirik took my hand. I wrenched it from him and led the way down to the basement, shifting the shelving unit and opening the door. Eirik moved it back into place behind us and we headed on into the tunnel system down the slope to Eirik's home.

I'd forgotten about Mama and her disdain for me until we entered the back door of the house. There she was in the dining room, face turning tomato red as her eyes fell on us. She started yelling. Elisabeta peeked around the corner from the living room, her eyes slitted with suspicion and warning. I'd had enough of this family and their drama. I turned on my heel into the maid's quarters and slammed the door behind me.

Mama yelled into the door of the maid's quarters. Clearly, she blamed me for her precious Eirik being gone so long. She thumped and wrestled with the doorknob, but I had my feet pushed up against the door. I was not leaving this room until morning. Until Valki said it was time to see Mr Cuthbert.

Things quietened outside. I relaxed my legs onto the bed.

The door flew open and Mama was grabbing at me, her eyes nearly bursting from their sockets. She got a hold of my wrists and pulled me from the bed. I tumbled onto the floor and into the kitchen, sending a roar of pain through my still-injured shoulder. Eirik was by her side, yelling at her while she was yelling back at him, pointing at me struggling against her hold. She reached up her hand, open-palmed, and brought it down across my face, tanning my cheek. She reached back again but Eirik slipped between us, her hand connecting with his forehead instead. Mama let go of me. I fell and slammed my shoulder again. Eirik toppled onto me. I cried out in pain.

He separated himself from me. I opened my eyes warily as the feeling of pounding blood thumped in my shoulder. Mama was pacing the kitchen, still red-faced and fuming. Elisabeta had slipped closer to the confrontation and was now in the doorframe between the dining and kitchen. She shook her head and walked away.

Eirik made a few calm remarks and Mama responded with a final word of indignation and stormed off behind Elisabeta.

Eirik had never defended me in front of his family before.

He gave me a strained smile, got to his feet, and reached out to help me up but I ignored his offered hand. I struggled upright by myself, cradling my arm.

"She's the head of the household. It's her prerogative. Until tomorrow anyway."

Was he really excusing her behaviour?

"We were gone for a really long time after all," he continued. "And she has every right to be mad—I almost missed my Overgangsrite tomorrow. And she thought we'd run off together."

His hand reached out, fingers brushing mine. I whipped my hand away and ducked past him back into the maid's quarters. I couldn't face him anymore. My stomach constricted; my heart ached. It hurt too much. I shut the door and locked my legs into place, feet against the door once more, just in case he decided to invite himself in. No matter how I still felt about him, he wasn't welcome anymore.

I stared at the roof of the maid's quarters. There were fourteen spiders of varying sizes that inhabited the ceiling of the room and seventy-three mud tiles that ran across the two rafters.

My stomach grumbled for breakfast, but I persisted with my protest to wait for Valki's signal, refusing my maidly duties. Instead, I holed up in the maid's quarters counting.

Fifteen days had passed for Dad while only one had passed for me. But so long as Dad and I got out alive, it didn't matter.

What would I do if things fell through with Heidelbert? What was my next option?

I could equip myself with the daggers and, wearing mum's locket, I could threaten the *hlif* to let my dad go. Except they didn't speak English so they wouldn't know what I was saying.

If Heidelbert wouldn't do as I asked, I could threaten him at dagger-point until he did it anyway. Which would make me no better than William, forcing people to do what they didn't want to do. But it was for a good cause.

I'm sure William thought that too.

There was a knock at the front door. The bread girl was right on time. No way was I going to face her today. Moments passed. She knocked again. Eventually, someone answered it. Mama's sickly-sweet voice that she reserved just for Freja rang throughout the house. They exchanged a few words, whereby Freja's girlish tones sounded a mix of relief and excitement. The voices stopped and the front door closed.

I shook my head.

The horn echoed down the cavern, signalling that it was time for the next sacrifice. The maids' quarters door swung open before I had a chance to brace myself against it. Mama was standing there, hands on hips, looking down on me with pursed lips. She said some stern words and stepped aside, waiting for me to get up. When I didn't budge, she grabbed me under the armpit and pulled me out into the kitchen and shoved me in front of her, prodding me in the back all the way out the front door. I pulled the bloodied arm of my coverall back over my shoulder and tied it up. I should have showered.

My stomach grumbled again. I should have had breakfast too.

Eirik moved into step with me up the slope and shoved a bread roll into my hand. I gritted my teeth. Didn't he realise that I didn't want anything to do with him? But passing out from a hunger protest wouldn't get me anywhere. I sighed and gratefully chewed on the bread.

Eirik opened his mouth but I cut him off.

"I don't know if you've noticed but I kinda don't want to be around you right now."

I watched him from my periphery as he ducked his head and slumped his shoulders.

"It's so hard to go through with all this," he said. "Evelyn, I want to be with you, but I have a duty to marry Freja."

My heart did a double-beat; my face felt hot. I swallowed a lump of bread not quite chewed enough and sped ahead of him up the slope. He had no right to say stuff like that. Didn't he realise that's what hurt the most? That if it were another situation, we would be together.

I found a gap halfway down the crowded field behind the prison and filled it, Eirik, then Elisabeta, and Mama squeezing in beside me. We were right on time because the horn blew just as I shuffled as close as I dared to the elderly man on my other side so that I wasn't skin to skin with Eirik.

The masters filed on stage followed by the Gothi to his podium. Two of the chairs remained empty—the ones on the far right by the eldest master. The cornrow whiskers master and the master with the gleam in his eyes were both missing. The Gothi noticed the error and hastily ordered a *hlif* to remove the chairs. I counted the remaining masters. Eighteen, including the Gothi and Heidelbert. Why were two missing?

The *hlif* processed down with the next prisoner, a woman.

The Gothi turned to the crowd with a toothy smile and named her charges, his *hlif* beneath the mirrors echoing along after him.

"She disobeyed her husband," Eirik whispered, his arm touching mine.

You went to jail for that here? So, if Freja refused to follow Eirik out of Verja, she could end up a sacrifice? Did Eirik think that was just?

The woman stepped forward and spun the Norns. I held my breath. It spun round and round until it settled on the white segment—'set free'—but then slowly ticked back one section in a queer way to the black one—'hanging'.

The Gothi quickly spoke up in an overly cheerful manner and the crowd responded with a cheer.

"Is it just me or did that look rigged to you?" I whispered.

"It happens sometimes. The Gothi said that the gods are playing with us—that they want to remind us that they have the final say," Eirik whispered back.

The old man beside me gave us a funny look. The noise of the crowd settled down, so I resumed my silence as the *hlif* strung her up and did their song and dance with the incense. They hanged her, her body writhing about silently above the stage.

How could I be so selfish and preoccupied with my desires when this was the potential fate that my dad faced? How could I allow anything to consume my brain space other than troubleshooting his freedom? I'd wasted fifteen precious days on Eirik in the Hidden Grove when I could have been attempting Dad's rescue.

A cold wave washed over me followed by the heat of

shame.

The woman stopped writhing, hanging limp and silent as though there had never been any life in her. The Gothi turned to the crowd with a satisfied smile and gave an animated final speech before processing out with the other masters.

As the crowd started to disperse, Valki's face flitted about, making a beeline for us. Mama and Elisabeta had already started to move away but I stayed still. I didn't want him to lose me in the crowd—who knew what news he had to bring. I waited expectantly. Eirik had seen him coming too and stayed beside me. The old man on my other side gave a disgruntled murmur and pushed past us.

Valki whispered in Eirik's ear. I watched his face for a response, but it remained neutral. Before I had a chance to do anything, Valki had turned and disappeared into the crowd.

"After the ceremony," was all Eirik said.

"What ceremony?"

Did he mean his wedding? And what was after it?

He gave me a deathly stare to be quiet, the celebrating crowd still thick around us, and started back to his house.

9

MAMA SHOVED A pail and scrubbing brush in my hands and pointed at the living room floor before leaving the house with a basket tucked under her arm. Elisabeta went to bathe and I was left standing alone with Eirik for the first time since we'd kissed. My cheeks flushed hotly at the memory, so I switched into task mode.

"What is the ceremony?"

"I'm becoming a man," he said.

I stifled a laugh. I was glad he agreed that he wasn't one yet, the way he'd been behaving.

"At the wedding?"

"No. My Overgangsrite is this afternoon. The wedding is tomorrow on Frigg's Day … erm, Friday. Weddings are always on Fridays."

The same day as my father's scheduled sacrifice.

"Okay, and what was Valki saying is happening after you become a man?"

"He said we could come to him. Mr Cuthbert is back."

I relaxed a little. Good. We could finally move forward.

I knelt down, dipped the scrubbing brush in the soapy water, and set to work. Eirik continued to hover silently in the corner of the room, watching. Of course, it didn't cross his mind to give me a hand. The sound of the bristles swabbing the floor filled my mind, but I couldn't shake the feeling of his gaze. I gritted my teeth. He cleared his throat.

"What do you want, Eirik?"

He hesitated. I continued my scrubbing, refusing him the satisfaction of piquing my curiosity enough to stop and look at him. Not to mention that I couldn't look at him.

"I was wondering if I could have the gold now."

I slipped, the scrubbing brush flipping out of my hand, and whacked my palm on the ground. I gritted my teeth once more. The nerve of him!

I grabbed up the scrubbing brush and took it in both hands, scrubbing back and forth loudly and brashly. I used to use art as an outlet for my emotion, but today all I had was this scrubbing brush. It would have to do.

"I don't feel comfortable going through with a ceremony that would make me a man if I don't have the means to act like a man and secure my kin's future."

He meant the bread girl's future.

"Does Freja know what you plan to do with her after you make her your bride?"

"She doesn't know. But she's a good girl and will be an obedient wife."

My jaw dropped open. Was he listening to himself?

"And does Mama know? Elisabeta? Do Freja's parents know?"

"I will tell them all when the time is right. I can't risk the *hlif* finding out."

Who was he to decide everyone's future? What if they were perfectly happy here?

"Look, when I become a man, I will be the head of this household. It will be my responsibility to take care of my kin's welfare—which I believe I can only honestly do outside of Verja."

"You haven't even figured out where you're going to take them."

He mumbled something about the "contingency"

worlds. I sighed.

"The answer is no, Eirik. We had a deal."

"And I'll still keep my half of it. You can trust me."

I slammed the scrubbing brush down and watched it bounce across the floor and settle by his feet.

"You can't do that. You can't say that!" I yelled. "It's all your fault and you've hardly even tried to help me and you talk about being honourable and 'the man' of the family but really you're just completely selfish and want to make your own life perfect no matter what happens to the people you crush along the way. You could stand up and fight, like Valki, but instead you're running away!"

I took a breath and got to my feet to face him.

What on earth did I ever see in him? He was an ugly coward.

"Does that mean your answer is 'no'?"

I narrowed my eyes and glared at him, then turned and walked out of the room.

"You can finish up here," I said over my shoulder.

I would not let another drop fall from my eyes for a man who traded his fears for lies.

I stood to attention in the clean living room beside Elisabeta and Mama, Eirik kneeling down before us. It didn't look like he was going to run along hot coals or go walkabout. All I knew was that I had to be quiet and stay still.

He was wearing an old silk embroidered two-piece tunic. It was a bit tight. Must have been an heirloom. He gave a deep bow to Mama and then turned to the family altar to do the same. Mama approached the altar, lighting incense, and Eirik removed the tunic shirt. Long lines of pink mangled skin covered his back, like he'd been slashed or whipped. Scars like the ones across the palm of my hand.

Mama moved behind him and stopped for a moment to gaze upon the scars, sighing. She said something with a hint of sadness in her voice and Eirik and Elisabeta looked to one another knowingly. Pacing around him with the incense, she began to chant.

I looked straight past him, out the window, determined to not let him get into my head again. I couldn't afford to be distracted. And he didn't deserve my attention anyway. I was furious with him. And disgusted by him. But why did he have to look so damn wonderful?

Despite reason and resolve, my eyes flickered upon him. He was looking at me out of the corner of his eye. Was that grief? Longing? Confusion?

If only things were different.

But my desire was covered in darkness—jealousy, bitterness, injustice, anger. A darkness that wasn't there before William. I felt it swelling up inside of me. I was angry with Freja for getting in the way. At Eirik for choosing her over me. And at myself for being a fool for falling for another guy who knew nothing about real love. Had I learnt nothing? Even after the betrayal and rejection, how could any desire for him still remain? Was I really so desperate? So desperate to be wanted, to be loved, that I took it no matter what form it came in?

I saw what Eirik was capable of from the start—a thief, a liar. He hadn't hidden who he was like William and led me to some false pretence. No, I went into this one with my eyes wide open and yet allowed myself to fall for him anyway.

But no more.

I would be stronger. I would be wiser. I would be patient. And I would not settle for anything less than real love. Because what Eirik had to offer Freja was not love but enforcing duty upon her for his sake. Gosh, was he really any better than William? And if he had chosen me, it would have been nothing more than lust. We had no logical hopes of a future together and any relationship would only hurt both of our families and ultimately one another. We were two different people from two very different worlds and though Eirik was trying to leave Verja and its ways, he would inevitably be bringing that culture along with him.

I didn't want mere affection or sexual attraction. No, what I really wanted was someone who could give their whole self to me, freely, faithfully, unreservedly. Someone who had my best interests in mind always. Someone I respected enough that I could do the same to in return.

That was possible to find, right? I think that's what my parents had.

Mama finally put down the incense and bowed deeply to Eirik. She moved behind him and undid his hair, letting it fall down his back. Taking a pair of sharp, shiny scissors with engravings and moulded shapes across the handles, she began to trim it, starting with large rough handfuls around his shoulders and slowly moving into smaller sections around his neck and ears in a more ceremonious manner.

He was still glancing at me every so often. And his look was definitely that of longing. I returned to looking out the window.

He wasn't allowed to look at me like that anymore. He had made his choice. And I had made mine.

My calves and lower back had gone from aching to numb and back to aching again by the time she was done. A circle of platinum hair lay on the floor around Eirik. His face looked different now, framed with a short crop of hair on all sides. A new man. Apparently.

He stood to his full height, with even greater hubris than usual, and faced us in our line. Both Elisabeta and Mama bowed low. He raised an eyebrow at me, but I stood my ground, head held high.

Eirik motioned for me to clean up the hair and dismissed the family. Mama and Elisabeta left the room and so, body stiff and resistant, I promptly did too. He may have been head of his family, but he was not going to control me.

I went to the kitchen instead and started picking around for food. After a few minutes, he followed in behind me and disposed of his old hair.

Before he could tell me to get into line or ask me for the gold in advance again or express how hard it was to go through with marrying Freja, there was a firm knock at the door. I left him to answer it.

My stomach flipped over as I opened the door on two *hlif*. They looked disgruntled and on a mission to find me. The one on the left held up three pieces of parchment paper—one with a crude drawing of Mr Cuthbert, one of Eirik, and one of me. Speaking in their Scandinavian tongue, I couldn't understand them. Getting impatient with my apparent obtuseness, they pushed past me into the house and started yelling. Eirik came running into the room, eyes wide in shock, but quickly recovering to a blithe dominance, speaking to the *hlif* as though they were beneath him.

He was lucky he'd just had a haircut—for the authority it gave him in the household and that it removed any likeness to the image in the *hlif's* hand.

Mama and Elisabeta had returned to the living room at the noise. Mama went ghost white and looked to Eirik for direction, taking her new inferior role seriously.

The *hlif* with the papers was surveying each of us and in turn the images. He paused for a long moment on me. I held my breath, keeping my face as neutral as possible, like I was being inspected by Dad for lying.

Eirik was trying to say something but it took a moment before the *hlif* paid him any attention. He was pointing to my weak hand, explaining. They didn't look convinced, so he left the room for a painstaking moment and returned with papers of his own. Identity papers. I joined Mama and Elisabeta in watching Eirik curiously. How was he going to explain that I didn't have any?

My heart thudded in my chest, my stomach in knots. I was standing closest to the door, the pair of *hlif* in the centre of the living room, Eirik nearest the hall, Mama and Elisabeta between them. I could turn and run out the door right now, while they were distracted.

Pointing to himself, Eirik read out the first: "Eirik Mörsugur Eik."

He pointed to Mama next. "Una Sigrid Eik."

Then Elisabeta. "Elisabeta Astrid Eik."

And then, lastly, to me. "Evelyn Harpa Tyr."

Elisabeta raised an eyebrow and Mama seemed to put to bed her concerns about me. I internally relaxed, the knots loosening in my stomach.

Eirik passed the papers to the *hlif* and they rifled through them, taking extra care to scrutinise the paper with my given name on it. Eventually, they conceded and shoved the papers back in Eirik's hands and left the house with a stern warning.

Mama relaxed and gave Eirik a comforting smile. I suppose he'd passed his first test as head of the household. She left the room but Elisabeta stayed behind. She addressed Eirik, looking to me every so often. Eirik seemed to be trying to quell her concerns. She didn't look convinced but eventually huffed and walked away.

"Is my cover blown?" I asked.

"No."

"Good. And the ceremony is officially over then?" I asked.

He nodded.

Somewhere along the way, he'd thought to get identity papers for me, something I hadn't even known I needed. It was the only thing standing between Fengsel and me. Trying not to meditate upon the fact that he had saved me, I headed out the front door for the trinket shop, Eirik a few steps behind me.

"You better not blow this meeting," I called back to Eirik.

"Mr Cuthbert needs to answer for what he's done," Eirik said, falling into step with me.

"We don't know if he lied to you."

"No, we don't know *why* he lied to me."

"You promised to help get my dad out. If you blow this

meeting, you're essentially signing his death warrant because I have no other way of getting him out at this point and we're running out of time. Take your anger out on Mr Cuthbert another time."

Eirik pursed his lips and we continued up the slope in silence.

Valki was standing behind the counter of his trinket shop as we entered. He was fidgeting agitatedly and had deep bags under his eyes.

"Everything go okay last night?" Eirik asked.

Valki nodded.

"And the tunnel, how's that going?"

"Getting there."

He didn't meet Eirik's eyes. I straightened my back as the feeling of residual tension from the previous day hung in the air.

Valki moved from the room and we followed. Once more he led the way through the secret passages up to Mr Cuthbert's hidden office.

Mr Cuthbert was behind his desk, as on the previous visit, but this time wearing a white silk tunic with long white gloves. He was clean and manicured and hardly recognisable. I hadn't taken him as the type who would employ dress-ups.

"I had presumed your demise," he said.

Or perhaps my capture at William's hands.

"We were about to send out a new volunteer to retrieve the daggers. Were we not, Mr Unfrid?" Valki nodded. "But we have the daggers now?"

Valki nodded again. "*Fjórtán* daggers."

Mr Cuthbert's forehead crinkled.

"Fourteen? But where is the fifteenth?"

Heat flooded my cheeks at the memory of losing it in the river upon my return from the castle to the standoff with William.

"I lost it," I said.

Mr Cuthbert gave me a deathly stare. My heart started to beat quickly. Was he about to back out of our deal?

"You never said you needed a particular number. You only said to retrieve the ones in the castle. Which is what we did."

"Are you lying to me, Miss Evelyn? Are you, instead, keeping one for yourself?"

The thought hadn't even crossed my mind. I wished it had.

"No. Honestly. I lost it in the river—last time."

I avoided Eirik's eyes. He still didn't know what had happened in Purlieu previously.

Mr Cuthbert pursed his lips and considered me. I must have passed his test because he stood up and wrapped a large ochre hooded cape around himself, concealing the delicate white. He nodded at the three neat piles of clothes across his desk: a matching white tunic and gloves, and two *hlif* uniforms, batons included.

"After Master Heidelbert's last failed excursion, he has been unable to leave Bornholm except for the sacrifices, to avoid suspicion. So, we must travel to him, I am afraid."

"What happened last time?" I asked.

"Why, of the two people the *hlif* managed to capture at the Uppreisn meeting, of course one of them had to be Master Heidelbert himself. He almost uncovered our entire operation and his own intended coup."

"So, he's definitely expecting us?" I asked.

"With great anticipation," Mr Cuthbert said. "Get changed and we will be on our way."

"What did you tell him?"

"Enough to get you in the room with him."

Mr Cuthbert stood and left the room, closing the door behind him.

"If we get caught in *hlif* uniforms, they won't hesitate to put us in Fengsel," Eirik said. "It could be a trap."

"I wouldn't put it past Mr Cuthbert," I said.

"Mr Cuthbert does this all the time," Valki said, motioning to the clothes.

"Well, it's worth the risk," I said. "For me anyway. You two can do what you like."

I grabbed the pile of white clothing, left the room, and got changed in the empty basement. The tunic slipped on easily and had a light, airy feel to it, breathing in a way the cotton coverall never could. I took up the gloves and was slipping them on just as Mr Cuthbert's office door opened and Valki then Eirik walked out a moment apart. They'd both apparently decided to come. Eirik's guard uniform was still undone at the back, exposing his scarred skin. Valki seemed to be wilfully ignoring it, disinclined to help him, having managed his own fine.

"Would you?" he asked me.

I sighed. He wasn't putting the moves on me. I wouldn't let him. Especially with the buffer Valki's presence provided.

"Fine," I said.

I passed him the wraparound ties of the jumpsuit.

"What happened?" I asked, eying the disappearing scars as he pulled the fabric tight around himself into a belt at the front. Eirik glanced at Valki.

"Lashings," Eirik said.

"I forgot about that," Valki said.

"Like with a whip?"

Eirik nodded.

"Why? And why didn't it heal from the Epli?"

"Remember how I told you I tried to get my father out of Fengsel? Well, I was underage when they caught me, so I got ten lashings instead of becoming a sacrifice."

His eyes became fierce as he chose to look at Valki while he responded to me.

"That's when I swore I'd get my kin out of here," Eirik said. "I don't ever want to forget what they did—it drives me on. That's why I refuse to take Epli."

I looked at my weak hand and nodded with

understanding.

Eirik whipped the cape around his shoulders and flipped the hood up to match Valki.

"It won't be like that, under my rule," Valki said.

Eirik looked like he wanted to reply but thought better of it.

"Let's find Mr Cuthbert and get this over with," I said.

He was waiting upstairs and moved straight into action when we reached him, passing me a matching cloak, and guiding us out the front door of the house and across the street.

"Hide that until we get there," he said over his shoulder, glancing at the locket around my neck. It was dangling openly upon the white tunic, which I'd missed in my rush to get changed. I replaced it safely beneath the fabric of my clothes as it usually resided.

In the neighbour's house, we went straight to the basement and into the tunnel system. Up and up we travelled through a maze of tunnels, in and out of basements, until we reached the end of the line and exited into a backyard at the upper caverns. The suburban mud hut house was beside the main thoroughfare and also directly across from the corner of the sheer-faced limestone wall with the gate to Bornholm. The wall reached the cavern roof and was spattered in moss and ferns, and birds nested in the many cracks and crevices that went along it. It was old and glorious and terrifying to behold up close.

Mr Cuthbert directed us from backyard to backyard, following the wall away from the towering corridor entrance and the gate of Bornholm. Almost at the wall's end, Mr Cuthbert had us stop and watch the pair of *hlif* doing the rounds, up and back along the wall. When they were halfway back to the gate at the corner, Mr Cuthbert got up and motioned for us to follow, crossing the road to one of the larger ferns. He slipped around it and disappeared on the other side. I followed behind him and found a fissure running through the wall. I stepped inside, hearing music and merriment coming from beyond the gap. It was a deep fissure, rough and difficult to navigate. At one point I had to turn side-on, careful not to snag the light fabric that hung from my shoulders. Ahead of me, Mr Cuthbert exited the fissure and rounded another fern.

Daylight spilled through, filling my sight, the full brunt of Bornholm's prosperity hitting me. Mirrors had been strategically placed all around the city to reflect light onto pockets of flora that draped across the walls and all around us. The smell of sweat and sewage was replaced by the sweet fragrance of flowers and the damp dirt smell of a rainforest.

We were located in the back corner of a vast garden, hidden from view by the curated growth of flowers and fruit trees. I could hear laughter and singing nearby.

Mr Cuthbert shed his cloak and stuffed it behind the fern, indicating for me to do likewise.

"You beside me," he pulled me in next to him. "And you two follow behind closely as our escorts."

We weaved our way through the garden, following the neatly trimmed paths, the blossom fragrance intoxicating my senses. It was unsettlingly perfect, just like the deadly flower planet.

The hedges made way for an open plain of lawn where a party was taking place. Men and women alike wore their silky hair in complicated braids, bodies draped in delicate white cloth and gold chain. There was a carefree joy about them, a glisten in their eyes that didn't exist in the rest of Verja. Perhaps it was that curfew clearly didn't apply here.

The revellers didn't take any notice of us as we moved past them and took in the unobstructed full vision of Bornholm. It was a clean and ordered city of limestone buildings, streets lined with alfresco dining. White-clad locals lazed about with glowing smiles and plates piled high.

My stomach turned over at the affluence. It was a stark contrast to where I'd just come from and something told me these people would not take kindly to a change in leadership and lifestyle. Valki would have his work cut out for him.

We moved onto the main thoroughfare and made our way through the city. My stomach grumbled at the smell of hearty stews and sweet stone fruit–based desserts. I tried to console myself with the promise of making whatever I wanted to eat when we got back home again. Even a fruit pie from the freezer would suffice.

We came to another limestone barricade. Rounding the corner, it turned into a metal fence with a gate halfway down and a pair of *hlif* standing guard. The road that continued past the guards led into a less affluent part of the town, with smaller houses. Though they were made of mud instead of stone, they were painted shades of pastel and decorated with metal trimmings on the eaves. Young women in white with babes in arm chatted from their doorsteps whilst *hlif* came and went from the area.

In contrast, on the other side of the fence to our left, empty lawns surrounded an expansive mansion compound of multiple enormous buildings and not a soul could be seen inside.

Upon approaching the *hlif* at the gate, Mr Cuthbert produced a parchment scroll. They smiled at him in recognition, entirely ignored Eirik and Valki, but peered curiously at me. I tried to look as regal as possible, straightening my back, elongating my neck, and looking down my nose at them, assuming that was what I was supposed to do. They broke the seal, unfurled the scroll, and glanced over it briefly. With a nod, they opened the gate and promptly stepped aside to let us through.

As we travelled down the empty pavement that carved a path through the lawn, I let out a sigh of relief.

"How did you do that?"

"Master Heidelbert always supplies me with new

entrance papers for my next visit each time I leave him."

"That's the one thing I don't understand," I said. "Why is Heidelbert on the side of the Uppreisn when he's a master? After all, he'll be on that stage when it collapses."

"I had hoped he would be able to convince his father to let him conduct the final sacrifice of the season, which would mean he would be on the podium, not the stage. Something tells me I will need to find an alternative to spare him from that bloodbath, which were the terms of our arrangement. Not that it is any of your business."

The mansion compound was broken up into separate dwellings with a maze of paths running between them. We passed the first cluster of four, which opened up a view of the next cluster, where the manor nearest us was in a wreck of rubble and ruin. The stone structure had collapsed in on itself, the contents and building indistinguishable from one to the other. No-one had attempted to rifle through the remains or begin the task of cleaning up. The only sign of acknowledgement of the disaster was the addition of two clay effigies where the door used to be.

"Do not stare," Mr Cuthbert said. "As a Bornholm resident, you should be on top of what happened here."

"But I don't know what happened here," I said.

"Locally, they are calling it the result of a quarrel between two masters. Amongst the masters, they are calling it an act of insurrection. The Gothi himself has suspicions that Master Heidelbert was at the heart of it, but has not been able to decipher a motive."

"So, which one is true?"

Mr Cuthbert thought for a beat.

"You see, when one becomes a master, the power is not so easily wielded. It is a craft that is acquired over time. Master Heidelbert was supposed to make the death of his uncles look like an accident, but he got a little overzealous. I have been attempting to teach him control ever since."

The two empty chairs at the sacrifice made sense now.

"But why?" I asked.

"So that he can be of use."

"No, why did you have him kill his uncles?"

"Because they were particularly troublesome. And besides, they were going to die anyway. The actual revolution would be all the easier if we could pick away at the masters in advance, however, with the Gothi suspicious of Master Heidelbert, we have had to put a stopper in those plans."

We were approaching the manor in the heart of the paths. It towered over the rest, with limestone pillars too wide to wrap my arms around. A pair of *hlif* were on guard at its entrance. Mr Cuthbert surrendered another parchment scroll and we proceeded through the double doors.

Up a wide staircase our shuffling steps echoed, muffled only by a high pile burgundy rug that ran the length of the corridor left and right. We followed it left, passing door after door until we reached the one at the very end. The wall and door were covered in gold leaf, paired with a gold plated doorknob barely discernible from the rest of the wall. It was like a fortress made of gold, which didn't make sense because gold was a soft metal, but for a family of masters, I suppose it was the best protection they could have from one another.

Mr Cuthbert stopped and turned to face each of us.

"Follow my lead and accept whatever the child decides," Mr Cuthbert said. "I need not remind you that though he may not look it, he is a master and can use his power at any moment as he pleases."

William's face too close to mine flashed before my mind's eye. How he had forced me to smile, to kiss him, for my body to respond to his as though I wanted him. I shuddered.

Mr Cuthbert knocked on the door. After a moment a small hesitant voice responded from the other side.

The room was large enough to fit Eirik's entire house inside and appeared to function as a bedroom, bathroom, and study, like a studio apartment. Layered rugs covered the floor, a golden net hung from the four-poster bed, and the furniture occupying the room was not made of stone or clay, but wood.

Mr Cuthbert had swiftly entered the room proper whilst the rest of us hung back. Seeing Mr Cuthbert, Heidelbert rushed and fell at his feet, sobbing and blathering. Mr Cuthbert neither comforted nor rejected him, merely tolerating the dependent behaviour. He spoke to him in a calm manner, looking down upon him with a neutral face.

Valki shut the door behind him with a click and Heidelbert noticed for the first time, through a tear-streaked face, that more than just Mr Cuthbert had entered. He backed away quickly, wide-eyed, and pointed to Mr Cuthbert in an accusatory manner. Mr Cuthbert put his hands up defensively and continued to speak calmly, occasionally pointing to the group of us by the door until he managed to pacify him. Heidelbert wrapped his arms around one of the poles of his four-poster, peering from behind it to us. The tension in the room released a little.

Mr Cuthbert turned to me and motioned for me to come a little closer. I gulped and stepped up beside him. Heidelbert was like a ticking time bomb—one wrong step and he would be inconsolable, uncontrollable, the death of us all. I had to choose my words wisely.

"Master Heidelbert, would you free—" I began. Heidelbert flinched and said something loudly, but I powered on. "—my father from Fengsel?" I finished.

Heidelbert looked around in a panic and quickly paced across to the closed windows on three sides of the room and checked outside. Mr Cuthbert was saying something that sounded like reassurance. When Heidelbert returned to his bedside, Mr Cuthbert turned to me, encouraging me to continue. Heidelbert watched me with caution.

"My father and I came to Verja by accident and we just want to go home. But he was captured by the *hlif* and now he's last in line for the Ofre Arstid. He's got darker skin and eyes, is really tall. Can you get him out?"

Mr Cuthbert chimed in, translating to Heidelbert.

"That's not what she said. You promised you would translate correctly," Eirik said loudly.

Heidelbert flinched again and shouted something at Eirik but Eirik continued, face red, a vein pulsing in his neck, "Just like how you lied to me about the perfect world to take my family to."

Heidelbert's eyes darted around the room at each of us as if looking for answers. His brow had furrowed, and life seemed to be draining from him at a rapid pace. He took a deep breath and mustered his strength, turning on Valki this time, yelling something at him.

My stomach dropped—he was confused and frustrated because he'd used his power on both Eirik and me, but it hadn't worked because we were wearing gold. So now he was flexing his power on Valki. I whipped around to Mr Cuthbert to get him to rectify the situation just as coughing started coming from behind me. Valki was grappling at his throat, unable to form words or even breath.

"Please excuse Master Heidelbert, he is still learning to harness his powers and forgets," Mr Cuthbert said.

Valki's face started to turn a purplish-blue. Why wasn't Mr Cuthbert doing something? Why was he acting so calmly as though this was just a minor inconvenience? Valki was dying!

Heidelbert was on his knees, sobbing again. Mr Cuthbert sighed and strode over to him and spoke softly but forcibly, in an instructive manner. Valki stopped coughing, a strangled noise now coming from his throat. He fell to the ground.

I moved in unison with Eirik to Valki's side, not knowing what to do. Valki had become silent, his eyes shut, his body still. I checked his pulse and breathing but he only had the former, a tenuous dull throb. He was unconscious. I tried to recall how long someone could go without oxygen before they became brain dead. Was it a minute? Five? Thirty seconds? Either way, he didn't have much time.

"Stop it! Stop it now!" I yelled at Heidelbert, but he was still on the ground in inconsolable tears.

The last beat I'd felt from Valki's pulse was over a minute ago. His last breath perhaps three. I removed the clasp that held his cape and placed the heel of my hands at the edge of his breastbone to begin CPR, wracking my brain for the one hour we spent on the subject in Phys Ed.

Heidelbert's sobs had reduced to a hiccup. He stood and was walking towards us, speaking calmly but firmly.

"*Anda*," Heidelbert said. "*Anda. Anda.*"

"What are you doing to him?" Eirik asked me.

"What's he saying?" I asked, ignoring Eirik as I began the compression.

"He's commanding him to breathe," Eirik said.

I checked Valki's airways, desperate to hear something, feel something, but there was no breath either in or out.

"Why isn't he breathing?" I said, tears forming in my eyes.

I pumped his chest, putting the full force of my weight upon him.

"*ANDAAA!*" Heidelbert said.

"Five, six, seven," I said under my breath with each compression, trying not to lose count with Heidelbert's voice amplifying as he attempted to command Valki to breathe.

If not even Heidelbert with his power could raise him, what chance did I have?

"It would appear that he is gone," Mr Cuthbert said.

"No!" Eirik said.

I fell back, exhausted, defeated, but Eirik turned on Heidelbert.

"Make him wake up," he said in English and then started yelling at him in his native tongue.

"Master Heidelbert still has much to learn," Mr Cuthbert said. "But one thing is for sure: he cannot bring someone back from the dead."

Heidelbert had collapsed again, his eyes wide and empty, staring at Valki in disbelief, no tears left to shed. Eirik started pacing, rubbing his hands to his face as he feverishly talked to himself, a sob escaping his lips every so often.

If I'd not been wearing gold, that would be me lying on the ground, the life sapped from me in a matter of moments. Same for Eirik. The power of the masters was just so great. How could we possibly hope to overthrow them? Just one newborn master could kill a man at the whim of his hormones. Imagine what seventeen fully matured men could do collectively. Perhaps Eirik had been right to say the revolution was an impossibility, a fool's errand.

Mr Cuthbert had started speaking to Heidelbert again. Still shell-shocked, Heidelbert nodded, got to his feet, and left the room.

"Where is he going?" I asked.

"To get a servant to dispose of Valki's body," Eirik spat with bitterness, translating Mr Cuthbert's words.

He eyed Mr Cuthbert with slitted eyes of distaste.

"You know I am right," Mr Cuthbert said. "If someone were to find his body here, Hilda would answer for it. The revolution, an impasse. Valki's work undone."

Eirik knelt at Valki's side, squeezed his lifeless hand, and spoke to him in their native tongue. Tears streamed his face.

Their last conversation had been an argument. I couldn't even begin to conceive what he was feeling. If it were Tiffany, I think I'd want to die along with her.

The door opened with Heidelbert returning, a manservant moving zombie-like behind him, pushing a linen cart. In one swift motion of strength greater than I would have anticipated from the servant, he hoisted Valki's limp body onto the linen cart. He piled white silk-like sheets and felt towels over him, draping down the sides, and left the room.

Eirik stood and watched as the servant pushed the cart the length of the corridor until Mr Cuthbert cut in front of him and shut the door, locking it with a click.

"Back to business," he said.

"How can you be so heartless?" I said.

"Do you want his help or not?" Mr Cuthbert asked.

I bowed my head and collected myself, "Of course I do."

Heidelbert returned to his position by the bed and Eirik mustered himself back onto his feet and came to my side, facing Heidelbert. Mr Cuthbert moved to the middle ground.

"Let us try once more," Mr Cuthbert said.

He spoke to Heidelbert at length, glancing at Eirik every so often. Eirik was nodding along, tears trickling down his face in silence.

"What's he saying?" I asked Eirik.

"He's translating your request. Correctly."

Heidelbert started pacing the room, externally processing. He sounded hesitant.

"He does not wish to upset the gods," Mr Cuthbert interpreted. "For their rightful gain of your father's death. However, he could manipulate the Norns, as his father does when he does not get the result he wants. But he is not sure the gods would be convinced and could punish him for it, which is not how he wishes to begin his reign as the sole master."

I knew there was something up with the Norns. Of course the Gothi manipulated the result—he had the means and the motive.

"Please," I began, speaking to both Heidelbert and Mr Cuthbert collectively. "Can't you do something? Anything?"

The doorknob of the room began to rattle. A gruff voice came from beyond. The voice sounded familiar.

"The Gothi," Mr Cuthbert said.

Heidelbert looked at Mr Cuthbert, his face pale, his eyes wide. Mr Cuthbert stepped forward and squeezed his shoulder, the first sign of any affection. He then moved towards the windows at the back end of the room. Heidelbert ushered Eirik and me to follow. Mr Cuthbert was out the window before we even reached it. I looked outside and saw him sliding down a limestone pillar. The door rattled again. Eirik gave me a gentle push. I climbed out the window and wrapped my arms around the pillar, looking back upon Heidelbert's blotchy face with regret as I slid down and out of sight, Eirik following suit.

Hedges and fruit trees surrounded the back of the manor. Mr Cuthbert carved a path before me into a hiding place by the building, out of sight from the windows above. Eirik and I followed closely behind as muffled yelling came from Heidelbert's room.

"How long do you think we'll have to wait here before we can go back up there?" I asked.

Mr Cuthbert furrowed his brow.

"What do you mean? We will not be returning."

"What? Why not? Heidelbert didn't get a chance to answer my question, to come up with a solution."

"But we have already received his answer: Master Heidelbert said it was too risky."

"He didn't say that. He hasn't exhausted all the options yet."

"He did," Mr Cuthbert said. "He said he did not wish to upset the gods by withholding a death that belonged to them."

"But Heidelbert was my best option for saving my dad. And you promised to help me."

"No. We made a deal that I would set up an audience and bring you to him to plead your case and I have gone above and beyond by also acting as translator."

I wracked my brain, trying to recall our previous conversation and the terms of the deal. I needed to be more careful with Mr Cuthbert. He was razor-sharp.

"Now, I believe I have more than fulfilled my share of the agreement," Mr Cuthbert said. "It is time we part."

Mr Cuthbert started looking about, readying himself to

leave our hiding place.

"You slimy piece of garbage. You haven't done squat," I said. "Eirik and I risked our necks getting those daggers back and all you did is line up a meeting for us to be murdered and then leave us high and dry in one of the most dangerous places in Verja!"

I tried to wrap my brain around the fact that this trip had in fact been a fool's errand and that I'd gambled my dad's life on it. And lost.

"Please calm yourself, Miss Evelyn," he said, shaking his head. "Perhaps you would like to arrange another deal then?"

I tried to relax my shoulders but at the sight of the twinkle in his eyes, I bit my lip. His deals never seemed to run in my favour.

"What did you have in mind?"

He smiled.

"I could personally persuade Master Heidelbert to set your father free."

If anyone could persuade him, it would be Mr Cuthbert. Hope bubbled within me, but I gave him a dirty look.

"You couldn't have thought to do that before."

"But what was there in it for me?"

"Very well, what's in it for you this time?"

I composed myself and braced for the worst.

"I have happened upon a significant opportunity in real estate and have a buyer in mind, however, the only problem is that the original occupant still has proprietary."

"And?"

"And it is a master, of course. Who can only pass the title through declaration or inheritance through death. I merely need to track down the original master and have him make it official."

"Okay. Where do I come into this?"

"I want your help in tracking him down."

"Why can't you find him?"

"He has left his world."

"So how could I possibly help?"

"There is no pleasant way of saying it."

"Just say it."

"As bait."

My heart pounded. I couldn't tell if this had always been his plan or if he was just an opportunist.

"The piece of real estate is Purlieu, isn't it?" I asked.

Mr Cuthbert gave a twisted smile.

"I always thought you were one of his brighter choices."

William. He wanted to offer me as bait for William. But William would either kill me or imprison me for life, using me as a breeding machine. And then when I'd outlived my usefulness, he'd probably kill me. It was suicide. I couldn't do it. I wouldn't.

"No. No deal," I said. "Anything but that. What could we trade instead?"

"You offer no other value to me."

"I could do more paintings for you, for you to trade!"

"Miss Evelyn, I do not think you appreciate the mountainous task of persuading Master Heidelbert. It is something your little paintings could never outweigh."

"Even if I dedicated every painting in the rest of my life to your use?"

"Even if," he said with finality.

I slumped against the wall, utterly defeated.

He was asking me to trade my life for my father's. There had to be another way. Without Mr Cuthbert. Without Heidelbert. There had to be.

"I guess we don't have a deal then," I said.

"I guess it is time I left, then," he said.

"You're not just going to dump us here to fend for ourselves, are you? How are we supposed to get out without being caught?"

"You are a clever pair. I am sure you will figure something out," Mr Cuthbert said.

I squared off against him and looked him straight in the eyes.

"I will scream. I will blow your cover," I said. "Unless you get us out of here."

Mr Cuthbert tensed his jaw, pursed his lips, and surveyed me.

"If you scream, we will all be caught."

"If you leave us here, Eirik and I will probably be caught anyway."

"You are learning, Miss Evelyn," Mr Cuthbert smiled. "Very well. But you had better pull yourself together, boy," he said, looking at Eirik. "*Hlif* do not walk around like they are at a funeral. It is already suspicious that you are without a partner."

Tears were still spilling from Eirik's eyes, his bottom lip quivering, his shoulders rounded. He sucked in a deep breath and nodded. This was not a side of Eirik that I knew. He was usually so well held together, a sly smile always on his face as though he were up to something, a joke not far from his lips, discord and strong emotions running straight off him like water off a duck's back.

"Your hood," I said, helping him to tug it back over his head, my fingers brushing the side of his face.

I wished I had something to hide beneath, for I felt my face betraying me in its many emotions: anger at Mr Cuthbert, injustice at Heidelbert's cowardice and despondency, grief for Valki plus the trauma of watching his death and not being able to save him, anxiety for my father, and an ever-raging battle over Eirik. I was so mad at him, so profusely embarrassed at having thrown myself at him, and still hopelessly yearned to be with him. It hurt too much to face him, so I turned away. I focused my energies instead on walking as graceful and entitled as possible, acting as though I belonged in Bornholm and knew exactly where I was going. I set aside all escalating fears about the fate of my father now that there would be no help from Heidelbert or Mr Cuthbert, determining that it was something to be dealt with once we reached the safety of the secret tunnels below.

Eirik wiped his face on the back of his hand and sucked in a deep breath.

"You can grieve for him when we get out of Bornholm," I said. "For the sake of your family and mine, let's make it out of here alive."

He nodded and pulled his shoulders back, his eyes becoming steely.

By Mr Cuthbert's side with Eirik a step behind, I followed his lead, rounding the building and returning to the main path that led out the gate. We exited the compound without question, just a small nod of the head from Mr Cuthbert to the *hlíf*, and headed back into the main thoroughfare of Bornholm. It was largely unchanged, people still eating, laughing, drinking.

A gaggle of plump, well-endowed middle-aged women were moving along the path in the opposite direction to us, forcing Mr Cuthbert and me to part ways and go around them. A commotion came in our wake and I turned to see Eirik on the ground with the one in the middle, clearly having collided. She was scrunching her large forehead, her white tunic now covered in dirt tightened as she shrieked at him. He scrambled to his feet, subtly flashing me a toothy grin, and then stooped down to help her up. She batted him away, but her anger subsided at the moment Mr Cuthbert stepped into her view. She gathered herself together, and with the help of her friends, got to her feet and they scurried away.

Mr Cuthbert led us into an alleyway and turned on Eirik, pinning him against the wall.

"If you—either of you—get me found out or get in the way of my plans, you will not survive to do it again," Mr Cuthbert said. "Watch yourself."

Eirik pushed back.

"Your plans? What about my plans? You lied to me. You told me there was one perfect world to take my kin," Eirik said. "I only ever tried to help you. What did you have to gain for lying to me? And now you've gotten Valki, my best friend and your supposed comrade, killed. What do you have to say for yourself?"

"I only gave you what you needed."

"And what is that?"

"Hope."

Eirik gaped and then roared out in frustration and fury.

Mr Cuthbert had said that before—that he prided himself in knowing what a person really needed. For me it was getting my father safe and sound, no matter the cost. And if my dad survived, perhaps I'd have a chance to escape William after fulfilling the deal with Mr Cuthbert—because he never said anything about agreeing to go back as a wilful prisoner to William, just to act as bait for him.

People had stopped to gather at the entrance to the alley gawking at us and the yelling. A woman called out in distress in the distance. A beat later the woman with the large forehead appeared amongst the crowd, pointing down at us, at Eirik. She was saying something in an accusatory tone.

Both Eirik and Mr Cuthbert understood what she was saying and by the looks on their faces, it wasn't good. Eirik grabbed a hold of my hand and tugged me further down the alley, Mr Cuthbert hot on our heels.

"Mr Cuthbert! Mr Cuthbert!" I called. "I change my mind."

"Now is not the time," he called back.

At the end of the alley, we turned left into a long back corridor behind the main street boutiques.

"There may not be another time."

I tried to gather the right words, to make sure the deal was on my terms, without loopholes that Mr Cuthbert could weasel his way through.

"I will help you bait William," I called. "If you persuade Heidelbert to free my dad and he isn't sacrificed—he walks free."

My heart thumped wildly as I tried to keep the fear of what I was agreeing to at bay.

"Your father will not be sacrificed. Mark my words. And

once he is free, you will come with me to play bait for William," he called back.

Footsteps pitter-pattered behind, headed after us. Eirik in the lead, tugging at my hand, we zigzagged our way through the back streets.

"Deal?" Mr Cuthbert called.

The pitter-patter of feet giving chase died away. We'd lost them. The tunic clung to my sweaty body; I heaved for breath.

"Deal," I said, my stomach leaping.

I quivered. I'd just handed myself back to William on a silver platter. But I would not waver in my resolve. Anything to save Dad.

Around another corner and the garden sprung up before us. I gathered my breath and looked around, straining my ears to ensure we weren't followed. Mr Cuthbert was not there. I could only assume he'd returned to the mansion compound to speak with Heidelbert once more.

"Evelyn, what have you done?" Eirik asked, his face scrunched up in concern, the mark of tears long gone.

I shrugged with nonchalance, contrasting the mounting tide of fear and hope that was welling inside of me.

"Oh, just sold my soul."

I held my head high and moved out into the open, playing the part once more of a Bornholm resident who knew her way, and strolled through the gardens, past the party that was still amassed with revellers, all the way back to the fissure in the wall.

"In other news," Eirik said as he stepped up behind me. "Look what I found."

I swung the ochre cape tucked behind the fern over me and was about to step through the fissure when Eirik held out his hand and opened it to reveal a gold chain and ring. He was smiling his cheekiest of grins.

"That woman?" I began.

He nodded. I shoved him in the shoulder. He'd stolen it from her. No wonder she'd been upset.

"You could have got us caught."

"But now you can keep your locket—we don't have to melt it down. I have enough for my kin."

"Good for you, Eirik. Why don't you celebrate by going and telling Hilda that her brother is dead?"

My cheeks ran hot at the low blow, but I didn't care. I was tired and emotional and didn't care about the gold right now.

"I'm not going to tell her. If I tell her, it could spoil the entire Uppreisn operation," he said. "No, it would be better if she didn't know and they went ahead with everything without him."

I shook my head and stepped into the fissure, making my way precariously through the tight gap and leaving behind the sweetness of flower blossoms. I emerged on the other side and had to hold my breath for a moment as the contrasting smell of bodily excretions hit my nose. I paused at the fern to check for where the *hlif* were in their rounds and finally breathed in the smell. My stomach turned over. The coast was clear. Eyes fixed on the backs of the *hlif*, I crossed the road into the backyard opposite.

Thwack!

A petite figure knocked the wind from me, and I fell to the ground.

10

ELISABETA'S ANGRY FACE was bearing down upon me, eyes wild with hysteria. Eirik pulled her off me and put her on her feet. He held his finger to his lips and tried to calm her. She snapped at him and pointed her finger at me with accusation. Eirik's palms went into the air defensively as he continued to placate her, but she didn't seem to be buying it. She stomped her foot and started threatening Eirik. He was pleading with her; hands clasped together, eyes desperate. She turned on her heel and ran away through the backyards and into the shadows.

I got to my feet, warily, brushing the dirt from me.

"She must have followed us here," I said. "But what was that all about?"

Eirik's eyes were wide with panic. He gulped.

"She thinks you're getting between me and Freja. She said she's going to put a stop to it."

I raised an eyebrow. She needn't bother.

"I'll meet you at home after I stop her from getting to Freja's house."

Eirik turned on his heel and sprinted after her.

Freja's house? She was really going to out her own brother?

It made sense, though. Eirik had said how seriously they

take betrothals in Verja and how much Elisabeta was relying on Eirik's marriage to secure one of her own.

I shook my head. It was none of my business anymore.

Slowly, I moved from backyard to backyard along the line of the wall, returning the way we'd come, this time as a party of one.

I couldn't bear to face Hilda, to be the one to share the news with her about her brother. I'd need to find a new set of clothes and another way to Eirik's. That's if I was welcome to stay there after Elisabeta's shakeup.

What would Eirik say to Freja to counteract Elisabeta's accusations? And how would Freja respond to finding her fiancé had a supposed lover? Would her parents nullify the marriage agreement because of the infidelity?

It would suddenly free Eirik of the burden of his promise. It would mean that there was nothing standing in the way of us being together. Except me. I would not let it happen, no matter how the circumstances may change. He was not worthy of my love.

I shook the silly thoughts from my head and turned instead to the more pressing matter at hand: my father. We had but one night. One night. How could I have been so stupid as to hinge so much on that one imperfect plan? If I had not been following Eirik around like a puppy while he looked for a new world to take his family, we would not have lost so much time and we could have seen Heidelbert days ago, inevitably fail in the endeavour, and then have more than enough time to come up with a new plan, instead of having to cut a new deal with Mr Cuthbert that put my life on the line.

Keeping my head low below the fence line, thinking about next steps, I reached the corner backyard by the main road.

What if Mr Cuthbert was unable to convince Heidelbert? I couldn't just sit around idly expecting it to happen. And besides, if I could get Dad out another way, it would void my deal with Mr Cuthbert.

The locket. If I could get it to Dad, he would be able to resist the power of the masters.

It wasn't much, but it was something if all else failed. It would give him a fighting chance to escape when they released him from the prison to take him to be sacrificed.

I had to get the locket to him now.

From the clothesline in the corner yard, I pinched an ochre coverall and singlet and transferred the whistle to the new pockets. I stuffed the flowy white satins and the hood within a pile of rubbish. In the basement of the house, I stepped into the tunnel system and headed down the cavern for the prison precinct.

I navigated through the tunnels using the mirrors along the top edge until I found my way to the space beneath the market square. On tiptoe, I watched for the *hlif* circling the prison and timed my exit from the tunnel into the market with them rounding behind the building. Up the stairs and through the trapdoor into the vegetable stall, I stepped as quietly as I could until I was directly opposite the open bars of the prison and the locked door. A large stone spice jar provided me with the physical invisibility and stability I needed as I propped myself in waiting for the *hlif* to circle round again.

There was Dad, around halfway down the building, lying down with his back to the bars. I was about to shift across to the right to align myself with his location but the *hlif* came into sight again. I held my breath, inciting encouragement to myself, bracing for the moment that they were out of sight and it was time to run for the prison.

The *hlif* stopped walking just as they neared the farthest corner of the prison. One leaned against it and rubbed his face. The other was looking around warily, speaking sharply to his partner. For how many hours had they been running rings around this building?

It was dead quiet and there was not another soul in sight. No other *hlif* marching up and down the main streets. Just me, my dad, and a pair of tired *hlif*.

The one looking around started gazing more intently at the marketplace, frowning as his eyes swept across my path.

I froze as I stared at him, commanding my eyes not to blink and my body not to so much as breath for fear of any movement catching his eye.

He continued to gaze past me and across to the rest of the marketplace.

The weary one finally obliged and stood up straight again, giving himself a shake, gathering the attention of his partner, and they continued around out of sight. I let out my breath.

This was my chance.

I slipped out from behind the jar and slunk as quickly and quietly as I could up to the bars where Dad lay, feeling very exposed.

"Dad," I whispered. "Dad, it's me."

I knelt down, reaching through the bars to squeeze him. He didn't stir.

I squeezed him again, my heart pounding against my chest. We didn't have much time.

"Dad," I whispered.

"Yes sweetheart," he mumbled in his sleep.

I jostled his shoulder.

He rolled over, the chain of his shackles tinkling, and opened his eyes. His jaw dropped open and he moved swiftly onto his knees, the shackles moving about noisily.

I hadn't timed the guards, but I was sure they were not far off rounding the corner of the prison again, perhaps their feet moving more hastily after hearing the stirring noises of the shackles.

I pressed my finger to my lips, squeezed his shoulder once more, and dashed back to the marketplace to my hiding place behind the jar. I peeked out from behind the jar to see Dad lay down facing the bars as though he'd merely rolled over in his sleep. The *hlif* rounded the building, the more alert of the two looking in through the bars suspiciously. Anxiously I watched the *hlif* walk past him more slowly, consideringly, and then round the prison once more.

I waited a beat and slunk across the open area once more feeling even more exposed this time now that the *hlif* were a little more alert. Dad's eyes were on me as I reached the bars and he quietly moved to his knees once more to take my face in his hands.

"Evelyn!" he said hoarsely.

I gripped at his shoulders, feeling tears well in my eyes. We shared a watery smile.

I let go of him and took the gold locket off, passing it through the bars.

"Hide this," I said.

He gave a sad smile and placed it around his neck and beneath his clothing.

"Don't worry," I said. "The wheel is rigged."

I gripped him once more, and then scampered back to the shadows of the marketplace, headed for Eirik's home.

Eirik was just finishing getting changed out of the *hlif* uniform as I reached the backyard. His eyes were wide, his forehead creased. He looked scared.

"I lost her along the way and she never went to Freja's," he said. "I couldn't find her."

My mind started to turn over the different possibilities.

"Will you go back and help me find her?" Eirik asked.

I gritted my teeth. I wasn't going to spend more time on him when I should be thinking of Dad.

A loud thump came from inside the house, followed by hostile voices, both male and female. Eirik whipped around and entered the back door of the house. I stepped in gingerly behind him, not wanting to get caught up in their domestic drama.

Eirik's shoulders relaxed at the sight of Elisabeta standing by Mama's side, but he immediately tensed up again. I peered around him to see a pair of *hlif* huffing and puffing at the door looking menacingly at Elisabeta. One had beady eyes and the other a snarl for a mouth. My breath caught. Everyone turned as we entered the room and Elisabeta shot her hand in the air, pointing it at me, saying something accusatory. The *hlif* with the beady eyes pulled out a piece of parchment paper from his pocket and held it up, looking between it and me. It had to be one of those posters from the marketplace again.

Elisabeta hadn't gone to Freja's house—she'd gone to turn me over to the *hlif!*

She had warned me that if I ever did anything to harm her family, that she would tell everyone about me—that I wasn't from Verja, that I was the intruder. Because in her eyes, getting in the way of Eirik and Freja's union was harming her family. And the only way to make the marriage go ahead was to get rid of me. To out not her brother, but me.

Mama spoke up and stood between the *hlif* and me with her arms crossed over her chest. Was she defending me? Eirik yelled something and pushed past her, headed through the dining and living rooms, down the hall. The *hlif* started moving forward. They were talking to me, but I couldn't understand them. I stood there, stock-still, staring back at them blankly. Eirik returned and shoved identity papers at them. Elisabeta was yelling at Eirik now and the *hlif* with the snarl had barged past Mama, straight past me, and threw open the door of the maid's quarters. He flipped the mattress on its side, revealing the only thing from Earth I'd still had on me when I'd arrived at Eirik's home: a pair of bright blue ankle socks that clearly didn't belong in a place like Verja.

He turned back on me and gave me a rough pat-down, stopping with triumph upon the pocket by my left thigh. He reached in and pulled out my silver metal whistle.

Eirik's eyes widened. Sweat trickled down the side of his face. Elisabeta and Mama looked confused. My heart pounded in my ears as the *hlif* shoved the whistle in my face, demanding something of me. An explanation, I assumed.

Eirik said something with a small, stumbling voice. The *hlif* jumped back from me, dropping the whistle as though it had grown hot in his hands.

My stomach turned over. They thought it was a weapon. Because Eirik thought it was a weapon. They thought I was armed and dangerous. That I was an armed and dangerous intruder that needed to be sent to Fengsel for sacrifice.

The *hlif* with the snarl grabbed at my wrists and the one with the beady eyes wrapped his arms around me from behind. They were turning me towards the door, half lifting me as they went.

"No!" I yelled. "It's just a whistle!"

I knew my cover was already blown and it made no difference whether they believed I was armed or not, but I continued to scream anyway.

"It's just a whistle!"

I writhed and screamed and slipped in their grip, trying desperately to call upon my aikido training but everything I did only increased their hold on me. They promptly took me from the family home and up the streets of Verja.

11

RÅDHUS WAS CLINICALLY bright and white on the inside but its holding cell was not. The darkness made my hands so invisible that I would have forgotten they existed if they weren't attached to my wrists.

Sharp discomfort told me that dirt clung to them from when I'd hit the ground falling from the arms of the *hlif* into the cell. They felt bruised, scraped. Might even leave more marks.

I paced the four walls of my tiny temporary home, feeling for the corner at each turn, grappling onto it for fear of forgetting which way was up. I counted the steps: One, two, three, four. One, two, three, four, five. One, two, three, four. One, two, three, four, five. I wasn't going to think about it. About the darkness. About what would come with the morning when they took me to Fengsel. About whether Mr Cuthbert had managed to convince Heidelbert to set my dad free and what that would mean for me, as next in line to be sacrificed. About whether Mr Cuthbert would get me out too—because he needed me as his bait for William. Or would he consider it "good riddance" and leave me for death?

My heart started to pound; my breathing became

laboured.

No. I wasn't going to think about it. I wasn't going to focus on where I was, or where I was going. I just needed to get through this dark night with these rough walls with gouges in their surface as though someone had been driven crazy and tried to scratch their way out. I didn't blame them.

It was one thing for me to lock myself in the maid's quarters in Eirik's home or for me to close the door of a bathroom while I bathed. It was a whole other experience to not be able to wilfully open that door. It was like Purlieu all over again and that glass cage and those locked doors of the cottage, William making me his prisoner.

No, I wouldn't do this. I wouldn't let the darkness, the walls, the locked doors, take me.

One, two, three. One, two, three, four. One, two, three. One, two, three, four.

Had the room suddenly gotten smaller?

My stomach constricted; my breathing became laboured once more.

I shoved my hand in my pocket to wrap around the whistle for calm, but it was no longer there, perhaps still sitting suspiciously, cautiously, on the floor of the kitchen in Eirik's home.

My heart pounded hard, like it was going to explode from my chest.

I was trapped, stuck within the impenetrable walls of this shrinking cell. No-one was coming to save me. Just like in Purlieu.

I started hyperventilating, my skin going numb. The walls were closing in on me. I crouched down into a ball, making myself as small as possible.

I'm going to die. I'm going to die. I'm going to die.

It was like the day William had raped me, he'd set his darkness upon me and I'd never actually escaped it. But now in the thick darkness of this cell, I could do nothing but face it, accept it—that I was now one with the darkness. There would be no more waking from the nightmares of William raping me. Here on the floor of my cell, he would do it to me again and again and again.

I scratched at my skin, desperately trying to get him out from under it. The surface broke, stinging sharply in runs up both my arms.

I have to get out of here.

I rolled onto my feet and charged at the door, ignoring my pitiful weeping as I threw myself again and again at it. I banged at it with open hands, I rammed at it with my shoulder, I jostled at its hinges.

"Let me out! Please let me out!"

I heaved for breath, my heart pounding, my entire body tingling and numb.

I'm going to die here.

I crumpled once more on the floor, my face meeting the ground, and shuddered with tears.

I awoke with a start, a sharp pain running through my shin. Harsh light shone in my eyes and gruff voices filled my ears.

Two *hlif* were trying to get into the cell but I was blocking the door with my body. I scampered out of the way, my back against the wall. My eyes felt clogged with dried-up tears, as I shielded them from the light from the hall beyond. The light was too bright, always too bright. They were yelling at me, pointing at my body, yanking at my clothes. One dumped a fresh white jumpsuit on the ground. They wanted me to change.

I nodded in understanding and picked up the jumpsuit, waiting for them to let me change in private, but they continued to tower over me. I stood and turned around, my fingers shaking as I took off my clothes and replaced them with the jumpsuit, ignoring the dry blood that lined my arms and the sting that came as I knocked the fresh scabs. I finished tying the jumpsuit around the middle and a hand gripped my shoulder. I was shoved down onto a little stool that had been placed in the centre of the cell. They took my old clothes and shoes as a new *hlif* with stained teeth entered, brandishing a blade.

I whimpered and tried to wriggle away but the hand on my shoulder only tightened.

"No. Please. Please," I said.

None of the other sacrifices had knife wounds. What if I wasn't going to Fengsel? What if they wanted to be done with me here and now?

The *hlif* with the stained teeth reached out and took my chin in his bony fingers, forcing my mouth shut. His eyes glinted. He chuckled and said something, his hot breath hitting my face making my stomach turn. The other two *hlif* sniggered.

He let go of my chin and held up the blade. I leaned away from him and squirmed and kicked. The spare *hlif* took my head in his hands and the one with the blade grabbed a fistful of my hair and sawed it off.

He wasn't going to kill me or maim me. He was going to shave me bald just like the other sacrifices.

"Please!" I cried.

Tears spilled over and ran down my cheeks as he continued to hack at my hair. It fell in clumps. Great frizzy orange clumps. In the harsh light from the hall, it appeared golden. How could I ever have wished it away?

The hands on my head and shoulders loosened as I wept, defeated, broken. This was it. This was the end. It was not like in the mountains of Purlieu or the glass cage of the Hidden Grove where I could find a way out. There was no way out from this. There were too many of them and they were too powerful. And I would die in bald humiliation, hung as a sacrifice to made-up gods.

He took the blade to the skin of my scalp now and shaved all that remained. Every so often the blade caught, nicking my skin. My whole head felt raw and exposed, stinging and aching. Heavier, not lighter.

He stood back to admire his handiwork and I hung my head in shame. They took me under the armpits and forced me to my feet. Shackles were placed around my wrists and I was marched out of the room, a *hlif* either side of me, and down the glaring halls of Rådhus. I shut my eyes tight, desperate not to welcome this day.

The sound of jangling keys cut through the shuffling of our feet and the tinkle of my chains. The *hlif* to my right held the keys to my cuffs and the prison.

The horn for curfew breaking echoed dully down the hall. A door opened and I squinted out to see that we were exiting Rådhus, heading into the open yard that led to Fengsel.

I should have been intentionally caught. Why hadn't I thought of it sooner? We could have rallied a pack of men and set an ambush upon my prison transfer while those keys were out in the open, free for the taking.

I looked to the edge of the marketplace, expecting to see Eirik's eyes pop up from behind a stall or a spice jar or a cart, ready for an ambush. But as we edged closer and closer to Fengsel, my heart sank. Eirik wasn't coming. No-one was coming. I couldn't rely on anyone. I was all alone.

I started to thrash about, twisting my shoulders erratically, and ducked out of their hold. I lunged at the keys, but just as I did, their hands were back on me again and the keys were ripped from my fingers. I turned on the spot, flipping around behind them. A sharp pain sank through the back of my head. My eyes were filled with the night.

My body ached all over, culminating in a dull throb in the crown of my head. I shifted my arm and the ache pulsed through my limbs. I lay still once more beseeching the spread of the pains that started at my skin and delved deep into my bones.

"Evelyn?"

I cracked my eyelids open. Friendly, brown eyes were looking down upon me. Dad gave a warm smile like a ray of sunshine, yet it had grief around the edges. It reminded me of a Van Gogh painting.

I could see that we were in the shadowed corner of Fengsel and realised my head was in his lap. He rubbed his thumb over my forehead and cupped the side of my face. The cool metal of his shackles rested on my shoulders.

"Dad," I said. Pushing through the ache, I sat up, chains tinkling, and navigated a hug despite the restrictions of our shackles. "I'm so sorry. I didn't mean to get caught," I cried into his shoulder.

"Evelyn, sweetheart, don't be so hard on yourself. This place is insane. You did so well to evade them for so long."

"But if you die, it will be all my fault," I said. "If you die, I won't blame you if you hate me."

He gave me a quick squeeze and pulled back to look me in the face again.

"You could never do anything to stop me from loving you."

I looked him square in the eyes, searching. He meant it.

All these months since I stumbled out of Purlieu, he had stayed true to his promise to not pry. Even when he was looking across the dinner table at me with a freezer fruit pie between us, eyes full of longing to bridge the gap and unravel all the secrets I'd kept from him, he held his tongue. He was a man whose actions matched up with his words.

"Oh Dad," I said, and began to shake, tears spilling over and gushing like a tap down my cheeks and pooling on his jumpsuit.

He was the one man who I could trust—who had earnt that trust. The one man I could let into my heart without reservation. He had my best interests in mind. He would fight for me without concern for himself. He would love me no matter what.

Not all men were bad.

I sucked in a deep breath and closed my eyes, my hands shaking. It was time I stopped hiding—time I stepped out of the darkness and into the light.

"Dad, I need to tell you something. I need to tell you

everything."

I came clean to him about where I had gone with William, how it had been good at first—that William had been good at first—but then the control crept in until I was his prisoner. I told him about the power he had openly wielded over me to keep me trapped there while I tried desperately to escape. But then I stopped short of the day he raped me.

Could I really say that word aloud?

He had listened quietly the whole way through, not wavering in his support of me, but nodding along, encouraging me to keep going.

"And then when Mr Cuthbert ran off, William turned on me. He used his power to get me back into the cottage, up the stairs, surrender my bobby pins and all the things in the room so I couldn't use anything to try escape again, and then he forced himself on me." My voice shook.

I lowered my eyes and picked at the non-existent paint on my hands.

"And used his power to make me have sex with him."

I braced myself for Dad's response—whether it be repulsion, disownment, or anger for putting myself in such a position. A beat passed. Tears welled in his eyes.

"Oh, sweetheart," he said and wrapped me in his arms once more, rocking me back and forth. "You've been battling this all by yourself, this whole time?"

I nodded. "You're not ashamed of me?" I asked.

"Of course not."

"And you believe me?"

"Believe you? Evelyn, look where we are. How could we be in a foreign city beneath a desert and still be in Mianjin? The Hidden Grove is real. Of course I believe you."

I felt lighter, like I was hovering just above the ground. Like William had less of a hold on me now. Perhaps withholding my story from Dad, from Tiffany, whilst well-meaning, hadn't been the best idea.

"Evelyn, what you went through in Purlieu was not your

fault. The man you loved deceived, manipulated, and abused you. What William took from you was not his to take."

I looked up. Dad's eyes were fierce and firm. Ever the protector, the defender. Why hadn't I told him sooner?

I let his words sit. Let them sink down into my bones.

I had been deceived by William. I knew that—his lies had been prolific from the start.

I had been manipulated by William. I knew that too—it was how he got me to the Hidden Grove in the first place.

But abused by William? Like I was pitiful and weak and couldn't defend myself?

Numbness washed over me but dissipated in a flash.

I didn't want the label. I rejected the label. That wasn't me. I wasn't a victim. I was a fighter. And I would not be boxed or branded.

To my dying breath—even if it were going to be tomorrow on the gallows—I would be a fighter.

Dad cleared his throat, breaking my thoughts.

"Please forgive me for any part I had to play in you going off with him. If I drove you away," his voice broke.

Tears gathered in his eyes.

"Dad, I forgave you a long time ago," I said.

He nodded and gave a grim smile. He wiped his face on his sleeve.

"Have you forgiven yourself?" he asked.

The numbness returned and a pit formed in my stomach. Again, I let his words sit and the comfortable silence cling to us.

How could I even begin to forgive myself?

He wrapped his arm around me, and we sat, watching the Verja people bustling about in the marketplace to begin their day. They were frail and weary but content, unburdened by the worries that hung over both our heads about what the day ahead would bring.

The crowd was starting to gather in the space behind

Fengsel. I was pacing, trying to communicate to Dad everything I could think of that had happened since the day I escaped from Purlieu with the power-blocking gold to our time in Verja. No matter what happened, he would be prepared.

"I know it sounds really far-fetched, but for whatever reason, a master can't control someone who is wearing gold. And you've got Mum's locket and they don't know it."

He nodded slowly.

"Is that why the thief wanted it? Is that how you got away when I was arrested?"

"Yes. It's also how I escaped from—from …" I trailed off. It still wasn't easy to say his name aloud.

"William?"

I nodded and refocused.

"And the revolution was meant to start today—just before the last sacrifice: you," I said. "But now that I'm in here, they will probably do it tomorrow. Especially because Valki died. Which means that if Mr Cuthbert doesn't follow through on his end of the deal—"

"What deal?"

"I agreed that if he can convince Heidelbert to spare you, that I'd be his bait for William."

Dad's mouth dropped open. "You agreed to *what*?"

"I ran out of options, okay? It's not easy to break someone out of prison. Even in a world like this."

"You are not putting your life on the line for my sake."

"Well, it's too late. I've made the deal with Mr Cuthbert. We'll find out soon enough if we're gonna live beyond this and whether I have to follow through on the deal."

"What exactly did you agree to?"

"That Mr Cuthbert could use me as bait to find William so he could sell the mastership of Purlieu to someone else."

Silence fell over us. I could feel Dad's mind ticking over.

"If it comes to it and you have to uphold your end of the deal, I'm going to be there. There's nothing in that agreement that says I can't be."

He was right. I was intentionally vague on the terms to leave room to wiggle.

"If we both survive the next two days," I said.

We sat in silence once more and continued to watch the crowd gather. A pair of *ómagi* approached the prison bars and placed two cups on the ground through the door. I got up and ran to meet them, not really sure what I could do or say and how it might help our situation, but they had already turned and left by the time I reached the spot they had placed the cups.

I looked down on the stone cups, filled to the brim with translucent red liquid. Epli. My aching body could do with a bit of healing. I picked them up, brought them back to where Dad was still sitting, and lifted one to my lips. He jumped to his feet and knocked the cup from my hand. It fell and smashed into two pieces, the red liquid staining the dirt and sucking away into the ground.

"Don't!" he said. "It's not just some drink that tastes nice."

"I know. It has healing properties."

"It's more than that, Evelyn. It's a numbing agent. It makes people compliant."

I cocked my head to the side, eying the cup in my other hand.

"The first time I had it, I felt it: it reminded me of what it was like to be on antidepressants."

"When were you taking medication?"

"After your mother died," he said, looking guilty. "But I didn't like the way it made me feel, so I dug into my time with the counsellor until I didn't need them anymore."

"I had no idea," I said.

"I was embarrassed. And I didn't want to burden you. And talking to the counsellor was one thing, but talking to you was a whole other thing."

He grimaced.

"I'm sorry you felt like you couldn't tell me," I said.

"There seems to be a bit of that going round, doesn't

there?" he said.

I grimaced back.

"But no more, right?" I asked.

He nodded firmly, "No more."

He squeezed my shoulder then took the other cup from me, pouring the Epli over the dissipating red stain in the dirt.

"Maybe that's why Eirik wants to leave," I said.

"What do you mean?"

"Well, he doesn't drink the Epli, so he's not just going along with the rules the masters have set. Same with why Valki started the Uppreisn. Because he sold the Epli he was given when his parents were sacrificed. Just like the other Uppreisers did."

"Yeah, exactly. Like the other prisoners, they seemed perfectly fine about the fact that they were walking to their deaths," he continued. "Because they were drinking it."

We nodded together.

"I've been pretending to take it this whole time," he said. "So that they would assume I was compliant when it came to my turn. But instead, I will have my wits about me. I'm going to try to evade the guards when they take me from here to the gallows."

"But Dad, it won't be enough. They'll have their guards out in full force and all their eyes will be trained on you. You'll be outnumbered—just like when you were arrested in the first place," I said. "Well, except that this time you'll have the gold on your side—they won't be expecting that."

He nodded along.

"How about you wait to see what the wheel lands on. If Heidelbert doesn't step in and rig the wheel, then I think your best bet is to start the revolution and run."

"But they're not ready yet, right?"

"They might be. We don't know. Maybe they need a little push over the line now that they've lost their leader."

I picked up one of the broken halves of the stone cup and passed it to Dad.

"Throw this at the nearest mirror. The breaking of a mirror is the signal. In the chaos and with the protection of the gold, you should be able to make it out."

"I'm not just going to just run off and leave you here."

"Why not? I'm doomed either way."

What was I saying? These weren't the words of a fighter.

"Evelyn, don't say that. I won't let it be true. We will find a way."

"I know. You're right. There's just so many 'what ifs', you know? Like what if the Uppreisn win, they might just let me go from here and tomorrow's sacrifice won't even happen. But if they fail, who knows what might happen?"

"Then we work with people that we can trust. Like each other."

I stared out into the crowd at the blank faces gathering and found Eirik and his family amongst them, close to the front. Mama looked like she was pretending she hadn't seen me. Elisabeta was giving me dagger eyes again. Eirik stared wide-eyed at the sight of me. I was sure I wasn't a very nice thing to look at with my bald and wounded head, the starched white jumpsuit, the fear. Would he offer some kind of reassurance that everything was going to be okay? That he had a plan, and I just needed to trust in him and be patient? Or was Dad right and we could only rely on one another?

Eirik looked away.

The *hlif* started moving about systematically to their guard positions and below the mirrors. It was starting.

"Okay, so how are we going to do that, Dad? We're running out of time."

"I don't know yet, but I will get you out. No matter what happens today, I will get you out."

It didn't sound like much of a plan, but he said it with such assertiveness that I couldn't help but believe him.

The masters were processing down the cavern, past Fengsel. They, with their power, were too close for comfort and I felt naked without gold to protect me. But they weren't here for me today. I moved to the bars again and tried to catch Heidelbert's eye, but he kept his gaze steady and forward.

What did that mean? That he was trying to pretend he didn't know me so that he could get away with tampering with the sacrifice? Or that he couldn't bear to look at me because he couldn't help me? Or that he didn't recognise me at all, and I was nothing but another sacrifice to him?

I returned to Dad's side and gripped at his hand. Sweat quickly gathered on our joined palms. Dad was just as nervous as I was.

The masters rounded the building and stepped up onto the platform to take their seats, the *hlif* to their stations, and the Gothi headed for his podium.

A hush came over the crowd and he began to speak. My heart pounded. This was it. This was the moment when we would know if Dad had assured freedom.

He gave me a quick squeeze as a pair of *hlif* approached Fengsel.

"I love you," he said.

"I love you too."

Would it be the last time I heard those words come from his mouth?

He let go of me and got to his feet, willingly moving towards the door. He offered his cuffed wrists to be taken and glanced over at me, a lopsided smile on his face as they took a hold of him. It sent a shiver up my wet back. He was playing the role of compliant sacrifice all too well.

If Heidelbert were going to step in, how would he do it without the Gothi knowing? Without everyone knowing? He could barely control his power. How did he hope to use it without being caught? Had Mr Cuthbert agreed to an impossible task?

This was all my fault. If only I had shared with Dad from the start, we never would have gone into the Hidden Grove and Eirik never would have taken mum's locket. And then after Dad was captured, if only I were quicker on my feet, I could have come up with a plan that would really work. And if only I'd stayed focused, I would have had more time to enact it.

My heart beat uncomfortably in my chest as tears formed in my eyes. This was entirely my fault. He was a good man. He didn't deserve to die.

"No," I sobbed. "Please, somebody, anybody. Please don't let him die."

I wrapped my hands around the bars of the prison and leant into the cold metal for strength, watching through slitted eyes as the proceedings unfolded. Dad placed his hand on the wheel of the Norns and gave it a good push. I held my breath and braced myself as the tears streamed down my face, watching it tick, tick, tick over. Everyone onstage had their back to me, except the Gothi, who was side-on, watching the Norns with hunger. I searched the crowd for Eirik's face, hoping he might give some indication of what it landed on, but I couldn't find him.

The wheel slowed. The crowd was silent, holding their breath just as I was. Heidelbert's back was stiff, giving no indication where his intentions lay.

Tick. Tick. Tick. It slowed to a stop.

There was Eirik's face. He looked strained, concerned. His shoulders dropped. He locked eyes with me and gave a slight shake of his head.

Hanging. It had stopped on hanging. Of all the luck—a one in five chance—it stopped on hanging.

"No!" I yelled, my voice piercing through the silence.

The wheel shifted. It swayed. It ticked unnaturally forwards one place.

Eirik's eyes widened and his jaw dropped open. A wave of movement and a murmur went through the crowd. The Gothi's face fell, turned livid, and quickly cleared to an amiable smile. He turned completely around, hiding his face from the crowd, and eyed each of the masters in turn. Heidelbert remained stiffly in his seat.

My stomach flipped over. It had ticked over to 'set free',

and the Gothi knew the Norns had been tampered with. Heidelbert had done it, surely.

Dad was free. After all this time, all this anxiety, and Dad was a free man.

But would the Gothi let him walk?

The *hlif* didn't seem to know what to do. And the crowd's eyes had returned to the Gothi, waiting with anticipation for how he might explain this act of the gods.

The Gothi sent another look across his masters, finishing on Heidelbert, fixed a big, false smile on his face, and then turned to face the crowd once more. He spoke with exuberance and good humour, and directed the *hlif* to release Dad.

I could hear my heartbeat in my ears and held my breath once more.

A *hlif* with a protruding jaw approached Dad and undid his shackles. Dad stepped back from him, free, but looked around for a moment, unsure what to do or where to go. Everyone's eyes were on him. The Gothi said something to him and pointed up the cavern. I think he was trying to tell him to leave Verja.

Dad ran from the stage and up to me at the prison, reaching for my hands.

"Oh Dad, you're free! Go! Go now while you still can!"

"I'm not leaving without you."

"I don't think you have a choice. They want you out of here."

I hadn't had a chance to think this part through. I mustn't have really believed it was possible.

The Gothi said something, a little more forcefully, still pointing up the cavern. *Hlif* started coming towards us.

"Dad, I think if you don't leave, they're gonna make you."

The Gothi made another stern pronouncement and several *hlif* moved into a run towards us.

"I'm going to get you out."

"Dad, I'm either going to get hung tomorrow or be bait

for William another day. There's no hope for me. Save yourself."

"Trust me."

The *hlif* were upon him; the nearest one took a dive, but Dad whipped around and sidestepped and the *hlif* crashed into the bars of the prison. I staggered backwards and watched blood spill from his skull, mingling into the dirt like the Epli. Dad leant down, grabbed the baton from the *hlif's* hips, and knocked the next one over the head with it, dodging around another.

"*Stans! STANS!*" The Gothi was yelling in a commanding way, becoming red in the face. He was trying to use his power, but it wasn't working because of the locket.

Dad slipped past the *hlif* who had paused, anticipating that he would stop moving at the Gothi's commands, and sprinted into the shadows of the marketplace. The *hlif* charged after him.

On tippy-toes, I peered as far as I could through the marketplace, over the heads of the *hlif* giving chase. Would they capture him and return him to the prison? Or send him straight to the gallows despite the result of the Norns? Or expel him from Verja, leaving me stranded to the whims of the Gothi?

The *hlif* disappeared into the shadows after him. A few moments passed. The Gothi seemed to be waiting for some finality to the situation but the murmur through the crowd was increasing. The people were animatedly talking to their neighbours, a sense of triumph amongst them. The Gothi was losing his grip on them. He turned back upon the crowd, thundered out the last of his speech, and signalled for the horn to end the proceedings. The horn blew and he quickly began the procession back up to
Bornholm, Heidelbert still avoiding my eye as he passed.

12

FROM THE SHADOWED corner of Fengsel the smell of hot food wafted across to me. My stomach grumbled as I watched the locals at work in the marketplace selling their produce. If Dad could survive a few weeks of this, I could survive one day. And just like Dad, I had no idea what lay ahead of me, no real indication of being saved in time, no certainty that I would be alive at the end of all this.

It had been probably two hours since the masters had processed back to Bornholm and nobody had come to visit me and tell me what was going on. If anything was going on. Not Dad, not Eirik, not Hilda.

The *hlif* also had not returned in victory or defeat. Had Dad evaded them? Or did he quietly get kicked out of Verja? Were the *hlif* now guarding every possible entry to Verja to prevent him from returning?

I hoped he got out; otherwise, I made the deal with Mr Cuthbert for nothing.

Would the revolution go ahead tomorrow despite Valki's death? Would they get the tunnel finished without him? Would Heidelbert save me like he saved my father? Or would Mr Cuthbert have another plan for getting me out of here so he could use me as bait for William?

I thrust my hand in my pocket and fished around for my whistle but came up dry. My hands started to shake, my breathing uneasy. I clutched at my chest and gasped for breath.

There were too many questions. Too many players with hands clasped around my neck, controlling me, controlling my future.

Numbness washed over me followed closely by tingles rolling across my skin.

I never used to have this problem. Of debilitating fear. This smacked-in-the-chest-frozen kind of shut down.

Nor did I used to fly off my wheel at people trying to control me.

I grimaced, thinking of how I'd attacked Vân. I shouldn't have done that, and I deserved the punishment the school had dished out to me.

I couldn't remember how I used to respond to that kind of stuff. Or perhaps I just hadn't previously put myself in those kinds of situations. Not before William.

Now that I knew what it felt like to be under someone's control—both with their magic power and with their authority and persuasion—I didn't want to ever feel that way again. Like my body had an aversion to it. An allergy.

But there would always be times where someone would have influence over me. That's what parents do. That's what teachers do. That's what the government and law enforcement do. I could hardly shut down every time they tried to impress their will upon me. And besides, not all control was bad. Miss Daniels had told me to use an art journal to process my feelings because she wanted to help me. She was doing it for me. That's the difference, right? Whereas William was controlling me for his sake. His intentions weren't pure. His manipulations were selfish.

I needed to be able to differentiate between the two. To not shut down at every instruction, but determine the motives and act accordingly. If I were to survive beyond tomorrow, I needed to find coping strategies, because I couldn't live like this anymore.

What William did to me wasn't my fault. He chose me because I was vulnerable, and he manipulated me when I was at my lowest to get me to Purlieu. Yes, I freely chose to go with him, but if he had really loved me, he would have tried to help me repair my relationships with my dad and with Tiffany. He would have encouraged me with my schoolwork. He would have defended me against Cameron.

And yet I chose to go with him, and I chose to stay when I had multiple opportunities to leave. Things wouldn't have been so bad if I had left when I had those chances.

My stomach knotted, my throat became tight, heat flushed my cheeks and neck. The burden of my shame weighed down upon me. I had a part to play in all that had passed in Purlieu.

I had been wronged, yes, and though I took it out on Cameron and Vân and Eirik, deep down, I really just blamed myself.

I closed my eyes, took a deep breath, relaxed my shoulders, and let all the memories of Purlieu wash over me. They played out in my minds' eye like flipping through a stack of old Polaroids. From the days by the art gallery as I fell for William's charm, to those early experiences of Purlieu and William revealing his true self, to agreeing to stay when he threatened suicide, to being trapped and openly controlled by him, and finally to the day he violated me when I had chosen to stay and help Mr Cuthbert instead of save myself. So many foolish decisions, so much naivety. I had been utterly played by William at every turn, despite having grown up with Dad's wisdom in my ear about abusive men and how I thought I knew better because of it. But I was blinded by William, wooed by his charm and interest in me because all I wanted was someone to show me some semblance of love.

Yes, William had done wrong by me. But *I* had also done wrong by me. And it was time I let it go.

I let out my breath and took another one, a deeper one. The air whooshed out of me.

I forgive you.

The burden lifted; my stomach loosened.

It was like I had been in a cage with the door wide open. And all this time I had been the only one keeping me there.

I opened my eyes and got to my feet, leaving the dark corner of Fengsel. I would no longer cling to the darkness but welcome the light.

I took to pacing. I had to do something. I couldn't just sit here and await my fate. I refused to allow other people to control my life—past, present, or future. If I were going to die tomorrow, I would not go willingly. I wouldn't allow myself to just surrender to the whims of false gods.

I tripped and fell, dirt smearing across my face, grazing my arms. Dusting myself off I looked back upon the ground. I'd tripped on the other half of the stone cup. I picked it up and ran my finger along its edge. It was sharp. A potential weapon against the *blif* during the sacrifice ceremony. I shoved it in my pocket and returned to pacing.

I didn't need to hide the fact that I wasn't from Verja anymore. I didn't need to hold my foreign tongue and bite back my English. I could appeal to Heidelbert on the stage. But with what? What could I possibly offer him that no-one else could?

I could warn him about Mr Cuthbert because surely his intentions weren't in Heidelbert's interest.

I could threaten to tell Hilda that he killed her brother.

I could—oh, what was I thinking? Heidelbert didn't know English. He wouldn't understand a word I was saying.

Dread washed over me.

Think, Evelyn. Think.

I had to come up with something.

I wrung my hands together to stop the shaking. It was morning and people were starting to gather in front of the gallows. A lone *ómagi* approached the gate into Fengsel and put a cup of Epli on the ground. I raced over to the bars and called out to her.

"Wait! Please wait."

She looked over her shoulder, eyes wide with fear, and picked up the pace away from the prison. She wouldn't have understood me anyway.

My stomach grumbled. I stared at the Epli as it splashed down onto the dirt.

The masters had started processing down the cavern past the prison block. My stomach turned over as I searched the line. Heidelbert wasn't amongst them. Had the Gothi realised it was his son who had manipulated the Norns? What would he do to him? What had he done to him?

I dropped the cup and it clattered to the ground.

The masters filed onto the stage, a *hlif* stepping forward to hurriedly remove the empty chair at the Gothi's stern eye.

My heart pounded and my palms became slick with sweat.

The horn blew, making me jump, and two *hlif* approached the jail, one slightly scrawnier than the other. I swallowed hard as they approached me. The bigger one grabbed roughly at my wrists and pulled, making me flinch as the metal dug into my skin.

I put a lopsided smile on my face, just as Dad had done, and allowed them to lead me out of Fengsel and around to the stage with the masters. The stairs were rickety, creaking with each step I took. I peered through the tiny cracks in the wood, looking for movement below, some sign that the revolution was on and any moment I would be saved from the gallows amidst the chaos.

But there was no movement below.

The *hlif* shoved me beside the Norns as the Gothi addressed the crowd with a grin from ear to ear.

I searched amongst the crowd for familiar faces—Hilda,

the men from the digging rotation, Eirik and his family—but came up dry.

The metal at my wrist was chafing now, the salt of my sweat seeping into the raw wounds. My breathing became laboured, erasing my lopsided smile.

The Gothi, with his bulging eyes, was looking at me expectantly now. The crowd had turned their attention to me too. Every pair of eyes stared into me, hungrily awaiting my death. The Gothi motioned to the scrawny *hlif* who promptly put my hands on the wheel.

My hands were trembling, but I refused to move. If I didn't spin it, the so-called gods couldn't reveal my fate, right?

The Gothi's lips were thin. He was nodding at the *hlif* again. The scrawny one placed his hands over mine and gave a good push, our hands collectively spinning the wheel.

A strangled noise left my throat as it ticked over in a blur of grey. Tick-tick-tick. As the wheel slowed, the sections became discernible. I set my eyes upon the white section and watched it go round and round and round. The Norns slowed and ticked round to 'set free'. With an unnatural jerk, it ticked back to the black section to 'hang'.

My stomach flipped over. The Gothi had manipulated it. He was always going to manipulate it. That's why Heidelbert had been left at home in Bornholm.

I looked desperately through the crowd. No-one was moving. The mirrors weren't being shattered. The revolution wasn't going to happen. Had Valki's death thwarted their plan altogether? Had they not finished the pit? There was absolutely no reason for them to wait any longer—they had almost all the masters in a neat little row on this stage just waiting to fall to their deaths. If they didn't do it now, they'd have to wait another whole year for a chance like this.

The Gothi gave a massive smirk and nodded to the scrawny *hlif* again. He grabbed my hands and pulled me over to where the noose hung from the platform, tugging it around my neck.

I was not going to die here. I couldn't die here. I hadn't given up yet. I hadn't had time to accept it.

As he tightened the knot around my neck I made a fist with my hands and elbowed him in the gut. He fell, holding his stomach. I shoved my hand in my pocket and pulled out the half piece of the stone cup and threw it as best I could at the mirror beside the stage.

"Stans! STANS!" The Gothi yelled.

My whole body froze, arms still in the air, pointing towards the stone fragment as it hurtled towards the mirror. It collided with the glass but bounced straight off, not even scratching the surface of the mirror.

My heart fell. Dread washed over me.

A moment later, something else much larger hurtled through the air and collided with the mirror. It chipped the surface, sending a fracture across it in two directions. The glass cracked and shattered, falling to the ground and raining down upon the *hlif* standing beneath it.

An uproarious cheer broke out across the crowd in several places, followed by a wave of movement. People were making their way quickly towards the stage, bowling others over in their haste.

I looked through my periphery for the source of where the second object had come from to no avail. But on the ground below the broken mirror was a shovel.

"Evelyn, get down! Get down now!"

It was Dad's voice. I was sure it was.

But I wasn't going anywhere. The Gothi had used his power on me.

A creaking came from below. The wooden panels shifted at my feet. I willed my eyes to see more, take in more, beyond the bounds of my periphery. If I couldn't move my body, if I couldn't see what was going on, how could I get out of this?

A small object flew through the air and smashed onto the stage. Smoke erupted by my side, clouding my vision further.

My body became loose, responsive. Hidden from the sight of the Gothi, I could move again. Eirik had been right.

The floor shifted again, creaking in protest. I clutched at the noose that still wrapped around my neck, pulling and grappling with the rope to loosen it. My hands shook as I fumbled. It slackened and I whipped it over my head. The floor gave way at my feet.

I fumbled again for the rope and gripped tightly with my hands, jarring my shoulder as my body dangled. A pit opened beneath the stage, exposing sharp jagged timber boards directly below me.

The masters tumbled down inside. Men armed with black daggers emerged from the broken shards of wood panels beneath me to my left and my right. Wild-eyed, the Uppreisn men turned and threw themselves, dagger-first, at the masters splayed in the mess. The elderly master, crumpled and pierced by the wood, had his hands up in feeble defence as a burly Uppreisn man stabbed him square in the chest with a dagger. The elderly master went limp.

Nearby, another Uppreisn man was making haphazard lunges at the beefy master. The beefy master sidestepped and the man plunged headfirst into the sharp broken end of a timber beam. He cried out in agony as blood gushed from the wound. The beefy master rounded on him to finish him off as the burly Uppreisn man jumped and wrapped his arms around the beefy master's neck, the dagger slicing through the purple robes and carving lines on his skin, soaking his robes with his blood, making them turn to look black.

I blocked out the screaming in agony mingled with the zeal of the crowd. I blocked out the bloody carnage below. I blocked out the splitting sound of the wooden frame that was now my lifeline. Instead, I moved about, pushing my legs out from under me to get some swinging momentum. Back and forth I swung, arms shaking, grip slipping, seeking just a little more arc to clear the broken platform.

Just a little more.

I swung back in full view of the bloodbath below, broken bodies impaled upon metal rods and split wooden beams alike, a murmur of movement from the survivors groaning and screaming in pain as they navigated their prison and fought off their aggressors. I swung forward again, towards the crowd where rioting between the Uppreisers and the *hlif* had broken out. Batons and knives crossed in battle. Some of the crowd fled for safety while others remained transfixed.

The *hlif* appeared to be winning, holding the Uppreisers at bay as they swung their batons in a mechanical, practised fashion in one perfect line. There were too many of them for the Uppreisers and they outmatched the pitiful kitchen blades and untrained combatants.

Out and up I travelled to the height of the arc. My hands unfurled and I let go of the rope. I sailed through the air, clearing the collapsed platform, and fell beside it with a deep *thud*. My knees buckled.

The ground began to rumble. Around the podium to my right, rock formations rose up on all sides, angled outwards to the height of the podium. The Gothi was completely surrounded. No-one could breach those walls. No-one could climb the rock at those angles. He was completely protected from the onslaught of the Uppreisers.

Hilda wheeled past me in a flurry of red hair, her eyes ablaze. She was aiming for the middle of the throng of *hlif*, propelling forward at full speed, shovel in hand. She bowled into them, several toppling at the force, causing a break in the line. The Uppreisn shoved through the break, clambering over the fallen *hlif*, and headed straight for the platform, straight for me. The *hlif* turned on their heels and gave chase, brandishing their batons.

The throng of Uppreisn and *hlif* surrounded me, engaged in battle once more, knives and batons flying over my head. Hilda sat at the rear, walloping *hlif* from behind with her shovel and cutting them with the sharp edge, no mercy written across her brow as she called out encouragements, or maybe it was instruction. An *ómagi* leading the revolution.

The high-pitched shrill of a whistle cut through the din. A blade swiped across in front of my eyes, missed its *hlif* target standing beside me, and slashed down the sleeve of my white jumpsuit, nicking my skin. I cowered away from it. The whistle shrilled again, this time closer.

There, on the lower cavern side of the clearing was Dad on all fours, dodging and ducking his way through the throng, baton in hand. His eyes were set on me, the whistle between his teeth. He swept at the legs of the *hlif* in his way, crashing them to the ground beside him.

Through the mass of bodies, I crawled for him.

A middle-aged woman fell across my path, the side of her face swollen, her hand wrapped around her own kitchen knife, which was thrust through her throat.

I scurried around her, following the call of the whistle as Dad blew it again.

I ducked my head as a baton swung before me, connecting with my neck. The *hlif* who wielded it, a wiry young man, whipped around and locked eyes on me. He drew back his baton again.

I reached my chained wrists up and grabbed behind his knee with both hands, pulling hard. He folded and collapsed in front of me. Two young men jumped on top of him and pinned him to the ground. I hurried around and dodged the weapons waving and legs stepping. The whistle blew again, and I followed its call. Someone stood on my leg just as a knee kicked me in the face, throwing my head into a spin. Through the stars that appeared before my eyes, I looked about for Dad's face again and strained my ears for the shrill of the whistle.

A hand wrapped around my wrist.

I whipped around. There he was, by my side, whistle still between his teeth, baton in hand.

"Dad!"

He dropped the whistle and gave me a swift kiss on the

cheek.

"Almost there now sweetheart," he said and turned and led the way back through the throng, carving a path before me.

I scrambled to my feet as we made it past the scuffle.

A metal screech cut through the shouting. The nearest mirror was turning, angling across the compound towards the upper caverns. Beneath the mirror, pushing and struggling at the pylons that held the mirror up, was Eirik.

"Hurry!" Eirik called.

Dad sprinted to the other side of the pylon and helped Eirik push it until the image reflected on it showed the entrance to Bornholm with gates open wide.

I ran up beside them awkwardly, my hands still linked by the heavy chain.

"You couldn't have started the revolution sooner, could you?" I laughed, and choked back tears.

Dad grimaced and held the chain between my wrists. He stood to his full height.

"I'll be back," he said and he walked purposefully back towards the battle, searchingly. His gaze rested on something near the stage. He ran head-on into the throng, beating at the *hlif* with his baton as he went. He bowled one over, the man toppling and not getting back up.

"We had to finish the tunnel," Eirik said. "And your *vater* spent most of the day and night looking for me, trying not to get kicked out of Verja by the *hlif*."

"I thought the revolution might have been called off," I said.

"It almost was. And then Mr Cuthbert found Heidelbert locked up in Bornholm," Eirik said.

Dad had set himself on target with a *hlif* with a protruding jaw. He wound up and knocked the *hlif* across the face with the baton. Blood sprayed from his nose. Dad grappled for something at the *hlif*'s waist. They tussled over it until Dad knocked him across the face again. The *hlif* turned from the blow and fell to the ground.

Dad spun back to return us. His face was like I'd never seen it, spattered in blood, fierce and grave and firm, as though it had never known good humour or peace or love. But it did know great love. He had just sacrificed himself to retrieve the keys to my shackles, determined to set me free.

He jogged up, unlocked my cuffs, and pulled my wrists free. I threw myself into his arms. Tears streamed my face.

"It's happening," Eirik said.

Dad and I pulled apart. Eirik was pointing to the mirror above. An image of Mr Cuthbert was reflected on it, standing at the gates to Bornholm with a dagger at Heidelbert's neck. Heidelbert was holding up a sign. My jaw dropped open.

"I thought Mr Cuthbert said he wasn't going to kill Heidelbert," I said.

"He isn't. It says: 'Surrender or I will kill him'," Eirik said. "It's how we make sure that Heidelbert is the last master."

"What do you mean?" I asked.

"He's just pretending to. It's a trap for the Gothi."

A cheer erupted from the collapsed stage. Four of the Uppreisers emerged triumphant, brandishing their black blades, attempting to scramble from the mess. The Gothi was the last remaining master and he seemed to realise it too. The ground rumbled as he commanded the rock formation surrounding him, protecting him, to return to the ground. He moved from his podium with a menacing look on his face, down the stairs and towards the ruptured stage.

He slipped between a broken segment of the stage and took up a black dagger in each hand. The Uppreisers looked unnerved, but returned to the carnage of the stage to take on the Gothi. The first stepped forward, the burly one who had killed the old man and the beefy master. He held his blade steady by his side, sizing up the Gothi. The Gothi commanded a piece of broken wood to fly through the air at him. He dodged it. The Gothi lunged forward, slicing at the man's thigh. He tensed his jaw but didn't budge, slicing back at the Gothi, missing. The Gothi plunged the other dagger into the burly man's side. He fell to the ground and the Gothi moved onto the next one.

"Let's get out of here," I said.

Dad and Eirik nodded.

Eirik had led most of the way, skipping through deserted streets as the locals boarded their homes, afraid of the rioting Uppreisers, or perhaps the vengeance of the Gothi should they fail. We'd reached the home stretch—the towering limestone walls and, to the right, the hidden Verja exit. From the next backyard over, three heads appeared with gold glinting from their necks: Mama, Elisabeta, and Freja.

My stomach turned over. I had forgotten about them. I had forgotten about her. I had been so focused on our destination: the Hidden Grove.

Freja's face was red and blotchy. She tugged at a metal medallion and length of purple ribbon dangling from her wrist. She'd been crying. Not the wedding day she'd envisaged, I suppose. Mama's face was also red, but from fury, not tears. Her eyes were bulging, her forehead crinkled. Elisabeta's arms were crossed, her lip pouting in defiance. I had warned Eirik that people didn't like to be told what to do.

Eirik gave an awkward smile, greeting them from afar, and nodded for them to continue up the slope to the right, past the towering walls and through the backyards.

The women led the way, followed by Eirik, and Dad a few paces ahead of me. I stared at the back of Eirik's head. How could I fool myself that it would not hurt just as much to say goodbye to him as it would to stay another day in his presence and not have him? I hated the way I was attracted to him. But I hated to let him go. Not that it made much difference—I'd lost his heart a long time ago. And there was Freja, his young spotless bride. They would be happy together, off in some unblemished world where they were free to raise a family how they saw fit.

"Stans," a young voice said from behind us and I stopped walking, my body frozen mid-action, muscles seizing.

I knew that tone and I knew that feeling that ran through my body. A master had commanded me to stop moving.

I was so close to leaving Verja, but someone was ripping my freedom from me, just when hope had found a home in me again.

My heart pounded hard against my chest. This was just like my many failed attempts to escape Purlieu. I was the only one not wearing gold. I should have learnt by now.

I pressed against the master's restraints on my body, forcing my limbs to move, pushing through the pain of muscle warring with bone. A whimper escaped me; my lip trembled.

I would not be overcome by this. I would not submit to my fears.

Come on, Evelyn.

I took a deep breath and swept the anxieties from my mind. I needed to think clearly.

The master had said *'stans'* which I was pretty sure just meant 'stop'. Stop moving. Stop escaping. But not stop thinking, stop breathing. Or stop speaking.

"Dad!" I called out with relief as I realised I still had full function of my mouth.

It took him a moment to realise I wasn't following him anymore. He looked over his shoulder and did a double-take, eyes looking past me down the slope to the master that was holding me captive.

"The gold. I can't move," I said.

He ran the ten paces between us just as *hlif* started surrounding me, surrounding us. Between their stern and obedient faces, I saw Eirik turn around and stop, his jaw bobbing open. He looked back up the cavern at his family moving away ahead of him and then down at me again. He looked at them again, and then back at me. His forehead creased. He shook his head and turned back up the slope, continuing after his family. They disappeared behind the cleverly placed stonewall.

My heart sank. He made his choice: Freja and his family. He left us to fend for ourselves.

I wasn't entirely surprised. He just proved why I needed to move on emotionally. He only cared about himself in the end.

13

THE COMMANDING VOICE spoke again and my body released its pose, arms slackening to my side. The *hlif* grabbed my wrists behind my back. They marched Dad and me down the slope and then back up again as we turned into the tunnel of towering walls to the open gates of Bornholm. There, between the gates was Mr Cuthbert and Heidelbert resuming their position in a fake hostage pose.

The one who commanded me to stop had been Heidelbert.

"You have a deal to uphold," Mr Cuthbert called out.

"You weren't at the revolution. I thought you gave up on the idea," I called back.

We stepped up to the gates of Bornholm, a few paces from Mr Cuthbert and Heidelbert.

"Master Heidelbert set your father free. Those were the terms, were they not?"

I pursed my lips. There seemed to be no way around it.

"Well, you seem really busy right now with winning Verja, I'm sure Purlieu can wait," I tried.

"You know, it is a shame you weren't sacrificed," Mr Cuthbert said. "It would have been much easier for me to manage both deals at once. Not to worry. I am wholly capable."

Did he mean that he didn't need me alive to play bait for William? I shuddered.

"I refuse to allow you to hand her over to him," Dad said.

"You are not privileged to have an opinion, I am afraid," Mr Cuthbert said. "If not for our little deal, you would be dead by now."

Grunting, yelling, and heavy footfalls came from behind. Mr Cuthbert's attention moved past us and Heidelbert spoke for the first time with a pathetic whimper. Tears dribbled down his face. I glanced over my shoulder. The Gothi was trudging menacingly up the slope towards us, slicked with blood. He had a black dagger raised in each hand, big eyes ablaze and set on Mr Cuthbert.

He reached our gathering and spoke menacingly at Mr Cuthbert. Mr Cuthbert nodded and motioned to the daggers in the Gothi's hands. He tossed them aside. With a smirk, Mr Cuthbert released Heidelbert, who ran whimpering into his father's arms.

The Gothi shrugged him off, his face upturning in disgust at the affection. Heidelbert staggered back from his father who swiftly swooped down and took a dagger in hand. Heidelbert mirrored him. They both faced off to Mr Cuthbert. A flicker of pride crossed the Gothi's eyes as he watched his son.

The Gothi started moving forward towards Mr Cuthbert. Heidelbert moved in behind him and with a few quick steps, drove the dagger into his father's back. The Gothi jerked and arched his back, screaming in pain. With his other hand, Heidelbert revealed another dagger and stabbed him with that one too. With a cry, the Gothi started falling. Heidelbert removed the daggers and his father hit the ground with a thump. A beat passed as the dust settled and then Heidelbert bent over his father and continued to stab him again and again and again, his robe becoming a tattered mess of blood and flesh.

A pool of blood seeped across the ground.

The *hlif*'s grip on my wrists loosened. They took a step back from us. Feet shuffled on dirt behind us. They were running away. One slipped around us and ran into Bornholm. The rest went down the cavern.

I rubbed at my sore wrists, watching Heidelbert. He left his father's body with the daggers sticking out of his back, and was shaking as he staggered over to Mr Cuthbert. He dropped to his knees, tears falling to the ground. Mr Cuthbert had a glint in his eyes. He spoke to Heidelbert.

Still shaking, Heidelbert got to his feet and started circling Mr Cuthbert, chanting, despite the tears that ran down his face and the blood that dripped from his hands.

My stomach dropped. He was making him a master.

This was what Mr Cuthbert had wanted all along. It was how he'd always planned on keeping control over the trade of Epli. Because the Epli created compliance. It was foolproof. All he had to do was give a little to any future client, falsely advertising it as a healing tonic, and suddenly they would be happy to do business with him.

"No, Heidelbert! Don't do it!" I called out.

Mr Cuthbert sneered at me. Heidelbert didn't falter, continuing to circle him as though we weren't even there.

Dad tugged at my arm, "Let's get out of here."

He was right. Who knew what Mr Cuthbert would do once he had the power? And he'd hardly stop Heidelbert in the middle of the proceedings just to stop us from getting away.

Heidelbert continued chanting as he touched Mr Cuthbert's eyes and mouth.

I allowed Dad's pull as I turned to run with him just as Heidelbert started touching his hands.

After a few steps, I dared a look back over my shoulder as I ran. Mr Cuthbert was now standing over the Gothi's body. He wrenched one of the daggers from his back and threw it at Heidelbert. Heidelbert's face was mingled with confusion and betrayal as it connected with his chest. He fell to his knees, blood immediately seeping from the wound. Mr Cuthbert returned to Heidelbert's side and watched him as he keeled over, a lone tear dribbling over his cheek with a groan, eyes fixed on Mr Cuthbert.

Mr Cuthbert wheeled on his heels, "Stop."

Ice ran through my body and froze my muscles. I was stuck mid-motion. Again. I could hear Dad continue a few paces on before grinding to a halt.

"You are too slimy, Miss Evelyn, and I cannot guarantee you will not try to run again. You will better serve the purpose dead," Mr Cuthbert said. "Pick up a dagger."

My stomach turned over and a chill ran across my face.

"Do not look so surprised, Miss Evelyn. You were always going to die."

He ignored Heidelbert groaning and choking at his side.

My legs moved for me, returning the few steps back up the slope and to the Gothi's body. I pried the dagger from his hand.

"Just so you know, Purlieu isn't exactly habitable at the moment. It's overrun by pterodactyls," I said, trying to buy time.

Mr Cuthbert only smiled, baring that gold canine at me. I glanced at Heidelbert. The light had left his eyes. He was dead. Mr Cuthbert was the only remaining master of this world. He had all the power now.

"Kill yourself," he said.

Dad's footsteps hurried up behind me as I took the dagger in both hands and reached out from my body, dagger pointed at my chest. Dad's arms wrapped around me as he fumbled to place the gold locket around my neck. My grip loosened and the dagger clattered to the ground. I had full control of my body once more. But now Dad was exposed. A wave of panic shuddered through me.

"Trust me," he whispered into my ear. "Run."

I did trust him. Gosh did I trust him.

He let go of me and I slipped around him to run, up the slope this time to the main exit from Verja.

"Never matter," Mr Cuthbert said. "You kill her instead."

Dad bent down to pick up the dagger and I picked up the pace up the slope, looking back over my shoulder as I went. Dad faced me and raised the dagger behind his head. He swiftly turned on the spot and brought his arm down, throwing the dagger at Mr Cuthbert instead. It flew through the air and hit him in the wrong side of the chest, slicing him and bouncing off to the ground with a clatter. Mr Cuthbert stumbled backwards with a grunt as Dad began to run after me.

"Run. Run!" Dad called out to me.

The tunnel was just ahead of me now.

"Stop," Mr Cuthbert yelled. "I command you to stop!"

I could hear Dad's feet, his huffing breath as he ran behind me. He wasn't stopping any time soon. Mr Cuthbert roared. A beat passed.

"Rise up, earth. Rise up rocks and mounds!" He commanded.

A great rumble echoed through the cavern. A jagged section of the path shot up in front of me. I dodged around it. Another section shot up on the side, taking a section of the limestone wall on the left with it. The cavern shook. Rocks skittered across my path as the ground moved beneath me. Thick dust flew into my face and I coughed and sputtered, squinting to see through it.

A boulder detached from the wall ahead and bounced down the slope as fragments fell from the ceiling before me.

I reached the main tunnel exit. Mr Cuthbert yelled in frustration.

"Down, rocks, fall down," he commanded.

The ground shook and rumbled precariously.

"Hurry, Dad!" I yelled.

I crossed the threshold of the tunnel and rounded the bend, listening out for Dad's footsteps behind me and hearing the thud, thud, thud, of his long stride catching on me.

Up and up we travelled, grasping at the walls of the tunnel for support and the ground shifted at my feet. I gasped for breath until I breached the stairs into the blaring light of the desert above and breathed clean air.

I put my hand up to shield my eyes but pulled it away, welcoming the light. I threw my arms open and let the heat wrap around my skin. I sucked in the fresh air. Dad emerged behind me and the ground continued to shift so we continued to the tree arch, into the Hidden Grove, and all the way to the Earth tree where we bent over, heaving.

"I guess the injury affected his aim, his power," I said between puffs.

Dad sucked in a deep breath and stood back up.

"This probably didn't help," he replied, holding his pinkie up.

Two gold rings, one with a princess-cut diamond, were sitting snugly on his pinkie.

"Mum's rings," I said. "But how?"

He smiled wryly and pulled me upright.

"They were in the locket, sweetheart."

I held the locket in my hand. He opened it to show two clips inside for holding the rings in place.

"That's why I gave it to her—so she could keep her rings safe while she was working at the hospital."

I shook my head and let out a laugh. He cracked a smile.

"Let's get out of here, Dad."

I looked up at the Earth tree, my mind sketching across its layered trunk, filling in the cracks and crevices in the bark. Never did it look so beautiful.

We began the climb up the Earth tree as I turned over this new revelation, glad I hadn't known about the rings sooner. I might have caved and given them to Eirik when he'd asked for the locket.

No, I wouldn't have.

I was strong. And I had stood up to him. I wouldn't have caved. Just like I wasn't going to start wondering where Eirik and his family had ended up in the Hidden Grove.

Because if I ever did stumble upon Eirik again, I would be considerate, like a neighbour would, but we were done. I had my father. I was going home. And I would start a new life where I wouldn't just say yes to the first guy who came along and showed me some semblance of love.

Eirik had his fair share of shortcomings—enough to write a list of red flags about, and I'd dodged a bullet by his decision to go through with the wedding. But he wasn't all bad. He was only trying to be a man; to take seriously the responsibility he had to his mother and sister and betrothed. To take care of them first and foremost, not put their lives at risk in the hope of maybe saving a stranger. He was just trying to do the right thing by them. To him, ultimately, the right thing was marrying Freja and leaving with her. Like most people, he was trying to be good. After all, he had stayed true to his promise to help get Dad out of Fengsel.

Not all men were bad. Just some were better choices than others.

I hoped that Eirik and his family had found somewhere safe.

"You know, Evelyn," Dad began from below me. "I've changed my mind about capital punishment."

"Doesn't feel so nice to be on the receiving end, does it?" I asked.

"Never in all my years in the force have I so directly intended to hurt, stop, or maim someone, as I did to Mr Cuthbert, let alone actually kill them. I've got no right to decide if someone deserves to die."

Something in me relaxed a little.

"Having said that, I would do it again if your life was on the line," he finished.

I paused in my climbing and stopped to look down at him. His face was tired, thin, and baldness didn't suit him, but there was warmth beneath his gaze, like life was being blown into him with every step we took closer to home.

"You know what else?" he asked.

"What's that?"

"I've had enough dirt between my toes to last a lifetime."
We shared a laugh.
"I love you, Dad."
"I love you too, Evelyn."
"You can always count on me too," I said.
He smiled.
"I know sweetheart. I know," he said. "And you know, Eirik was great and everything. But when push came to shove, he showed his true colours—leaving us behind like that."

I nodded, knowingly.

"You deserve better than that, Evelyn. A man whose actions line up with his words."

Yeah, it's not worth the heartache.

We reached the top of the tree.

"Dad, take my hand. We don't know how much time may have passed. We have to cross at the same time."

His big, calloused hands enveloped mine and we stepped across the bough together. My vision filled with light, glorious light, as we crossed the threshold back into Earth. Soft afternoon sunlight hit my face and I welcomed it. I would never live in the darkness again.

My leg hung over the window ledge, catching the winter sun, as I finished my second helping of apricot pie. It had been a few years since I'd last sat here, overlooking the garden below, watching. But it wasn't Mum's bent-over posture that I gazed upon this time. It was Dad. He was weeding her old garden, whistling contentedly in the shade of the trees.

I slipped a pencil beneath the scarf around my head and scratched at the short, itchy hair that poked at my scalp. It was going to take a long time to regrow it to an acceptable length but thankfully I had another week of school holidays plus my two-week suspension to learn how to do a proper headwrap.

The art journal Miss Daniels had given me was propped up on a pile of books on my bedside table. I licked up the final crumbs of apricot pie, took a deep breath, and swapped the plate out for the journal, flipping to the first page. The pencil hovered above the page as I hesitated. My phone rang. It was Tiffany.

"I just got your message," she said. "Tell me everything."

I took another deep breath and let the words tumble from my mouth—from Purlieu to Verja and back again. And then something unexpected happened. She shared too. About following me into Purlieu, about being manhandled by William, about the days she spent confined to that small space behind the bookshelf and how she didn't understand why and didn't know if she'd survive and didn't know what to do. And then the harrowing anxiety of leaving me behind in Purlieu. We laughed, but mostly cried, and everything seemed just awful but lighter; always lighter. As the hours passed and the tears dried and my arm hurt from holding the phone for so long, my heart opened, and it didn't seem so bad after all.

"You're going to be okay," I said.

"No. *We're* going to be okay," Tiffany said.

I smiled and promised I'd see her tomorrow and she promised we'd learn the headwrap together.

I hung up the phone as Dad moved to a spot just beyond the awning of the house. The sunlight shone golden across his back, and an aura of haziness clung to his edges. I pulled the pencil from the scarf around my head and took yet another deep breath. The pencil connected with the paper and I began the first downward stroke of his back.

Everything was better in the light.

Pronunciation Guide

Eirik Eik = EYE-rick EYE-ck
Elisabeta Eik = E-LIZ-a-bet-a EYE-ck
Epli = EP-li
Fela = FEE-la
Fengsel = FENG-sell
Freja = FREE-ya
Gothi = GOTH-thi
Gull = gool
Heidelbert Sol = HIDE-el-BURT SOLE
Hlif = hill-FF
Ofre Arstid = OFF-reh ARR-sted
Ómagi = OH-mahjii
Overgangsrite = OVER-GANGS-RIGHT
Rådhus = RAD-house
Spill-ehal = SPILL-e-hall
Stans = stanz
Una Eik = YOU-na EYE-ck
Uppreisers = UPP-rize-ers
Uppreisn = UPP-rize-en
Valki Unfrid = VAL-key UN-frid
Vân Vũ = VAN VOOH
Verja = VERR-jah

Translation Guide

Verja word	Direct translation	Meaning
anda	to breathe	
Bornholm	wealthy area of Verja	
daufi	stupid, dumb	a curse word
Epli	'Idun's golden apples'	elixir drink
fela	to hide	gas vials
Fengsel	prison	
ffjórtán	the number fourteen	
fimtán	the number fifteen	
Gothi	political and religious leader	head of Verja
gull	gold	
hallo	hey!	like 'oi!'
hlif	shield; protection	guards
kápa	coverall	
Mánis	moon	
Norns	female gods of fate	wheel of fate
ofre	sacrifice	
Ofre Arstid	Sacrifice Season	
oke	okay	
ómagi	dependent	disabled, 'the damaged'
Overgangsrite	rite of passage	manhood ceremony
Porri	spring	
Rådhus	city hall	
sextán	the number sixteen	
skjule	to hide	
spill-ehal	gambling room	the gambling den
stans	to stop	
Uppreisers	revolutionaries	
Uppreisn	rebellion, uprising, revolt	revolutionary group
vater	father	
verhaftet	to be arrested	
verja	to defend/guard/protect	

What did you think of Verja?

LOVED IT? HATED IT?
LOVED TO HATE IT?

Or go to:
tinyurl.com/HiddenGrove

Stay tuned for the final book in the series:

~

Mianjin

THE HIDDEN GROVE SERIES: BOOK 3

Michaela Daphne

In a seaside warehouse of the Hidden Grove,
Evelyn is forced to honour her deal with Mr Cuthbert.
Will she be taken prisoner by William once more?

Coming soon.

ACKNOWLEDGMENTS

To *Shawn* for being my best critic, *Kathrina* for your faithfulness, *Jen* for your enthusiasm, *Lorraine* for your eagle eye, *Megan* for helping me believe in Pigfarts (see you on Mars!), and *Hayley* for re-inspiring me of the mission.

ABOUT THE AUTHOR

Michaela Daphne is an Australian writer who has penned several short films, TV scripts, stage plays, and fiction stories and authored sections in the books Learning to Love and The Word Made Flesh. She's spent the last ten years volunteering and working with high-schoolers and young adults in Australia and Singapore and her passion lies specifically with helping to equip young women for healthy relationships. The Hidden Grove series is inspired by personal experiences of her own life and the lived stories of the young women she's encountered.

Follow Michaela Daphne on Instagram @michaeladaphnewriter

or visit her website at www.michaeladaphne.com

www.ingramcontent.com/pod-product-compliance
Ingram Content Group UK Ltd.
Pitfield, Milton Keynes, MK11 3LW, UK
UKHW041301180426
11947UKWH00009B/598